Soul Boundary

BY KATARINA STENSTEDT

Paperback: ISBN-13: 978-1-7326047-0-4
E-book: ISBN-13: 978-1-7326047-1-1

This is a work of fiction. Names, characters, businesses, places, events, and technologies are either the products of the author's imagination or used fictitiously. Any resemblance to actual persons, living or dead, or actual events, is purely coincidental.

Cover design by Gene Anderson

Published by Katarina Stenstedt
www.SleepOnTheHearth.com

PART 1: EARTH

PART 2: BETWEEN

PART 3: PATIENCE

Part 1: Earth

Extraction

My soul tethers me to my selfs.
—Pixi Romano

Stanford University

Everyone knows a body can't survive without a soul and a soul can't survive without a body, and of course a soul can't be cloned. But can a soul be moved from one body to another?

Tensel Brown considered this as he rummaged the fridge for his leftover Chikin' cup. Why did whatever he wanted to eat go missing just when he felt like eating it? He shrugged and grabbed a carton of chocolate emulsion with "Jason's" written across the front as he returned to his thoughts about souls.

And why did scientists have to use that old word? *Soul.*

His Adam's apple bobbed up and down with each swallow as he emptied the carton. The emulsion tasted faintly putrid, but it would take more than that to make Tensel sick. Like most of his friends, he hosted innerbots that could make even the nastiest emulsion into something digestible — or at least harmless. He was tall, with long muscles and a rolling stride and wavy dark hair that looked greasy, even when it was clean. His forehead was high and his face was curved, with strong cheekbones and hollow cheeks beneath. It was a serious face.

He dropped the carton into the regenerator, which needed a tune-up. Was it his turn? No, Jessica would've reminded him. Jessica wanted him to ask for better housing, a big double where they could live alone, where she could control who tuned up what, and when.

But the material world didn't leave a big impression on Tensel. When he found crusty dishes in the sink or ants in the

3

desalinator, he felt a moment of vexation, then forgot about it. If he pestered Dr. Kendel for a favor, it wouldn't be for better housing.

Meanwhile, he couldn't sleep, so here he was again. Awake in the middle of the night.

He slipped into the tattered fabric chair in front of the living room workstation. Six augmented-reality headsets were piled on the desk, cords tangled. He freed the one marked "T. Brown" and pulled it over his head, then scooted the chair close to the data screen. The implants in his head transmitted data from the cloud to his optic and auditory nerves, so the AR headset wasn't required, but it optimized signals and blocked ambient sights and sounds.

He pictured his personal research files, then imagined them opening. They opened, visible only to him. He gave an eye signal to turn on ocean sounds, then took a deep breath as the white noise of the surf and the cries of the seabirds did their calming work on his nervous system.

Could an organism's macro quantum pattern, the biological attribute people called the *soul*, be moved from one organism to another? He had a hunch the answer was yes.

But how? His expertise in post-quantum soulistics told him it wasn't possible, but what about recent improvements to quantum teleportation? Some lines of inquiry that were abandoned centuries ago seemed worth reopening.

He both loved and hated wondering about soul transfer. Many people believed that the soul was impenetrable to science, or if not impenetrable, then a Pandora's box, not to be meddled with. And every time the question of manipulating the soul came into his mind, his stomach dropped.

Why did he love to wonder about a topic that made him feel sick, Jessica had asked when he told her this. She was an undergrad, and sometimes Tensel wondered if she was too young for him, but she made him laugh and helped him remember that he had a body, and that felt good. Plus he was less forgetful when she was around.

But Tensel's real home was his mind. He could shift ideas and emotions around in there as if he were arranging furniture. Breathing slowly now, eyes closed, he sank into the ocean sounds and pictured himself holding his queasiness and superstition in his hands, placing them into a wide, safe drawer, and closing the drawer. In his imagination, he considered his empty hands. He imagined them filled with the bright, warm light of a new idea.

His meditation complete, he switched from ocean sounds to a drum and synth piece that matched his brain's EEG readings at his peak concentration level. He began to think. Tones at different frequencies in each ear moved his brain waves into synchronization with an optimized pattern, the drumming faded into the background, and his mind settled into a fast groove.

Tonight, finally, a plan began to take shape in his notes and sketches. Using the novel quantum teleportation technique that was occurring to him now, he would try to remove an animal's macro quantum pattern and store it, even briefly, without decoherence. Then he'd store the pattern for longer periods.

But where could he store these patterns? What material could act as a database for soul? And what would happen to an animal whose soul was impressed into the database? Or—and this was sheer fantasy, given the regulations around human testing—what would happen to a human?

Oakland, California

Just after 2:30 a.m., Rachel stepped into the train car, examined a seat near the door, and wiped it with a tissue before she sat. She pulled a protein roll out of her purse and took a bite, chewing and thinking. She tried not to stare at the man across from her, who seemed to be doing a yoga routine in his virtual-reality gear.

She fingered the gold cross around her neck and the speck of emerald, her birthstone, embedded in the center of it. A birthday gift from Sam. Her easy child.

Blackness lay behind the reflection of her face in the window, and she glanced at herself, then looked away, not wanting anyone to see her so self-absorbed. But no one cared, so she looked at herself more closely. Her steel-gray hair was sleek and gently curled, as always, and her clothes were neat and well-mended. She slept in soft rollers every night, which her kids said was crazy. Well, was that crazier than spending a fortune on high-tech shoes, like Sam? Or sleeping in VR gear, like Sam's sister Miriam?

Her eyes unfocused and settled on the darkness behind her own face as she thought of her daughter's face. The bags under Miriam's eyes, the crunchy spikes of her hair, the scornful set of her mouth. How did her little girl get so tired? So angry?

At 19th Street, Rachel left the train and hurried down the night-darkened sidewalk. She remembered the day's air-quality rating and held her breath for a moment, but that was silly. She had to breathe the outside air like everybody else, at least until she got to work. She didn't have the luxury of in-nerbots, complex nanobots working to filter toxins out of her lungs and blood, protect her skin, patrol her intestines . . . .

She stepped around a few bundled forms in sleeping bags and paused in front of a burnished metal door marked "Employees Only." Invisible tech verified her ID, and when the light over the door turned green she rushed ahead, the door whooshing open and shut as she passed though. She paused for a long breath, eyes closed, savoring the clean weight of the filtered air in her lungs. *Sorry,* she whispered, thinking of the bundled forms out on the sidewalk. And had she seen a few children out there tonight? *Dear God,* she whispered. *Mercy.*

"You just made it, two fifty-*nine* a.m.!" called Bernadine, with an emphasis on the *nine*, as Rachel passed her supervisor's office and slid into her call booth.

On autopilot, she attached a sensor to each fingertip, then snapped on a pair of rubber gloves to hold the sensors in place. After decades at Human Converse, she knew by feel whether her fingers were lined up correctly against the damp, felty squares of soul fabric, though she had no idea how the technology worked, and no interest in learning.

She was senior enough that she never *had* to take a graveyard shift, and she kept forgetting how hard it was to interrupt your sleep like this. It might take her a week to get her schedule back on track. But this was what love looked like, wasn't it? She'd offered to switch shifts with Anya, because she assumed she could afford the emotional cost more easily than Anya. Anya never said she was having trouble, but Rachel worried anyway. Anya and Sam were friends, and Rachel had helped Anya get this summer job. She didn't want the girl to flounder.

"Rachel Anna Deimos," said Rachel in the direction of the voice-verification mic.

"Low volume," said a bland voice. It entertained Rachel to imagine the voice going off script and having an existential crisis. "Who cares who *you* are? Who am *I*?" But today was not that day.

She repeated her name more loudly.

"Identity confirmed," said the voice.

Soul fabric was semi-organic, so a bit of earthiness came with the territory in this line of work. She slipped off her shoes and socks, then hesitated before pushing her feet into the sheer booties that held the humid fabric against her feet during calls with clients. She'd run out of the antifungal powder that she sprinkled in there at the start of each shift. Ugh — couldn't Human Converse replace the soul fabric more often, or at least clean the booties more convincingly? God only knew what kind of fungus might be crawling around in there, itching to find a home between her toes.

She opened a panel in front of her and took out a gelatin capsule stuffed with digestible soul fabric and time-stamped nanobots. Pinching the large capsule between the finger and thumb of her rubber glove, she dropped it into her mouth and choked it down with water.

What a hassle. But she was used to it, and clients paid good money to know what it was they were talking to when they heard Rachel's voice. The interior probe inside the capsule, plus the finger and foot sensors, relayed a crucial fact to her paying clients during their conversations: here sits a human being, alive and well, talking for herself, ensouled from head to toe.

Only one type of being has a soul and can carry on a coherent, spontaneous verbal conversation with a human, and that's a human. Terrific conversationalist with no soul? It's a machine. Soul, but limited conversation? Could be a human, or maybe a souped-up chimp or dolphin, or even a dog. Terrific conversationalist and certified "yes" by the patented soul-check technology used by Human Converse? Guaranteed human.

She tapped her foot to the side twice to signal her readiness to take a call, and her first call came in. The client software received its proof that Rachel had a soul and was conscious, and the conversation began. She hoped for easy callers, unlike that guy last week who'd tricked her into staying on the line for five minutes before she realized he was angling for phone sex. Human Converse was only licensed to provide human-voice service for everyday *information* needs.

Her first caller identified as a non-binary humanoid named Pandaria, and the royal blue face that Rachel saw on her screen made a vivid contrast to the avatar's large golden eyes. The gleaming electronic image was only centimeters from the camera, and a wide blue nose dominated the picture.

She knew she might be talking to a pimply teenaged girl named Emily who had unlimited access to her parents' search account and enjoyed using it to kill time in the middle of the night, but it didn't matter. Pandaria the avatar was researching famous 26th-century heroin addicts, and Pandaria wanted information, along with the companionship of a patient, personable human.

The call took almost 45 minutes, and Rachel was halfway to her first break. Being busy was a great help in forgetting her troubles, she reflected.

Then her stomach clenched as she thought of Miriam, home alone with the baby. Was it going okay? Would Miriam get Eliza to childcare early enough in the morning to make it to her own job on time?

Rachel knew it wasn't hers to worry about, but she had a hard time letting it go.

Stanford

Tensel didn't notice when Jason came in the front door at 4 a.m., made himself a sandwich, left an open jar of peanut butter and a sticky, used knife on the kitchen counter, and disappeared into Room A. Nor had Tensel realized that Alison was asleep on the couch a half a meter from his workstation. He didn't hear it when she got up, said goodnight, and joined Jason in Room A. The day lights started going up in the common room at dawn, and at 6:20 a.m., a muffled buzzing sound came from Jessica's alarm clock in Room C.

Jessica opened the bedroom door and took in the scene. She'd slept in red boxer shorts and a T-shirt that said "Stanford Soccer," and a frizzy braid hung down her back. She walked the long way around the couch and came toward Tensel from the side, knowing it was best not to startle him when he was like this. She crept her hand forward and put it on his knee. "Sweetie," she said, "have you been at this all night?"

"What?" he said, refocusing his eyes to find her face.

"It's soul transfer again, isn't it?" She raised her hand to his temple and smoothed his dark hair, tucking it under the strap of his headset. "Aren't you tired? No. Of course not."

Tensel looked blank. "No. Of course not," he said, then returned his gaze to his interior world.

She took her hand off his face and walked into the kitchen area. "I have to get going. We'll talk tonight, okay? I'll leave the oatmeal out. Should I make coffee for you? You remember you're teaching a section this morning, right?"

She wasn't expecting answers.

* * *

Tensel was running later than usual. He pulled on jeans and a frayed sweatshirt he'd had since the eighth grade and slammed the front door behind him. As he strode down the moving walkway that sped him toward the center of campus, he estimated that each of his steps took him 17 percent farther than Jessica's steps would take her, given her height of 156 centimeters, plus the difference in the relative length of her legs. Done with these calculations, he left his legs to stride without conscious intervention and returned his thoughts to last night's soul-transfer idea.

Dr. Kendel didn't like him getting distracted from his thesis like this. "When you get a new idea, record yourself a note, then shrug it off," Dr. Kendel had said. "Think about your great ideas later." Here he'd leaned a little closer. "The point is to make it past the goal line! So for now, keep your eyes on the data. You've got to *whip* that data into a thesis." At the word "whip," he'd circled one of his beefy fists in a whipping motion, making the conversation a hard one to forget.

Whipping the data into shape seemed like an okay plan, but Tensel usually felt more like the data was whipping him. His funders had given him access to data from 82 slightly different manufacturing machines, each etching patterns onto synthetic-carbon fiber substrates all day, every day. So far he'd collected three quintillion data points, and adjusting his machine-learning algorithms to find useful results was tedious beyond belief.

Engineers were forever designing more efficient 1,200- and even 1,300-qubit chips, but maybe it wasn't worth the effort. Was there a limit to how much a soul-fabric manufacturer's bottom line could be improved by a better chip? This was Tensel's research question, and even *he* found it a bit dull. If he proved the existence of a limit, then the corp that provided his grant money could spend less on chip research, which would save them a bundle.

After he finished his thesis, he'd have to move into industry work proper—after all, that's why they paid him a stipend and kept him in the program. But his heart called him elsewhere.

Fortunately, he had a few student assistants to lighten his load. He smiled as he thought of Jessica's friend Sam Deimos, a fresh face in the department, and the only undergrad invited into the Biophysics work-study program. Sam could set up hundreds of calculation runs per hour when he was on task. And Sam laughed at Tensel's jokes, even when other people didn't know they were jokes.

The Post-Quantum Soulistics building was in sight, then the classroom door. Ten strides away, nine, eight, ...

Tensel jogged into the room and whisked his tall frame into the seat behind the podium. Before he could speak, a wiry man in the second row raised his hand. Tensel sighed. "Yes, Mr. Dobbik?"

"Do cloned animals have unique souls?"

Leave it to Mr. Dobbik to ask a stupid question half a minute into section. "Well," said Tensel, staring out the window, "what might you expect, if you were doing the testing?"

Mr. Dobbik sat up straighter, glowing in the light of the attention. "Hmm," he began, "a clone of a mammal, let's say, is in all aspects a living being, which would make me expect it to have its own soul. On the other hand, it isn't a unique being, if genome is all that's in question. You'd need to exercise extreme care to make it epigenetically identical to its original; but if it could be identical in that way as well as genetically, well then, maybe it wouldn't be unique. And uniqueness . . . umm . . . ."

"I don't know that it needs to be so complicated," said Tensel. "Anyone remember the tests run by Alistair and Ramda, 2641? Or what about Ramda's Axiom of Soul Viability?"

While the students were looking blank and using their in-eye displays to rummage the cloud for an answer, Tensel had an abrupt insight about his soul-transfer puzzle. Clone cells! Maybe a batch of stem cells cloned from a mouse could hold a mouse's extracted macro quantum pattern. Fully developed clones had quantum patterns of their own, but a petri dish of cloned stem cells wouldn't. And with no quantum pattern of its own, this group of cells might be receptive to a pattern belonging to its genetic original. A soul database! How could you hope to find a better, more habitable place to store a soul than within cells copied from its original host?

He was physically present for the rest of the class, but mentally elsewhere. Mr. Dobbik followed him after class, asking about symbionts and their souls. "If that interests you," Tensel called over his shoulder as he accelerated, "look it up."

When he reached his dorm, everyone was gone. He put on his running shorts and shoes and set out on his usual 7 km route up to the Dish, a rusted old radio telescope in the foothills above the university. His idea about clones had the ring of truth and clarity that he knew from experience to be the hallmark of a good idea. It felt beautiful and excellent to him. He smiled as he circled around the back side of the water tower, the halfway point of his run.

But how would he get funding to work on this excellent new idea? Dr. Kendel would never go for it, but there was a way around that obstacle: he wouldn't tell Dr. K what he was doing. He'd create a proof-of-concept on his own time and pay for the materials himself. Dr. K would know nothing about it until the prototype was complete, tested, and reproducible.

He blinked open his work files, his fingers twitching and his lips moving as he manipulated design specs, machine sketches, and equations. In spite of his built-in navigation safeguards, it was a wonder he made it back to his dorm without twisting an ankle.

Oakland

At noon, Rachel was on the train home. At the Coliseum station she transferred to a dingy electric streetcar that shot down the middle of Hegenberger Road between pedestrians, bikes, and a few domed electric vehicles. She emerged from the dimness of the streetcar and stood with her eyes closed, turning her face toward the sun. She spoke aloud as she walked up 105th, thanking God for the sun and the beauty of the day, polluted air be damned, and for her job at Human Converse. Then she thanked God for Sam and Miriam and baby Eliza, who was two months and four days old, and even for Miriam's wildness (or as Miriam preferred to frame it, her *creativity*).

"If anyone can weave a tapestry out of this mess of threads, it's *you*," she said, pointing heavenward. She rarely hesitated to speak loudly and emphatically to God in public, given all the other folks communing with real and virtual companions no one else could see or hear.

Home was a room she shared with Miriam and Eliza. It was in a post-consumer bioplastic house at the corner of 105th and Jalquin, a two-minute walk from San Leandro Creek in the south part of Oakland. The house had a postage-stamp yard with a real tree and real grass, which would have been a pleasure if Springy, the Schnauzer mix who lived in Room 2, wasn't always tearing it up and shitting all over it.

Rachel opened the gate and stepped into the yard, pushing Springy away with her foot as he scraped his wet paws down her shins. Springy's owner Stan often just *happened* to be looking out his window when Rachel got home from work. He opened the window and leaned out.

"Nice weather."

"Lovely."

"How's your kid?"

Rachel chose to assume he meant Sam. "Oh, Sam loves school," she said. "Biophysics turned out to be the right fit for him, though we miss him every day now that he's moved out."

"Biophysics, wow. Unbelievable!"

Why was it unbelievable? She was used to mild, thoughtless astonishment about her son's accomplishments, but it made her feel more tired than she already was. She hesitated. "And how are you?"

Stan's gaze turned inward as he began a comprehensive answer to the question. Rachel fumbled in her purse, pulled out her house keys, held them with her arm bent in front of her— hints that Stan didn't take. After a few minutes she flipped to a large brass key on her keychain and opened the house's front door, then stood with the door open, smiling and nodding pleasantly. Stan had to lean farther out his window and almost shout now that Rachel was standing on the house's front step.

It was quarter to one before he paused. "You enjoy the weather, now," Rachel blurted as she ducked inside the front door. She rushed down the dim passageway and into Room 3, bolting the room door behind her.

Was that rude? She cringed against the door, tempted to go across the hall, knock on Room 2's door, say a few friendly words to Stan. His loneliness and sadness stuck on her like glue.

She tried to let go of whatever feelings might belong to Stan, turning to face Room 3 and her own life within it.

* * *

Room 3 was a rectangle with a door in the middle of one of the long walls and three windows on the opposite wall. In this house, rooms with windows on two walls cost an extra 45 credits per month.

A far cry from the space she'd shared with Jackson when they got married: an entire apartment to themselves, with two bedrooms, a fenced-in patio that Rachel covered with pots of tomatoes and herbs, and their own bathroom. A private bathroom! She thought she'd live that way forever. But his parents gave him that money for college, and when the money ran out, there wasn't any more. Not from Jackson, not from his parents, not then, and not now. Her fantasies had turned out backwards and somehow *she* ended up supporting *him* — along with the two children they had together — and then he was gone and they were divorced. How did it all happen?

She paused by the door to hang her keys and purse on a hook labeled "Rachel." The entire place was only 8 by 10 meters, but she and Miriam and the baby managed to share it semi-gracefully. Ironic that the space had seemed larger when there'd been three adults instead of two adults and a baby. She touched the hook labeled "Sam," which was empty now that Sam lived in a dorm at Stanford.

Her children, Sam and Miriam, were forces of nature—one sunshine, one clouds. A mixture of sunshine and clouds is fine, but nothing but clouds is hard work. Pregnancy and post-partum hormones hadn't improved Miriam's clouds, but Miriam never wanted to talk about it. Rachel had to make due with her own guesses and endless ruminations about what was going on inside her daughter's heart and mind.

Rachel's space was on the northwest side of the room, separated from the shared center area by two floral-print sheets hung neatly on a clothesline near the ceiling. The head of her twin bed was under a window, which she opened on hot nights to get a bit of air through the security bars that chunked up her view of the yard. A rose-patterned bedspread covered the bed, topped by an afghan that her grandmother, Rose, had crocheted for her 30 years earlier. Every morning Rachel made her bed, fluffed her down pillows, and positioned them on top of the bedspread. Real goose down, the most luxurious thing she owned. Geese were extinct, and Rachel reflected sadly that when these pillows met their maker, she wouldn't replace them. Even if goose down were available on the black market, she'd never buy it again.

She had a real wood table next to her bed, about knee height. It was just big enough to hold an oil lamp made of cobalt blue glass, a few dog-eared paper books, and an olive-wood figurine of the pregnant Virgin Mary with her arms folded across her belly. The table was Rachel's altar. She intended to pray there every morning, and sometimes she did. She'd sit cross-legged on the floor on one of her precious pillows and close her eyes for a few minutes, trying to slow her breathing and let her thoughts settle. Then she'd light the lamp, open her breviary, and read the day's short prayer to herself in a whisper, or speak it out loud if Miriam wasn't there. When she had time she'd linger, reading and thinking about the prayer, telling God her problems, and trying hard to listen for what God might be saying in response.

*
**

Miriam came through the door just before 2 o'clock, even though her shift at the school cafeteria didn't end until 4. She threw her keys on the kitchen table and disappeared into her part of the room, a bed and heaps of dirty laundry separated from the shared space by a Chinese screen and a big rolling display board that she'd found near a dumpster.

She didn't look at me, thought Rachel, who sat in her rocker with a half-embroidered quilt square on her lap. Virtual-reality gear squeaked and clunked behind the screen, and Miriam began to giggle and mutter, engrossed in whatever reality compelled her that day.

Rachel tried not to hear it, tried to return to her inner world. She was intuitive, and sometimes her intuition was on target, but even then, intuition had limits. Where intuition left off, it was tempting to let imagination take over and color in the details. She reminded herself of this; reminded herself that she couldn't penetrate the mystery of Miriam — not really, not ever. Only Miriam knew what it was like to be Miriam, and only God knew what Miriam needed. She intended to trust God with Miriam, and trust Miriam to find her own path.

Easier said than done.

A few hours later, Miriam stepped from behind the divider. "Somebody needs to pick up Eliza from childcare, but I promised Ex I'd come over," she said, leaving for the bathroom down the hall.

Surprise surprise, whispered Rachel, putting down her embroidery and fixing herself and Miriam plates of E-Z Prep Chikin'.

When the food was ready, Miriam chewed and swallowed mechanically, murmuring as she ate.

Probably talking to one of those fools she calls friends, thought Rachel. If Sam were here, he'd say something funny or outrageous. Maybe he'd talk about his latest adventure with the hair-washing bot that had its own (questionable!) ideas about the proper care of his shoulder-length locs. Or his plans to dress up as an entangled particle for his Post-Quantum final project. He'd know how to call Miriam back into the room.

Rachel wanted Sam to come through the door. She wanted a phone to ring. She wanted a twig to snap and break the tension, a lightning bolt to clear the air, *some*thing, *any*thing to let her and her daughter start over and take a deep, clean breath.

An abrupt clatter made her heart skip a beat as Miriam dropped her empty plate into the sink. Miriam plopped down in the armchair near the table and flipped open a copy of *Crochet World*.

After a few minutes, she tossed the magazine on the floor and rolled her eyes.

Rachel felt paralyzed, though now was the time to speak. What could she say? *Are you okay? I'm worried about you . . . .* Or maybe *I'm tired of taking care of your life, and you need to grow up!* But when she opened her mouth, out popped, "Don't worry honey, I'll pick up Eliza."

"Great," said Miriam. "I'm outta here." She grabbed her VR gear from her bed, then paused at the door. "You know mom, this place is depressing," she said, indicating the room. "If you weren't so nervous about tech, if you'd — I don't know, do some shopping and get yourself some gear, we could immerse together. You might enjoy it."

Done, she made her exit.

Rachel rocked in her chair, lost in thought, as her daughter's boots clomped down the hall. She scoffed, imagining herself and Miriam lost together in VR. Who'd do the dishes?

Miriam couldn't afford full-body VR gear, thank the Lord, but she spent countless waking hours and most nights in VR gloves and headgear, immersed even while she dreamed. Customized ads flashed into her consciousness during the day and into her dreams at night — sales pitches for gadgets, upgrades, and immersion experiences promising a bigger rush, a better high.

But as unhealthy as it seemed for Miriam to spend so much time and energy in her imaginary reality, it seemed worse for her to spend real time with the people she called friends. After all, you can't put real drugs in your body by means of a cheap VR headset and gloves, and you can't get bugs and diseases or become anything but make-believe pregnant.

She blinked to dial Sam, breaking her own rule about using video tech in the house. Sam, grinning, appeared in her mind's eye. It was his busy video. "I'm not available," he said. "You'll have to carry on without me."

She hung up without leaving a message, and the questions she'd been working not to think about crept back into her mind: why had Miriam, tech savvy as she was, let herself become pregnant? Why had she wanted to keep the baby, given the way mothering cramped her style?

And who was Eliza's father? Maybe that creepy Exscalibur boy, the one with the green eyeliner. It always looked like his face was molding. She shuddered and pushed her mind back to the topic of VR.

Rachel hated VR. She'd tried it a few times with Jackson, long ago, but immersing herself in a world where it was hard to tell what was real and what wasn't made her feel vulnerable. She was even uncomfortable with augmented reality, though AR was unavoidable if you wanted to get anything done. She spent every work day in an AR harness, and maybe that's why she was so anxious to be rid of the stuff when her work day ended.

Like most people, she had a cheap neuroprosthetic implant that the state-run hospital had installed in her head shortly after she was born. The implant fed into her optic and auditory nerves, and she used it to search the cloud and make calls, just like everybody else. The implant had rudimentary manual controls, tiny switches behind her left ear, and she kept hers in the Off position whenever she could, especially when she was inside her house. If you called Rachel while she was at home, you usually had to leave a message and wait for her to notice.

Organic flesh is the real you — that's how she saw it — and the real you didn't have synthetic implants when the Creator knit it together in your mother's womb. Enhanced reality is always just that; enhanced. It adds nothing to your true self. After you die, your gadgets are cut out, cleaned, and recycled, so why not try to keep them out of your body in the first place? But now she was just muttering to the empty room.

At this point Sam would probably quote Tensel Brown, his hero at Stanford. Sam and Tensel would say technology had become part of life itself; that your personal tech was part of your soul and helped constitute your personality. So-called experts considered the mind to be the brain plus whatever tools and resources the brain makes use of. The mind has always extended itself beyond the brain — it's normal for people to use tools, words, their own bodies, and even their relationships with other people to help them think, assimilate new information, and store memories. Why not also use more advanced technologies for these tasks?

But to Rachel, you end where technology begins. If it's engineered, it can never be part of you. Period.

*
**

Miriam hurried down 105th and boarded a streetcar toward downtown. Why should she do any Eliza-related chores when she'd probably get signals from her mom that she was doing them *wrong?* The more she thought about it, the angrier she got. It was as if mom *wanted* to do everything herself, even while quietly acting like a martyr about it. "Well mom," she said to Rachel in the rehearsal space of her own mind, "do you want me to take care of the baby, or don't you?"

Satisfied that she had no reason to feel guilty about Rachel picking up Eliza from childcare, she brought up a visual of Exscalibur in her peripheral vision. "I'm on my way," she said, staring past him. "Be ready to hook me up as soon as I get there. I am in a *mood*."

She blinked to close the connection, letting her face go slack and closing her eyes. Her thoughts went to the VR setup at Exscalibur's place. "Ugh," she whispered in the private space she'd claimed at the back of the streetcar, which she wished would go faster. "I need a break."

Stanford

The Stanford Soulistics labs were in Warehouse D, just off the south edge of campus in what had once been a quiet residential neighborhood of Palo Alto. Walking into the warehouse, you couldn't help but look up. Rooms topped with false ceilings ringed the edges of the space, and two soul-fabric imprinting machines dominated the open center. Grad students had named the two hulking machines, each 10 meters tall, Joker and Thief. Late at night when the place was dimly lit, Joker looked to Tensel like an enormous ancient manual typewriter turned upside down and balanced on its carriage. Thief was identical to Joker, but a bit newer and shinier. From what would be the keys of each one, support beams angled down, and thick ropes of cabling fell to floor level and snaked into the backs of workstations.

Tensel's favorite workstation was under what he thought of as Joker's "q" key. The machine's gunmetal-gray weight hung over him like a lead cloud, which comforted him in a way he couldn't articulate. He had a private lab of his own, partly by the luck of the draw, and partly because Dr. Kendel felt sure he'd produce money-making results one of these days. Even so, he preferred the shadowy space under the shelf of the great machine.

But now he needed privacy. He kicked out the undergrads who used his lab to study and installed a lock on the lab's door. He re-read his contract and discovered that he'd agreed to spend only 32 hours a week on teaching, research, and thesis work, and he began spending only 32 hours a week on teaching, research, and thesis work. During most other waking moments and some sleeping ones, he was in his lab with the door shut. Mysterious packages were delivered and strange noises came forth, but it was the Soulistics lab, after all. Soul physicists were a strange bunch, as everyone knew.

*
**

Fall and winter quarters passed, and spring quarter began. On Mondays Jessica had an 11:15 Cognitive Psych class on the south side of campus, and one Monday after class she biked over to

Soulistics with sandwiches in her backpack: tofu on wheat for Tensel, synthetic roast beef on rye for her. She twirled a finger in her ponytail as she walked across the warehouse, unconsciously ducking as she passed through the shadows of Joker and Thief.

What was the deal with her boyfriend's latest obsession? She hoped he wasn't doing anything foolish — brilliant as he was, he sure could be dense when it came to reality! Good thing he was cute.

She nudged his lab door, and it stopped when it hit the chest freezer that had been delivered the day before. "Oof," she said as she squeezed into the lab and climbed onto the freezer, "does that have to go right here? Jesus, you're lucky enough to have the biggest lab space in the whole department, and you've found a way to fill it up."

Tensel was at the end of the rectangular room, his long limbs askew in his workstation chair. He pushed his goggles up on his forehead, making a section of his black hair stand straight up, and looked around. Jessica followed his gaze and realized that with the addition of the freezer, there was hardly any space left in the lab. She sat down on the freezer and drew her legs up under her.

Her volunteer work at the hospital gave her an appreciation for germs, so she didn't plan to give Tensel his sandwich until he looked like he might be ready to eat it. No spot in the lab looked clean enough to put food down. Microscopes, a laser, robotic arms, and a row of culture hoods obscured one of the two counters. Smudged slides and used cleaning cloths were strewn everywhere. Anxious mice were suspended in a smelly cage over the sink. Glass-fronted cabinets on the walls above the counters held bottles of chemicals and gels. The second counter, opposite the mice, was covered with metallic equipment Jessica couldn't place.

"What's with all the new stuff?" she asked.

Silence.

"Oh come on, you've been keeping a secret for a while now. Maybe you should tell me. You spend more time than ever at work, but you never mention your soul-fabric research. And I bet this doesn't contain data-processing equipment." She patted the freezer beneath her.

Tensel exhaled. "You're right, I should tell you. This stuff is for cloning and quantum teleportation." As if that explained everything.

"Whoa. And those?" Jessica pointed at a row of petri dishes half-filled with a red substance, flat and translucent.

"Those are, well . . . handling those is outside my wheel-house, but I'm learning fast." He stood up to look more closely at the culture medium in the dishes. "I'm trying to grow a batch of cloned stem cells from Trixie to act as a macro quantum pattern database."

"Trixie?"

He waved at the mouse cage. "She's the gray one with the gold patches on the sides of her face, by the water bottle."

Jessica stepped onto and over a fume hood, unopened in its original box, to reach the sink. She considered Trixie's twitching nose.

"I'm modifying some old-school teleportation equipment to support my novel technique," Tensel continued. "When everything's ready, I'll send a stream of particles through a beam splitter to create pairs of entangled particles. I'll bombard those cloned stem cells with one of the streams. The other stream will go (along with Trixie, of course) into the scanner. To be measured." As he talked he stood up and pointed at the triangle of machines that were set up on the second counter: the particle gun that would emit the beam, the beam splitter that looked like a tiny and complicated set of mirrors, and the small, rectangular black box that was the scanner.

Jessica considered this for a moment, then clambered back to the freezer and sat back down. "So Trixie herself will go through the scanner."

"In a manner of speaking, yes. The quantum state of her particles will be disrupted."

"Meaning . . . ?"

"Quantum teleportation destroys the original. The measurements I get from the scanner will tell me how to irradiate the stem cells in such a way as to put their particles into a quantum state identical with the quantum state of Trixie's cells."

Jessica raised her eyebrows. "So your soul-transfer idea isn't just theoretical? You're really gonna *try* it? Whoa. Tests like this are illegal on living animals without paperwork and approvals, you know that, right? And anyway, what makes you think Trixie's soul will be teleported along with the quantum state of those particles?"

"Pattern."

"What?"

"It's not a soul, it's a macro quantum pattern. I wish you'd remember that. The word 'soul' is imprecise, and it triggers irrationality. Using it as a technical term has biased the way we study it, and I'd like to avoid that mistake in my personal work, even though there's no getting around it in public."

"Sorry." Jessica crossed her arms, thinking thoughts she decided not to say aloud. "So 'soul' equals 'pattern' to you, fine," she continued at last. "What makes you think Trixie's 'pattern' will be teleported along with the quantum states of her particles?"

"I don't know," said Tensel, "but it's my hypothesis, and that's why I have to conduct live experiments. I can't think of any other way forward."

"How many Trixies do you plan to use?"

"As many as it takes."

Jessica thought for a moment, her lips pinched together. "Well," she said, standing up, "thanks for telling me. I mean it, I'm glad you told me." She handed him his sandwich, kissed him quickly on the mouth, and climbed over the freezer to leave. "How can you think with all this stuff in here?"

"Just wait till I get the portable accelerator and target chamber. They're coming Friday."

"You're insane."

"We'll see," he muttered as Jessica squeezed out through the door of the lab and disappeared.

Gods

Rachel took a deep breath, then tapped her foot to the side twice. A familiar tingling alerted her to the soul checkers doing their work on and in her body.

In the break room, Anya had asked where she felt this tingling, and Rachel hadn't been able to produce words for it — that warm flash of solid aliveness, which maybe happened behind her breastbone, where she knew her heart to be. Or maybe it happened near her bellybutton, or behind her eyes.

The caller presented a rich, male voice, but no video. Not even a profile photo.

She glanced at the box in the lower corner of her screen to see which avatar she was showing. This time she looked like a young black woman, hair neatly arranged around her augmented-reality headgear, an artificial face that managed to look vacuous but fascinated at the same time, and the suggestion of an outsized bosom concealed beneath a snappy white professional blouse. She did a double-take and looked more closely. The avatar almost never resembled her — she'd been presented as a unicorn once — but this time it looked oddly like her younger self. A vacant, robotic, big-breasted version of her younger self.

She knew the machine selected an avatar based on the caller's likely preference, which made her feel exposed and a bit angry. She tugged her sweater higher on her neck and wrapped her arms across her chest, though this had no effect on her flirtatious-looking avatar. At least the caller would hear her real voice.

And on this call, she was probably hearing the caller's real voice, because although this voice was pleasant, it was too ordinary to be a purchased avatar. She looked at the stats. The call was paid for by Tiger Steers Investments, and she was talking to employee #8417, who had a 45-minute call limit. Evidently Tiger Steers didn't want #8417 spending all day on the phone.

"Good morning, fellow human," said the voice. "What's it like to be alive in your sector of planet Earth today, if Earth is indeed where you're stationed?"

"Good morning to you, too," she replied, hoping she wouldn't have to spend 45 minutes making goofy small talk. Her control screen showed her that this caller was in fact within 80 kilometers of her location in downtown Oakland, but she didn't mention it. "And your search query would be?"

"Sigh," said the voice. "Yes, sadly, we must get to it. Is that your real voice? I love it."

There was a short silence. "Are you looking for some sort of information?"

"Ah, right." The voice sighed again. "I'm doing some research into crop-seed genetics. I'm looking for possible correlations during the last 50 years between designed-seed production and the known incidents of rogue activity in the seed banks . . . ."

And so it went. Halfway through the call, the caller identified himself on Rachel's screen as "Jax." Jax wasn't phobic about talking to AI bots, as some of Human Converse's clients were, and he wasn't reluctant to search the cloud in the normal way, through his implants. He just enjoyed humans, and talking helped him think. No other human brokers at Tiger Steers were researching crop-seed commodities, so subscribing to a human-voice service was a cheap way for the company to boost his productivity.

"Have you already read about Et265?" said Rachel. "I'm pushing these old field reports over to you. Anything useful here, do you think?"

"That's *more* than 50 years ago," said Jax.

"I know, but it says here that the Et265 wheat fungus 'was seen by some as the first nail in the coffin of farmer-driven crop production.' Sounds like a social upheaval in the making. Food and Ag was telling people they could no longer control their own farming practices, so it makes me curious."

"And . . . you're thinking this might relate to the first of the violent seed-bank incidents in the late 25th century. I see. This also makes me think about the Earth Exodus movement. The stampede to get off this planet really started to pick up at about the same time." Jax's voice was quiet for a minute. "But that's what we'll talk about when I call again. Do you specialize in global food theory?"

"Not even close," said Rachel, "though I do keep a little kitchen garden in a window box, and my tomatoes and herbs are outdoing themselves this year."

"I'm glad it was you who took this call. Are all the voice workers at Human Converse so good at putting ideas together?"

"Oh, I don't know," said Rachel, chuckling.

"How long have you worked there?"

"Twenty-eight years this August, I'm embarrassed to say."

"So that means you started when you were, let's see . . . about three years old, by the sound of your voice?"

"Ha!" she said. "Though I *was* young. Seventeen, if you must know the entire truth, my age and all."

"I'm starting to wish I could know more than that," answered Jax.

Rachel hesitated. "Do you have more work to do on this call? It might be time to hang up."

"I have 63 seconds left, and I enjoy talking with you. Tell me how I can reach you — it might never happen again that you're the one to answer when I call, and—"

Rachel hung up. She was intrigued but tired, and she'd heard lines like Jax's before. She'd even fallen for them once or twice over the decades.

Not now, not while my life is so complicated, she thought as she tapped her right foot twice to the side to take the next call. Maybe later.

*
**

All his equipment was in place, and Tensel had a stable batch of stem cells cloned from Trixie. He imagined the cells in their dish in the incubator — alive, in a way, but with no macro quantum pattern of their own. The plan was to teleport the quantum state of Trixie's particles into those waiting cells. If the cells registered positive against soul fabric even for a picosecond, the trial would be a breakthrough. Tensel Brown would be the first scientist to change an entity from a non-souled state to a souled state. Stem cells with a macro quantum pattern!

He decided to run his first trial early on a Sunday morning, when he was likely to be alone in the warehouse. He wondered whether to anesthetize Trixie before the procedure, but decided not to. Maybe it would help the process for her to be conscious when her body was scanned. He'd need to bombard her with an intense laser beam, so she'd probably die quickly. He hoped so.

That Saturday while he, Jessica, and Alison ate take-out Thai and watched soccer on their wall screen, he told Jessica he needed to go back to the lab and wouldn't be home that night. She nodded, knowing what he planned to do.

Most people left the Soulistics department before 11 p.m. on weekends, but Jason seemed determined not to go home that night. He was tinkering with Thief's weft system and knocking on Tensel's door every half an hour to yell a joke through the closed door. Tensel began to get nervous. Did Jason suspect something?

But finally he left, and Tensel was alone. He could begin his real work for the night. He did a health check on Trixie, who nipped playfully at his fingers. 16.25 grams of Trixie's cloned cells lay in a wide dish of culture medium in the target chamber, ready to host the macro quantum pattern from her 16.25 gram body.

"Goodbye," he said to the small gray and gold mouse. "You'll be famous, if that's any consolation." He stroked her head a few times with his index finger, looking at her closely. She seemed relaxed, but he noticed that his own hands were shaking. In one quick motion he scooped her up and nearly threw her into the small black box of the scanner. He thought he heard a frightened squeak as he sealed the door and started the laser, or maybe it was just his imagination.

Turning away, he started up a stream of particles and sent it through the beam splitter, one half of each entangled pair aimed into the scanner, the other aimed at the 16.25 grams of stem cells. He knew that Trixie's body was being dismantled into nothing more than a collection of particles. He was frozen with dread as he turned back to the scanner, listening to the laser's placid hum.

He peered through the scanner's thick glass door, but he couldn't see anything that looked like Trixie. As data came in, his workstation performed calculations and began to irradiate Trixie's cloned stem cells, transforming the alignment of their particles to match the state of Trixie's particles at the moment of her death. All Tensel had to do now was wait.

He fell back in his chair and stared at the target chamber that contained the stem cells. His left knee quaked up and down, and he rested his hand there to stop it. Was some fundamental aspect of Trixie still alive within the cells? The filter on the back of the scanner was clogged with organic material that used to take the shape of Trixie. What should he do with it when he changed the filter? Toss it? Bury it? Cremate it? Ugh.

He pulled himself out of his morbid imaginings and queried the test results. Positive! The stem cells in the target chamber had a macro quantum pattern that originated 0.02 picoseconds after the teleportation was complete. The readings indicating Trixie's pulse, respiration, and brain functions had flatlined abruptly when her body lost structural integrity, but her quantum pattern still existed, and it was stored. And for now at least, it was stable—a better result than he'd dared to expect.

His anxious foreboding was gone. The quantum pattern was viable outside its original host. The stem cells thrived, or seemed to. They showed slightly elevated health readings, and their mass had increased by 1.4×10^{-5} percent, an exact match for his hypothesis. His first trial was a success! He threw open the door of his lab and sprinted around Joker and Thief, jumping to slap his hands against high bolts on the metal struts. Out of breath, his face shining with joy and sweat, he found a permanent marker and went back in his lab to write "MQP Database" on the side of the target chamber that held Trixie's macro quantum pattern within its stem-cell host.

Intoxicated by the terabytes of data from Trixie, he worked all day as the sounds of people and machines filled the warehouse outside his lab door. Late the next night, he nearly fell over when he stood up to stretch. Yawning, he realized he knew what to do with Trixie. He donned gloves and removed the scanner filter, careful not to dislodge any of Trixie's remains. He dropped the whole mess into a biobag, then walked it across the warehouse to Lab 28, where approved mouse testing happened. It was late, so no one was there to see him drop the bag into Lab 28's bio-disposal chute.

He walked the rest of the way home, thinking, glancing now and then at the clear sky above him as if in communion with the stars. He didn't stop to answer Jessica's questions as he passed her in the living room of their suite, but in the bedroom he paused to untie his high tops and pull them off, and then he fell across the bed in his jeans and lab coat, asleep like the dead within seconds. He didn't stir when Jessica pulled the sheet and blankets out from under him and snuggled against him under the covers, an arm thrown over his body.

A few hours later, he had a dream. In it, he extracted the soul from a small black mouse and felt his own guts sucked out of his body, then forced into the mouse's body to replace its lost soul. He had to wind into a tiny ball to fit into the tiny body. The smaller he got, the smaller the mouse's body became — cramped and claustrophobic. He woke up sweating and moaning, trying to get out, batting at the tangled sheets and Jessica.

Now sharply awake, he lay still and thought about Trixie. What had happened inside her when she died and her soul came out? "It's not a *soul*," he corrected himself in a harsh whisper. He wasn't anxious to go back to sleep and risk another dream, so he crept out of the bedroom in the dark, started a pot of coffee, and sat down by the window to think. What were the applications of his invention?

Was he creating the technology that would produce unending life? People and animals being migrated from one body to the next, like data chips moved from old gear into new? But where would these new bodies come from? Animal clones had macro quantum patterns of their own, and human clones did too, if reports from illegal human-cloning trials could be believed.

Could a body hold more than one macro quantum pattern?

Before anyone in the suite could wake up and start talking to him, he slipped into his running clothes and left. His intention was to clear his head with a run, but the questions kept coming.

What if a body and its quantum pattern were uniquely paired? In that case, what was in the target chamber back in the lab? Had he extended Trixie's existence, or had he ended it and created new life? Or could the thing in the target chamber be called *life* at all?

What, precisely, was he doing?

An intuitive dread washed over him, but he steered his thoughts back to the firm ground of logic and hard science — the stability of the scientific method. "Trust the process," he told himself. Examining moral principles was the work of the government ethics office — they determined whether inventions were safe, socially fair, and tested without coercion. Or they were *supposed* to, anyway. At some point bioethicists should also be consulted. But Tensel's field was soulistics, and his mandate was to push the limits of soulistic discovery. He had work ahead of him, and he needed a clear mind and a calm body to carry it out. Nightmares and emotional detours didn't help. He needed to get his head back in the game.

He used the rest of his run to puzzle over the technical intricacies of the next round of trials.

* *
*

Tensel returned to his lab and stayed there for the next three days and nights, sleeping only when his body made him do it, slumped in his chair or resting his head on a pile of pizza boxes and grimy paper towels. He was growing clones of all his mice in a cloning crèche that he'd borrowed from Jason. When he pondered the existential fate of the mice he felt sick, so he decided not to ponder it. The question was best left to others

— he wasn't a philosopher, ethicist, or theologian, after all. And if he'd already made an ethical misstep, maybe the next step in the pattern-transfer process would make up for it. Maybe Trixie could live again.

He left her macro quantum pattern in the database for a week. Several times a day he tapped the side of the chamber and whispered a few words of encouragement, though he knew this was irrational.

Early the next Sunday morning, he reversed his original process: he teleported Trixie's pattern out of the stem-cell host and into one of his clones, a mouse named Eixirt — "Trixie" backwards.

Science and intuition suggested that one body could hold no more than one quantum macro pattern, so he expected this trial to fail. It was rational to expect Eixirt to die, and he set up some bio-disposal equipment in his lab so he wouldn't need to sneak into Lab 28 when the time came. But even so, he was startled when Eixirt thrashed and squeaked, then died in a frothy, bloody heap half a minute after the transfer. Turning his gaze away from the bloodied eyes and ears, he lifted Eixirt by the tail and dropped him into the disposal chute, then wiped away the little patch of blood that the mouse had coughed up. "Male QMP recipient #1, probable pulmonary embolism," he wrote in his notes, leaving out Eixirt's name.

By the tenth quantum-pattern transfer, he was no longer aware of any feelings about the mice. They were lab supplies, nothing more, numbered and cataloged. He developed a systematic test plan and moved through it, varying the type and intensity of the lasers, the stem-cell cloning techniques, and the irradiation techniques that he used. Some trials went better than others, but the occasional successes fizzed in his head like caffeine and kept him moving. He hardly slept. He felt as if his energy would last forever, as if he'd found the source of it—the fountainhead. The world's mundane realities could never bring him down, not from an idea so exhilarating.

When he was at the dorm with Jessica, which was rare, he was silly and playful. But when she came to visit him at the lab, he was grouchy. It seemed odd to her that all he wanted to do was work, and yet work seemed to make him unhappy. It was confusing. After he snapped at her one time too many for interrupting him, she stopped bringing lunch to the lab.

*
**

At 1:15 a.m. the sound of soft classical guitar music roused Rachel from a chaotic dream. She'd been awake an hour before this, listening to Miriam heat up a bottle for Eliza, and she'd just now fallen back to sleep. She groaned and rolled over, pulling her comforter over her head, and at 1:17 the alarm's volume increased. Bernadine was having trouble filling shifts since the latest round of flu, and Rachel hated to say no.

At 1:20 the alarm switched from guitar music to muted horns repeating a distant call. It sounded like a fox hunt was moving this way, and she was rarely in bed long enough to hear what she knew would come in 90 more seconds: a horn blast loud enough to raise up a corpse—or maybe startle that fox to death. She shut it off, not wanting to wake Eliza or Miriam, who were cuddled together in Miriam's bed. She crossed the room to peek at them, Miriam snoring gently, Eliza wedged in the crook of her arm.

Rachel returned to her area of the room and threw a pillow down on the floor, then sat cross-legged on it. During her meditation she caught her head falling forward a few times, but she began to wake up in earnest once she turned on a tiny book light and reached for her breviary. The book contained traditional Judeo-Christian psalms and antiphons in the order they were chanted by the group of nuns who lived near St. Malcolm's. She loved the feel of the green leather cover that held the book — soft and worn, cracking and dark along the edges where her fingers had held it open several times a week for the last 20 years, ever since her divorce. It was the support and love of the people at St. Malcolm's that had gotten Rachel through it when she realized she needed to stop giving James second chances; when it became clear that she'd have to raise two small children on her own.

At St. Malcolm's she'd learned how to lean on the God she'd always believed existed, but hadn't integrated into her day-to-day life. What had been a vague assent to God's existence became a belief in God's trustworthiness and love, even when life was painful and unfair.

The day's reading was from Psalm 6, and she mouthed the words as she scanned them with her eyes: "My whole being is troubled, and my soul is in anguish. How long, Divine One, my Creator? How long?"

If the psalmist could ask God hard questions, she could too. She let her pain inhabit the words. Did God hear her prayers for her granddaughter Eliza, let alone act on them? Did God care that she worked extra hours to pay for better childcare than the scary places the state provided for free?

Anger flickered up. Screening tests showed a possible problem with baby Eliza's hearing. Did God care about the diagnostic tests the clinic wanted Eliza to get in a few months? The upgrade she might need to her neuroprosthetic implant? Speech therapy? Would God pay for all that?

Rachel spread her hands and held them open in front of her, palms up. Was she handing her troubles to God, or accepting whatever God was handing to her?

Her intention was to do both.

*
**

As Rachel settled into her call booth at Human Converse, she composed a text to Sam, asking him to do Miriam a favor by picking up Eliza and taking her to childcare. "And make sure she's been fed and changed."

Before she sent the message she stopped to think. Taking care of Eliza was up to Miriam, but Miriam would be exhausted in the morning and happy to see Sam, plus she needed to stop being late for work. Asking Sam to help seemed like the kindest thing to do, and Sam seemed to enjoy being involved.

Would Miriam be grateful for Sam's help, or would she be annoyed? Rachel's private feeling was that keeping the baby safe was more important than Miriam's feelings, but she would never put it to Miriam like that.

Or maybe Miriam would be right to be annoyed?

At times Rachel got carried away orchestrating other people's lives, and she knew it. She meant to stay grounded, stay inside her own skin, but it was just too tempting to try to help, even when people said no thank you. And too hard when a baby was involved. Miriam might do all the right things this morning, but then again she might not.

She saw with relief and a flash of guilt that the first caller in her queue was Jax, and she couldn't help but relax when she heard his warm voice over the line.

They'd talked a few times now, and Jax was becoming a friend. He liked to flirt, but he wasn't looking for romance—he was just lonely. In their last conversation he'd told her why he didn't turn on his camera: a diving accident had left him a quadriplegic, and his mind-controlled wheelchair made him self-conscious. "Good thing Tiger Steers lets me work at home," he'd said, "because with this rig it's a big hassle to get out of the house. And besides, I like to hang around in my pajamas."

Rachel switched her video output to a live view of her own face, knowing she'd see no more than a blank screen, or maybe an avatar, on Jax's end. "Stop calling me at work!" she said, only half meaning it. "If we keep this up I might get Bernadine in trouble."

"She'll manage," said Jax's voice. "So how are you?"

"Exhausted," she said, "but okay. Now we should hang up and go back to work like grown ups. Both of us. You shouldn't waste your employer's money like this."

"Talking to you a waste of money? Never. And besides, they don't care how much time I spend on the phone, as long as I get my work done. How's Eliza? What did the doctor say?"

Well, if he was willing to listen, she was willing to talk.

"They've narrowed it down to an inner-ear deformity. The doctor said our toxic world causes a lot of problems these days, and he could've stopped there, but *no*, he had to keep talking. He said that in Eliza's case, the problem might've been helped along by 'extra' chemicals she was exposed to in the womb, beyond the usual noxious stew that every baby gestates in these days if their parents can't afford innerbots." She paused, not wanting to say more about the recreational drugs that might've been the source of those 'extra' chemicals. She tried never to say anything negative about her children.

Trying to forget Miriam for the moment, she turned her focus back to her granddaughter. "On her next visit they'll do more expensive testing, and they mentioned a cochlear upgrade to her regular implant—"

Rachel started to cry, and as the tears flowed, so did the words. So much for restraint. "Miriam hardly notices what's happening with her own daughter," she continued. "I paid her VR bill this month, because I know she can't afford it. I took a look at her bank balance to make sure she really did need me to step in, because I don't like to meddle unless it's absolutely necessary. When I told my covenant group about it, Porsha told me it would be a gift to let Miriam experience the consequences of her own behavior. But how can I do that when the consequences affect Eliza? And won't Miriam learn how to handle life experiences by watching *me* do it?"

Rachel's rested her head against the back of the call booth and closed her eyes. "I'm happy to help her," she said, "but sometimes I need support too!"

She almost never let it all out like this. Damn, it felt good.

When she opened her eyes, she noticed with a start that a visual image was coming through from Jax's end. How long had it been there? It wasn't an avatar, but it didn't seem to be Jax either. What Rachel saw looked like a fluffy white fox with seal point markings: dark gray ears, legs, muzzle, and tail. It was on a table, standing up in a plush pet bed, leaning toward the camera as if examining her.

Had this animal been sitting with Jax every time they'd talked? She'd never actually seen Jax, after all, so she had no idea what, or who, was in the room with him.

"Oh!" said Rachel. "What's that?"

"It's Jasper," said Jax's voice, "and he and I are *both* supporting you. I thought you might take some comfort in meeting him. Jasper, meet my friend Rachel. Rachel, this is my familiar transgenic, Jasper. I think you'd much rather see Jasper than me."

Jasper's teeth were bared and his lips were turned up at the edges, like a grin. He lifted his paws and touched his nose to the camera as he was introduced, and Rachel leaned back instinctively as the wet black nose and blurry grey muzzle filled her screen.

"Your familiar *what*?" Sweet Jesus, were these two a couple of some sort?

"My familiar transgenic," he said, his pride obvious. "Jasper was engineered to match me; in fact, his genome includes selected genes duplicated from mine."

"You match." Rachel had heard about unnatural things like this, though she'd never met anyone with personal experience. "So is he some kind of . . . human?"

"No," said Jax, "not even close, as you can see. Though he seems more human than some people I know. And in case you're wondering, nothing, umm, *untoward* goes on between us."

"So he's a pet."

Jasper's "smile" dissolved and his ears dropped. His tail, which looked like a dog's, stopped wagging.

"Jasper is my second self," said Jax's voice. "He goes everywhere with me. He's a precious comfort, and I thought he might cheer you up. To me, he's a symbol of tech's power to help us with our suffering. It's amazing what can be done, and I thought he might give you hope."

Rachel had stopped crying.

"Tech isn't God," she said.

"What's the difference?" said Jax.

Transfer

If it's meant spiritually, don't interpret it physically.
Active imaginations cause a world of trouble!
—From *The Cloud of Unknowing (51)*

Tensel was on his way out of the campus Starbucks when Sam Deimos called to him from a table by the window. Sam's headset held his neatly twisted locs away from his face, and his T-shirt read "Quantum Biophysicists Entangle in the Lab." It seemed as if his fingers were covered with titanium and copper rings, though he wore only five, three on his left hand and two on his right. He retracted his face screen so his face showed clearly, etiquette not everyone followed when having an in-person conversation. Sam had inherited his father's intellect but not the man's snobby aloofness, so it was easy to talk tech with Sam, easy to linger, easy to take a seat, and before he knew it Tensel was explaining his idea of transferring macro quantum patterns from one animal into another.

After he described the results of his latest mouse trial, a qualified success with female QMP recipient #48, he stopped talking and took a sudden interest in his espresso cup, as if wondering whether it was to blame for his gush of words.

"So . . . ," Sam ventured, "it sounds like you want to do more testing. Maybe you want to explore what soul transfer could be like for humans? Your soul-fabric manufacturing research and all these classes you have to teach are a bit boring right now because you'd rather be working on this other thing, is that right?"

Tensel looked up. "Yes."

Sam had become more relaxed around Tensel since he'd entered the Biophysics work-study program and become

Tensel's assistant. But Tensel was still Sam's instructor, his employer, and way ahead of him in the field. Sam would stay awed, no matter how friendly he and Tensel became, but he also knew when the moment was right to offer a suggestion.

"If I may," he said, watching Tensel's face for a negative response, "I think I know what you might want to do." Tensel looked up with interest, so Sam continued. "I think you need to ask directly for what you want, even if it's uncomfortable. That's what I did. I wanted my senior thesis to be about a novel quantum communication system, and I asked Dr. K straight up. At first he acted like it was a stupid idea, but that's because he didn't understand it, so I had to play to his strengths and sell it to him."

Tensel was silent but paying attention.

"So what I'm thinking is that you need to *sell* your idea to him," Sam continued, "and to do that you need to figure a few things out. Let's start with this: what exactly do you want? What do you need?"

"Well . . . time and money for research. To be released from my other responsibilities. Someone to pay for human testing and cut through the legal questions and paperwork."

"Ah. Human testing is gonna be a big ask, but what I'd do is start small and ask for human testing later, after you get the money and time you need, and after you show Dr. K you mean business. If you want, I can help you make a plan. Want to role-play the first conversation you have with Dr. K on this subject?"

Sam saw a look on Tensel's face that combined terror and disgust, but he pressed on. "It's logical to practice, at least once. C'mon, I'll walk you through it. Make your mistakes on me. What might you say to him?"

Tensel glanced around, but everyone at the nearby tables was engrossed in their own virtual or enhanced reality. He began in a quiet voice. "Ahem. Dr. Kendel. I've successfully transplanted the q-node area of the macro quantum pattern of a mammalian subject onto a semi-organic database created from stem-cell conglomerates removed from—"

Sam stifled a laugh, then turned serious again at the look on Tensel's face. "Sorry, sorry!" he said. "It's just that Dr. K isn't a detail guy, he's a big-picture guy, and he likes to be involved. Let him feel involved, and he'll like the idea a lot better."

"Involved?" Tensel smiled faintly. "That's asking a lot."

"Well, talk about the kinds of things he understands and wants to hear about."

Tensel let out a single, quiet "Ha!" of a laugh. "VR porn? Immigrant jokes?"

"No!" said Sam, "I mean *practical* things. Tell him what your idea's good for. Tell him its uses, and how the ends will justify the means. What will *he* get out of this? Could it earn money for the department, and indirectly for him? Maybe even directly for him? And definitely use the word 'soul,' because you're the only person around here who refuses to say it."

Ah. Sam was clearly better at this kind of task than he was.

They kept talking, and half an hour later Tensel still wasn't sure he could convince Dr. Kendel to let him spend time on his idea, but he was determined to try. And Sam seemed to believe that if the conversation didn't go perfectly, he could learn from it and try again later.

*
**

Tensel bit his thumbnail and shifted on the hard bench where he waited in the hall.

Ten minutes later, Dr. Kendel swept into the building, beckoned for Tensel to follow him into his office, and motioned to a seat in front of his cluttered desk. "Sorry I'm late," he said, then added in a stage whisper, "My wife's lawyer couldn't wait a minute longer to tell me her latest demand."

He settled into his desk chair, which looked ready to give up on its attempt to contain him. Though he was a few decades past his last scrimmage, Dr. Kendel still had the physique of a linebacker. "Okay, there," he said, gripping the chair's arms as if holding the chair together. "What did you need to talk to me about?"

"Well Dr. Kendel," said Tensel, pulling his own chair closer to the desk, as Sam had coached him to do, "I have this, I have this, I have this data." He hated that he stuttered when he was nervous, and when he noticed he was doing it, it got worse. He took a long, slow breath, another idea from Sam.

Dr. Kendel frowned, a look that drew attention to his impressive neck, probably made of solid muscle like the rest of him. "So you've already spent time on whatever this is?"

"Yes . . . no! Not my sponsor's time, my free time. But listen: what if you could extract your own macro quantum pattern, then impress your pattern onto a clone of yourself? Later? What if you could store a macro quantum pattern for days or even years? Your, your, your soul, I mean. What if you could move it from one cloned body to the next? I've done it with mice, with . . . one mouse. I need to solve a few technical problems . . . ." He trailed off, remembering that he needed to cut to the chase. "But in short, it'll work, and it'll make money."

"What are you saying? People could do this, not just mice?" Dr. Kendel put his hands on the desk and leaned forward, narrowing his eyes. "Why?"

Tensel hesitated. "We're years from this result, but I can get there: individual humans can be re-created. Reconstituted, transferred from one clone of themselves to the next. Genetically closer to the original than a child could ever be. Soulistically closer to the original than a clone could ever be. Possibly with a macro quantum pattern identical to the original."

"You mean you can clone souls."

"No. I'm saying I can move a . . . 'soul' from one place to another."

"Ah. So the original becomes *uninhabited?*"

"Correct. The original body can't survive."

Dr. Kendel was silent. "You're talking about eternal life," he said, then lapsed into more silence. He frowned and pressed his fist into his chin, thinking. "I understand why you brought this to me. And soul cloning?"

"Not possible." Tensel's words came more easily now that he was out of sales and back to his idea. "The continual shifting of a macro quantum pattern is part of the pattern, and the pattern can only exist in one physical location, one host, across any given time span. It can't be copied, only moved."

"I see." Tensel could almost hear the train of Dr. Kendel's thoughts chugging along its tracks. "Human trials will be tricky," he said. "But you've done it with animals, you say? Mice?"

"Yes. One successful trial."

"Live mouse trials aren't exactly legal. And as for the experiments you've done on soul matter, well, some of the more conservative pastors in town would string you up for that, you know. Tampering with a live animal, and a live soul."

"Well, I, I, of course. But I hope you can help me get around any legal problems with the animal trials I've already done. And as for 'soul tampering,' this is a scientific question, not a religious one."

Dr. Kendel's train of thought was picking up speed, and he talked faster now, a grin spreading across his face. "Yes, and those religious folks are after eternal life too, aren't they? Ha ha. One successful mouse trial, you said? Well, with a potential upside this big, one trial done by a genius is a good enough start for me."

He stood up and came around the desk with alarming speed to clap Tensel on the back. "Tensel my boy, I've watched you during your time at Stanford, and if you say you can make it work for humans, then by God, you can make it work for humans. Getting you what you need is all about loosening up money and greasing wheels, and that is one of my gifts. Leave it to me."

"Thank you . . . sir." Tensel leaned away from the brawny hand thumping him on the back. He wondered if he was about to be offered a cigar.

Dr. Kendel returned to his chair, snapped his AR headset into place, and picked up an air stylus. "Okay. You have data, you say? I want it. And explain your technique to me in plain English, draw me some word pictures, and I'll write us a one-pager. Plus I'll need you to memorize an elevator pitch, because I don't want you fucking this up. Ha ha! What corp wouldn't pay big bucks for this?"

And then a look of wonder spread across Dr. Kendel's face, as if only now had the real upside of Tensel's idea dawned on him. "And too bad, Linda," he said in a low voice, looking down at his hands, "because *you* won't see a *penny* of it, given how fast you're making this divorce happen."

*
**

It didn't take long for Dr. Kendel to find a sympathetic ear at the Wolf Corp, which hired both him and Tensel into its philanthropic division, the Center for the Study of Post-Earth Arks. The Ark Project was a sleepy corner of Wolf that seemed to exist only for the tax write-off, but Tensel's discovery was what they'd been waiting for. As if an accountant in a back room had opened a valve, a river of money washed over everything involved in Tensel's idea. Tensel found himself with an annual salary larger than he'd expected to earn in years as an academic. On the Wolf campus, the island that dominated the artificial lake was renamed "Ark Island," and employees were moved out of its work spaces, labs, testing facilities, and corp apartments to make room for all things Ark.

Tensel was excused from teaching, and excused from finishing his thesis, and Dr. Kendel was pushing Stanford to give him an honorary doctorate. Ark hired eight research assistants for him, and Tensel made sure that Sam and Sam's friend Arjuna, a statistician already employed by Wolf, were on the list. He needed a few people who were easy for him to be around, and people like that were rare.

Applying this tech to humans was the most complex problem Tensel had ever faced, and the flurry of activity pushed away his nagging doubts and discomfort.

At least at first.

*
* *

At the weekly status meetings Tensel stared into space, eyes wide, leaving the agenda and action items to Sam. He was slightly more present when he, Sam, and Arjuna took over the corner conference room once or twice a week to consult with each other.

"I need more access," said Arjuna at one of these ad hoc meetings, absently running a stylus back and forth across his mustache. "I can't run my full simulation without some sensitive data on potential candidates. I sent you a list of what I need, Sam. It's blocked by the FCC. Somebody has to unblock me." His black hair flopped across his eyes, and Sam wondered how he saw anything but his in-eye data. Maybe he didn't.

"Sure thing," said Sam. "I'm guessing Dr. K can help. I'll figure it out."

Arjuna was 29, old by Wolf standards, and his genius was in coaxing the AI to find overlooked patterns in big data. His task was to find a pool of candidates for human testing, even though approval for any such thing would be a long time coming, if it ever did. The Wolf Corp hired competitive, compulsive people, then asked them to define their own idea of success, so Arjuna worded his 2646 first-quarter goal like this: "Identify at least 2,000 ideal candidates for soul transfer." No half-way benchmarks for him; only "ideal" would do.

Tensel was usually interested in the technicalities of Arjuna's work, but today he didn't ask questions and had nothing to say about his own work. Sam was worried. "You okay?"

Tensel nodded.

"You seem kinda low energy."

No reply, and Sam knew not to push. He'd hoped to ask Tensel for advice about a few challenges he had with his own lab work, but now wasn't the time. He stood up. "Okay, good job, guys. Let me know if you need anything else."

*
**

Two weeks later, Tensel was still in a funk. Dr. Kendel swept into the lab and waved a hand in front of his face. "I'm taking you to lunch on the corp credit card, off campus. Don't say no. We're going." Tensel *was* a bit hungry, so he disengaged from his gear and unfolded his tall frame from the workstation chair.

Dr. Kendel spent the first half of lunch firing volleys of small talk that weren't returned and indulging in a few complaints about Linda's bitchiness: was all this shit-flinging really good for the kids? And Jesus, he hardly ever got to see those kids nowadays anyway, which made him sad. But the upside was that he had pretty much nothing to do but work. Getting lots done!

Over his third whiskey sour, he got to the point of the lunch. "You're behind schedule," he said to Tensel.

"I don't work to minor milestones," said Tensel, who was concentrating on a beer. He hadn't shaved for a few days, and if it hadn't been for a 20-credit bill passed from Dr. Kendel to the maître d', his ripped T-shirt and flip-flops would've kept them out of the restaurant. "I work toward the end result. I'm doing fine."

"Well, we can flex with your distaste for schedules — hell, we're being as flexible as a pile of wet noodles for you," said Dr. Kendel, "but it looks to our investors like you're not on the ball. Your status reports are ridiculously sparse. How can I change that?"

Tensel just looked at him.

"Your sleep monitors show you getting less than three hours a night. That has to change. How can you sleep in that crazy dorm suite with all those nutcases? Do you want to move?"

More silence.

"Maybe Jessica wants to move? Maybe it would help. Privacy, room to stretch your limbs or dance a jig on the kitchen table or whatever it is you do in your free time . . . ."

"It's fine," said Tensel.

Dr. Kendel decided to take "it" to mean the idea of Tensel and Jessica moving to a quieter place.

"Wonderful! I'll make it happen, and Ark will pay, of course. Start packing. I have just the place for you two — the penthouse suite of the corp apartments. You can see it from here." He pointed out the window, toward the top of the high rise on Ark Island. "You'll like being closer to work."

*
**

The noise and chaos of roommates had always been more of a problem for Jessica than for Tensel. The silence in the penthouse unnerved him. He lay awake night after night, chasing thoughts around the track of his vast mind. He was haunted by the same intuitive dread that he'd had after extracting Trixie's macro quantum pattern, and he wondered about the rightness of what he and his team were doing. With so much money floating around, and so many people on the project, had it already gained more momentum than anyone could stop?

He could've taken sleeping pills, or even programmed the innerbots coursing through his body to incline him toward sleep, but he didn't. Maybe some part of him believed that he deserved these sleepless nights. That it would be wrong to take a shortcut away from his troubled thoughts.

One night, he lay turning from his left side to his right, then onto his back, then onto his left again — each time being careful not to pull the covers off Jessica or bounce the bed and wake her up. Every position felt awkward. He watched the clock obsessively — 2 a.m., then 3, then 4. He gave up on sleep, and his new goal became to lie there until dawn. Then, unexpectedly, he fell asleep.

He was awakened what seemed like only a second later when Jessica raised the bedroom lights and opened the blinds, revealing a painfully bright morning.

"Sorry, but you need to get up," she said. "There's only one way to cure your insomnia, and that's to reset your internal clock. It's time to be awake."

She sat on the edge of the bed, holding a cup of coffee toward him. "C'mon," she said, when he didn't move. "You can do it. You're getting up right now. I'm making you do this because I love you."

He groaned, then sat up and shook his head, running a hand through his tangled hair. He squinted at Jessica, his eyes taking on a silver cast in the glare. "Damn it!" he said, "I'd finally fallen asleep. Finally! Why would you do this?"

The smile left her face, and her eyes went blank. "Wow," she said, "I was just trying to help." She set the coffee down hard on the nightstand, spilling part of it, and shut the door hard behind her as she left.

Tensel fell back on the bed and closed his eyes. No way he'd be able to get back to sleep now.

*
**

Months passed, and Tensel's spiral continued its downward bend. One morning he woke before dawn, seeing in his personal stats that he'd slept less than two hours. Not unusual these days, as Dr. Kendel and Jessica never tired of pointing out. He lay on his back and stared at the darkness, resting in its emptiness. It had a comforting simplicity, darkness. It asked nothing. Said nothing.

Dim ceiling lights came up as Jessica's alarm vibrated, and Tensel closed his eyes before she could see that he was awake. He'd made it clear that he didn't want words in the mornings, but sometimes she forgot and talked to him anyway. That never happened when she thought he was asleep. He listened to her shower and dress for the day — probably jeans and a T-shirt, as usual. She'd probably spend the day at the library, or maybe in class. Was school even in session now? He couldn't remember.

He heard the microwave start up in the kitchen. He imagined Jessica with her sleek hair combed and wet, eating her bowl of steel-cut oatmeal in silence, alone.

The front door closed, and he exhaled with relief. He rolled to a sitting position on the edge of their king-sized bed, sat for a few minutes, then shifted into the living room and lay down on the couch. He brought up the house menu and blinked a command to close the shades, blocking out their million-credit view of the Ark lake and the foothills beyond.

It was afternoon when he found the energy to get dressed and leave the penthouse. He was outside only long enough to cross the street, but those few seconds of outdoor air, filtered into a delightful fresh-air mix by the nanobots in his lungs, lifted his mood. As he paused in the doorway of the lab, he felt glad to see Sam, who'd already swiveled his chair to face the door. "Heads up," Sam said. "Dr. K's in the reactor room."

"Great." Tensel sat down at the workstation next to Arjuna's. Arjuna's face screen was opaque, a privacy icon alight on its surface. His hair flopped over the top of the screen, making him look like a roughly smudged version of his regular self, with no nose, mustache, or mouth.

"What's Dr. K doing, anyway?" Tensel asked Sam.

"He's breathing on the animal-cloning crèches and acting like he knows how they work. I'll keep an eye on him."

"Okay." Tensel activated the face screen on his own headset, darkened it, and activated his privacy icon.

Sam turned his chair back to his own workstation. The webcam feed from the reactor room showed Dr. Kendel fiddling with dials, and Sam winced. Sandra would probably need half the afternoon to sterilize and recalibrate the equipment.

At six, Tensel pulled off his headset and stretched, refused an offer of dinner, then left without speaking.

Sam sat for a moment. Tensel never had much sense of humor, but what little he'd had was gone. He swore more. His cheeks looked long and empty, his eyes dull and flat. At first he'd worked on this project with quiet intensity, carried along by some life-giving current that was his version of joy, but now work was clearly something else for him.

*
* *

Tensel maundered down the hall, taking a slow lap around the third floor. In so many ways, he felt *off*. Was he doing the right thing by investigating quantum macro patterns, or was this whole line of inquiry immoral?

He didn't have a clear sense of what Ark intended to do with his work. He'd signed his contract with them so quickly, and it had changed his life in unexpected ways, and Jessica's too.

Jessica. Did he need to break up with her? But how? "I'm at Ark right now," he whispered to himself, reeling his mind back into the present. He turned his thoughts to work.

Maybe his ennui was caused by being stuck: how could he make it viable to transfer human macro quantum patterns if he couldn't test on humans? Every species has a distinctive type of quantum pattern, so no animal experiment could give him the data he needed—what he needed to test was humans. He thought of Sam. Brilliant, eager, ready to help with whatever came up. Would Sam agree to be a test subject? He stopped abruptly and leaned his forehead against the corridor wall, ashamed for thinking such a thing.

They needed the go-ahead for randomized human trials, and they needed it now, but Dr. Kendel kept giving him non-answers. We're working on it. It's complicated. It's a delicate political situation. Blah blah blah.

Dr. K's latest non-answer included a bit more detail: teams at Ark were making progress on political and legal issues, but the PR team's coordinated salvo of marketing probes had returned data that showed surprising resistance to soul-transfer tech. In fact, the team might *never* find a way to make the tech seem neutral, let alone desirable, from the perspective of John Q. Public. Human testing would mean political death for Wolf's lobbyists, even if they could find willing test subjects.

Why did Dr. Kendel talk about science in PR and political terms? And had there ever been any question of *unwilling* test subjects? The conversation made Tensel feel like he needed a run and a hot shower. He remembered that Dr. Kendel was currently in the reactor room, probably half hoping they'd started to clone humans on the sly. As if they could hide such a thing from the press.

Did Dr. Kendel and Ark's execs have private plans to move human testing forward? Were they keeping secrets from him? Dr. Kendel talked too much, and when he was on a roll he was liable to blurt out just about anything. Maybe he'd told Sam something! Tensel hurried back into the lab, stopping just short of Sam's chair.

"I'm losing control of my work," he exclaimed. "What's Ark doing with my idea?"

Sam retracted his face screen and leaned back, alarmed. "If anyone's privy to the details, it's you."

"I thought so too. But Dr. K and those Ark suits have a hidden agenda, I just know it. Secrets. Are people acting strange?"

"Umm . . . yes."

"I *knew* it," said Tensel, missing the significance of Sam's smile.

For Ark to care about the work it had to have a practical purpose, a money-making purpose. He knew that, and yet some part of him had refused to think it all the way through. Now that the idea was in the front of his mind, a more sinister question rode along with it: was Ark planning to use his technology for something unethical?

"Is it unethical?" he said, speaking only the tail end of his thought.

"No," Sam said, glancing at the door, "of course not." His smile was gone, and his hands were braced on the arms of his chair.

Tensel shifted closer and touched Sam's arm with his own. He didn't have much instinct about personal space, and he didn't notice that they were touching. "My colleagues think we're out of bounds, don't they?" he said. "I've heard that scientists outside of Ark think it's wrong even to consider using this technology on humans. Is that how you see it?"

Sam looked pained. He wished Tensel would back off and give him room to breathe. He always saw the good in people, and he liked Tensel a lot, but it was hard to think clearly with anyone so awkwardly close, let alone a person this intense. His mind went back to yesterday's conversation with Dr. Kendel.

Dr. Kendel had phoned when Sam was on the streetcar, away from the lab and away from Tensel. Sam blinked to answer the call before he stopped to think about the timing — this call was meant to be off the record. Even though he took the call audio-only, he arranged his face in a smile. Dr. Kendel was the type of person who might use one of those crazy high-end video setups. Some systems could infer facial expressions based on any nearby data stream that could be hacked — data streams like security feeds, retinal cameras belonging to people near Sam on the streetcar, Sam's bio readings, or who knew what else.

"What's up?" said Sam as Dr. Kendel's ruddy face filled his in-eye display.

Dr. Kendel was so close to his camera that it was impossible to see anything about his context. "Our favorite mad scientist is clinically depressed," he said without preamble. "Keep an eye on him. In fact, consider it part of your job."

Sam tried to stay fixed in his usual friendly smile, including the muscles next to his eyes. He knew it was hard to fool the affective software some people used to interpret other people's emotions. As for Sam, he was fairly good at reading emotions without a software assist, and he found the flow of affective data annoying, so he rarely used it.

"Well, that's a weird request. Tensel's my friend."

"That's why you're perfect for the job, Sam. Tensel likes you, and our latest psych scan shows that the nodes you activate in his psyche are more consequential than the ones Jessica activates, which is new. You now resonate almost 5 psi-specs closer to his conscious awareness than Jessica does. Congratulations."

"Whoa," said Sam. "Intrusive much? Can you scan my psyche too?"

Dr. Kendel chuckled. "Of course we can, and if you're wondering whether it's okay for us to do it, you might want to take another look at Ark's employee privacy policy. But you've got nothing to worry about; background-process psych scans don't come cheap, you know!"

"Glad I'm so important to you."

"Oh, you *are* important, and if we need more info you'll be on the scan list too, trust me. But one thing I like about you is that what's on your mind usually finds its way out your mouth. Seems to me our profile on you is already pretty good."

"I want to talk this over with Tensel," said Sam. "I'll have to tell him you asked me to keep an eye on him."

"I'm sure you can understand why that wouldn't be helpful," said Dr. Kendel. "We all want the same thing: a healthy, happy, productive Dr. Brown." Dr. Kendel insisted on calling Tensel "Dr. Brown," even though the honorary doctorate was still forthcoming. "If you tell him about this conversation it'll bother him, and that's the opposite of what we're shooting for. He has plenty to think about already, and he's happiest when thinking about work, not his own state of mind or big existential crises or whatever. We all know that."

"Given his depression, *shouldn't* he think about his state of mind?"

"Now's not the time. For now let's stick with what brings us the results we need. We'll feed him meds, distract him with work, and keep Sam nearby, our loyal Golden Retriever, ready to absorb his moods and handle the people stuff. Heh heh."

Dr. Kendel looked pleased with himself. "And voila, Dr. Brown back to maximum output. You should be proud of the role you play."

"Wow," said Sam. "So lemme make sure I have this straight: Tensel's depressed, but Ark needs him functional, so you won't tell him about his condition or get him proper treatment. Instead you'll sneak around and fix it behind the scenes. And you want me to help."

"Ha ha! Exactly. I knew you'd get it. Sounds like we have a deal. And by the way, this *is* proper treatment, in case your conscience bothers you. We're helping him get back to work, and what makes him healthy and happy other than work? Why burden him with something he's not good at, namely handling his own emotional state?"

For once Sam said nothing. His days and nights were already filled with all things Tensel. He set up and ran big-data calculations on Tensel's behalf, monitored animal tests, wrote status reports, reminded Tensel to eat and go to meetings, and he'd even reminded him that his anniversary with Jessica was coming up. When Tensel was unimpressed by the fact, Sam made reservations for two at Jessica's favorite restaurant, sent her a calendar invite from Tensel, and told Tensel to go to the restaurant when the time came. Maybe he was already doing what Dr. Kendel was asking him to do? But the way Dr. Kendel described it made him feel squirmy and unclean.

"And remember, you've got backup!" Dr. Kendel was saying. "We'll step in if we see him with a gun in his mouth or whatever, or if it looks like he's about to fuck up the project, of course. Otherwise he's all yours. You have two jobs now, your regular one, and handling Tensel. Don't worry, you'll see the adjustment in your next paycheck. Carry on!"

"If you say so," said Sam, unable to keep the disgust and anger off his face any longer. Clearly his disdain wouldn't make any difference to Dr. Kendel.

*
**

"Of course your work is ethical," said Sam, nudging Tensel's arm back to a comfortable distance. "You and I both know that every invention can be used to do harm, but harm's not inevitable. In the big scheme of things, Wolf's done a lot of good in the world, more good than harm, and we have no reason to think they won't stay the course with the Ark Project. At this point we need to do our jobs and trust others to do theirs." Sam hesitated, hating what he was about to say. "Your mind will clear if you just . . . get back to work."

"I'm sorry," Tensel mumbled. He sat down at his workstation, slipped a headset over his eyes and ears, and lit his privacy icon.

Sam was alone again. "No problem," he muttered, lost in thought.

*
**

That night Tensel had a nightmare that woke him up, shaking and disoriented. He stood facing a full-grown clone of himself, looking into the man's eyes to see if they were the same stormy gray-blue as his own. But there wasn't any color in the clone's eyes, only a distorted reflection, and behind it an absence like the vacuum of space.

He spent the rest of the night on the couch, and at dawn he messaged Sam with a priority beacon. "I'm wiped," he said. "Do the status meeting without me."

The beacon woke Sam from a sound sleep. With his eyes still closed, he sent a response from his in-eye display. "No prob. U still need to finish that pattern analysis tho."

Ugh. Covering for Tensel all the time felt wrong, and the famous "Dr. Brown" was becoming more of a myth than a presence around the lab. Sam coaxed him to do little bits of work, like a mother coaxing a baby to eat bites of mashed food. But in spite of Sam's best efforts, Tensel's productivity ramped toward zero.

Meanwhile, Ark's lobbyists were chipping away at human-cloning regulations, pushing for a crack in the law wide enough to let the FDA approve Ark's request for limited human testing. The day they succeeded, Tensel's morning message to Sam was longer than usual. "Migraine, puking. Dr. K won't let me control the testing. Says it's to give me a rest, says I'm more needed on other projects, but I don't buy it. Find out what you can."

For Sam it was easiest to read situations in person, so later that morning he found a reason to visit the 35th floor. "Hey Dr. K," he said, stopping in Dr. Kendel's doorway. "Need help reconfiguring the cloning room? Tensel has a small headache today, and I told him to take it easy. Plus having plenty of flexibility seems to help his mood. I know how he wants the tests set up, so until he can be here himself, I'd be happy to stand in for him in the planning meetings, or whatever you need."

"No testing-setup design for you, Sam," said Dr. Kendel, leaning back in his chair and putting his hands behind his head. "And none for Dr. Brown either. I know what you're after —he wants you to keep him in every loop, but we have enough people on human testing, so don't worry about it. Your job is to help Dr. Brown get back to theorizing."

"Sure, but it's his tech they're testing. Shouldn't he be involved?"

Dr. Kendel sat up and smiled. "Now that's an interesting thing to say, and technically incorrect. It's *not* his tech, not anymore, but we do need his brain up and running. His brain is one of our most precious assets, and one of our most expensive." He frowned. "So Dr. Brown's job is to get his head screwed back on, and a big part of your job, as you might recall, is to help him do it."

"Ah," said Sam. "Okay."

He was about to leave, then paused. He liked working for Tensel, but his own expertise was quantum entanglement. His idea was to create pairs of biologically active entangled particles, separate them, implant them in animals, and make use of the "communication" that the particles had with each other. What if one half of each pair was on Earth and the other half was light-years away? It wasn't every day that he had Dr. K's undivided attention, so he squared himself in the doorway and made his pitch.

"I realize that helping Tensel is key to my work here at Ark," he began, "but I'd like to work on some of my own ideas, and I'd like your support, maybe in the form of machine time and a few hours a week of tech help. You're familiar with my thesis topic, and it might interest Ark: I think I can solve real-time long distance communication, given time and some resources. I know that the subject interests Ark—how could it not? And if I develop it while I work here, it'll be Ark's intellectual property. So: a great deal for Ark, it would make me happy, and it would make you look *fantastic*."

He reacquainted Dr. Kendel with the specifics. "If it works," he concluded, "we can use it for real-time communication with the colonies on Io and Titan, the storage asteroids in the belt, plus any extrasolar expeditions Earth might launch. The key is that certain organic materials need to be in place at the receiving location. So if we want to communicate with, say, Mars, we have to send a receiver to Mars by classical means. But once things are up and rolling, we'll have instant communication.

Sound, images, VR immersion, the works — all with no lag. Think about it!"

"Sounds good, Sam. Too good to be true until you put hard data on it. I'm fine with you using Ark's equipment to run your tests, and I'm even fine with you getting help from the other techs, as long as it never interferes with anyone's regular work, of course. And if you get a working prototype, I'm all ears. Fair enough?"

Sam nodded.

"But when it comes to handling Dr. Brown, you can't delegate that. It's always your top priority, and I look forward to your next status report on his interior state." Dr. Kendel switched to a whisper and spoke behind his hand. "This is off the record, of course." He smiled and folded his hands across his lap.

Sam gave a thumbs up.

In the elevator back down, he relished his excitement about having the go ahead to research his own idea, then shook his head at his gift for getting in the middle of things. How did he end up not only trying to figure out Tensel for Dr. K, but also trying to figure out Dr. K for Tensel? Sometimes he feared being overwhelmed by the needs and emotions of the people around him — his sister Miriam, Tensel, and even Rachel, his mom.

But sometimes he felt both overwhelmed *and* left out. How could you feel left out when you were being overwhelmed? And yet, somehow, he did.

He called Tensel to check in. Better to be overwhelmed than left out.

Soul mate

Love and death are equally strong.
—Song of Solomon 8:6

Tensel skipped work the rest of the week. The first day he felt up to it, he arrived at 12:30, hoping everyone would be at lunch. He wanted to check out the human-testing facility and make it back to the penthouse without talking to anyone.

But before he'd taken his coat off, Dr. K messaged him. "Come see me. Now!" Damn those sensors — nothing came or went unremarked at Ark. He headed for the elevator, smoothing the front of his wrinkled shirt as he rode up to the 35th floor. Jessica had a few Vicodin tablets left over from her knee surgery, and he'd taken half a tablet before leaving the penthouse. Now that his already crappy day included face time with Dr. Kendel, he was doubly grateful for the little pill.

Dr. Kendel started talking before Tensel even sat down. "Dr. Brown, I'll get straight to the point. What the hell is wrong with you?"

Dr. Brown. Tensel cringed.

"You're not making progress," Dr. Kendel was saying. "Sam spins tales about your headaches and whatnot, and I know you've been depressed. We've tried to help. My sympathies, but frankly, given how much we pay you, could you find a way to move past it? You're not helpless, you're not a little boy."

Tensel hunched over in his chair and made a choking noise.

"Are you sick? What's wrong?" Dr. Kendel jumped out of his chair and came around the desk toward Tensel. He was crying. "Oh *shit*," said Dr. Kendel, returning to his chair. "What's the problem?"

Tensel didn't respond, and Dr. Kendel thought for a moment. The shrinks had told him not to confront Dr. Brown too harshly, and maybe they were right. Then again, *their* approach hadn't brought much in the way of results. What would make the ever-complicated Dr. Brown man up? He forced a smile onto his face. "Come on, let's talk, scientist to scientist. What's the problem? You can tell me."

Tensel choked back a sob, and then the words poured out. "I can't stay on the project," he said. "Experimenting with a living creature's pattern is, it's, it's morally questionable. Logic says it's a bad idea, a genie in a bottle, but I went ahead with it anyway on the mice, and now the rats are going through it, and soon we'll do it to *humans*. I wish, I wish I'd never started this chain reaction. I wish I could undo what I did. I wanted human testing, but I was wrong. We shouldn't do it!"

Dr. Kendel leaned back, on terra firma now that he knew what the problem was. "Ah geez. Nothing's even *happened* yet. Your conscience has nothing to worry about. The human trials are limited for now, as you know. We only have the go-ahead to create a few human clones and blast 'em with our thus far primitive soul-suppression tech — and what's wrong with that? In theory their own souls will reestablish themselves after we stop suppressing them, so they'll never know the difference once the tests are done. And you're not even *working* on the human trials, such as they are! If anyone should be queasy, it's those techs down in soulistics, refitting the crèches so they can grow humans — ugh, that's just gross. Am I right? Gross but necessary, heh."

He grinned as he continued. "Just don't think about it in too much detail and you'll be fine. That's how I handle it. And by the time we actually remove people's souls — if we ever clear these legal and PR hurdles, that is — it'll be perfectly safe.

We're moving forward in steps, baby steps. Safe, safe, baby steps."

Still no response from Tensel, so he plowed ahead. "Anyhoo, full human testing is a long way off. For now it's something that shouldn't bother you one whit. And you, my friend, have important work to do in the meantime. We know you're capable of moving mountains with that brain, and you're not done making the miracles. We need you to rev that engine of yours back up and think through your ideas about soul suppression—*that's* what we need from you now."

Tensel looked up at Dr. Kendel. His eyes were red, and his unwashed black hair stuck out at angles where he'd run his hands through it. Dr. Kendel wondered whether Dr. Brown might go on a rampage. Was he crazier than anyone knew? Maybe they needed a whole new angle. "Okay," he said, rummaging his brain for an idea, "let's try something different. Maybe you need a rest. Aren't you happy at home? Are things bad with Jessica?"

Silence.

"C'mon, what would bring a smile to your face?" Dr. Kendel continued. "Ark's in bed with you in a big way, and there's not much they can't afford. So what is it? *More* money? Oh, I know, something to change the Jessica story? Hey, how about Vegas, or maybe a fun robot? Heh."

Silence.

"Or how about a transgenic?" It was a long shot, but he was getting desperate.

To his surprise, Tensel looked up. "I always wanted one," he whispered.

Dr. Kendel slapped his hand on his metal desk, making Tensel jump. "My friend, we've got a deal."

*
**

The next day Dr. Kendel called Tensel with news: Ark would pay to have a high-end familiar transgenic designed for him. In fact, he could start the selection process that afternoon.

Tensel smiled, ever so slightly, for the first time in weeks.

"Why do you need a transgenic?" Jessica said that night, cuddling up next to Tensel on the couch while he read work notes on his slate. They wore matching gray Stanford sweats that she'd bought for them the year before. Her legs were tucked up under her on the couch, and Tensel's long legs were askew on the coffee table, his bare feet dangling over the far side. "What if I'm allergic? What if I don't like it? Or what if *you* don't like it?"

"That's impossible," he said, not taking his eyes off his slate. "She'll have a little piece of my genes spliced into her, but otherwise she'll be a lot like a cat. We both like cats, right? Her designers are working off a scan they have of me from five months ago, because they didn't want my 'crazy,' as Dr. K so tactfully put it. But I don't think my psyche is any different now than it was five months ago."

"Hmm. Maybe I'll like your transgenic better than I like you."

"What's that supposed to mean?" He dropped the slate into his lap and turned to look at her for the first time that evening.

"You've actually changed quite a lot in the last five months." Jessica was twisting and untwisting a strand of her hair, a habit that annoyed Tensel, though he never said anything. "You're just, you know . . . you seem absent," she said. "I feel like I live alone. You cancel on soccer half the time, and I have to go by myself."

"I'm busy, and you have other friends. Don't you like having enough money? This penthouse?"

"Sure, it's all good, but I feel cut off from you. You don't tell me what's going on at work anymore."

"It's boring. You wouldn't care. It probably always bored you—why would you care now?"

"Okay fine. How about this? You throw up every morning before you leave for the lab."

Tensel glared at her. "How do you know that?" he said.

"Look, I'm worried, mad, and lonely. You said maybe hearing about your work bored me, well, it never did. Bored is what I feel *now*. Maybe I don't even know you anymore, and I'm losing track of my own life. I can't remember why I wanted to be here in the first place."

"You don't have to stay."

They were quiet for a long time, then Jessica spoke. "Is that what you want, for me to leave?" Tears started down her cheeks.

"No!" he said, "no, of course that's not what I want. I just want you to know you're not trapped."

Maybe things would be better with Jessica once his transgenic came? He leaned toward her and put his arms around her, which made her cry for real.

"What if your transgenic — what if *she* — doesn't like me?" said Jessica.

He thought for a few seconds. "She'll be related to me. She'll be on my wavelength, and I like you. How could she not like you too?"

*
**

Belle wasn't a familiar transgenic herself. She was just a big yellow domestic cat. A surrogate mother — a plain school bus whose job was to carry kits, one load at a time, through their first few months of existence. She had strong teeth, clean fur, bright clear eyes, and a hearty love of cat kibble. When not pregnant, she weighed in at nearly 7 kilos — much heftier than the average domestic shorthair. She liked the humans who cared for her, and she was docile during her medical procedures, which were many.

She was often under anesthesia, and she never seemed surprised to wake up and discover herself to be pregnant. She formed a natural and life-giving bond with every embryo the designers implanted in her uterus. After each delivery she nurtured each transgenic newborn as if it were her own offspring, as if it were a cat, as if it had been conceived the way most cats are conceived.

Today's delivery, Belle's twelfth, was an easy one—only six kits. Zoë was the last one out, and when she slid out in a pile of gooey fluid and tissue, she weighed only 32 grams—about as much as a tulip bulb. Her eyes looked like they were sealed shut with gelatin. Miniature whiskers pressed back against her cheeks as she opened her mouth to let out her first mewling noise. She moved her head back and forth sniffing for food, and Belle licked her from head to tail with one sweep of her tongue, pushing her over backwards.

Zoë and her five littermates, all female, ranged in color from nearly white to a tawny orange. Zoë was the darkest, and as Belle licked her the techs noticed that her fur was marked with black spots, so tiny for now that they were almost invisible. Belle cleaned the other newborns, and other differences became apparent. Zoë was the smallest of her littermates, but she was the loudest and the most active. When she was three days old, she opened her eyes and began to look around her world, curious and intelligent. When one of the techs put a hand near her, she reared up to sniff it, her ears and whiskers forward.

The techs watched the kits, taking notes each day about the markings and behavior of each one. Each kit contained a small splice of genes copied from Tensel's genome, but only one of them would become Tensel's familiar transgenic.

The lead designer visited two weeks after the birth. Zoë's eyes were open and clear now, and beginning to change from their original deep blue into a greenish color. She'd just learned to walk and was teetering around the birthing-room floor when the tech on duty scooped her up and handed her to the lead for inspection. Though they'd keep watching to make sure, it seemed clear that Zoë was the one destined for life with Tensel. The others would be adopted by good homes, though their new owners would have to abide by the copyright, of course: no cloning.

*
**

Tensel was nervous. He knew Zoë was female and would weigh about 3.5 kilos when full-grown. He'd picked out the name, but now he wondered whether it would suit her. Would she like it as much as he did?

The receptionist at Familiar Transgenics United showed him into the greeting room and told him to have a seat. A minute later, a tech came in carrying what looked like a tiny cat. This couldn't be Zoë. Surely a familiar transgenic would look more . . . unfamiliar? It did have intense eyes, though, and intriguing spots on its coat. The tech held the animal out to him and Tensel looked at it cautiously, leaving his hands in his lap. The animal gazed at him with a worried expression and flicked its tail.

"Gods, I hate to part with this little darling, I really do," said the tech, looking at the animal. "But here we go. Zoë, meet Tensel." He smiled at Tensel. "And Tensel, meet Zoë. Go ahead, she won't bite. Or she'll never bite *you*, anyway."

Tensel reached out and took Zoë between both hands, then shifted her into one hand. She was still a kitten, so she fit snugly into his palm. He held her up to his face, and she leaned forward to sniff his nose. He held his other hand up to her, and she rubbed her cheek against his fingers. Then he cupped his hand gently over the top of her head, flattening her ears.

"Zoë," he said.

He heard a faint whirring noise and held her up to his ear so he could hear it. She was purring.

Check mate

soul *noun* \sōl\
: one having a good or noble quality in the highest degree
: *exemplification, personification*
—Merriam-Webster Unabridged

Tensel was dozing on the couch at home with Zoë on his chest. Sometimes when they were lying like this he'd forget she was there and stand up without giving her time to jump off. She'd grab the front of his shirt with her tiny claws and scramble up to his shoulder.

She weighed just over 2 kilos now, and her eye color had deepened to a vivid moss green. A tuft of fur over each eyelid gave her a slightly worried look, even when she was playful, and her empathic bond with Tensel gave her an eerie ability to mimic his facial expressions.

Tensel's watch vibrated and flashed, waking him up, which woke Zoë, and they glared at the watch with matching scowls. He'd used the small toggle switch behind his ear to shut off his neuroprosthetic implant so he could get some down time, but Ark had found a way to reach him. What now? The message was long, so he transferred it to his reading slate. It was marked confidential, which he knew meant that the system had just verified his identity with a retinal scan. It also meant that if any unauthorized readers came into the room while he was viewing the memo, his slate would go blank.

He looked at Zoë. "I'm kind of anxious about reading this," he said. She gazed at him steadily, then started to tread with her front feet, kneading his stomach, bumping her head up against the slate. He smiled and moved the slate farther out, holding it at the full length of his right arm while he rubbed Zoë's ears with his other hand. He began to read.

Respectfully posted from the executive desks of the Wolf Corp's Center for the Study of Post-Earth Arks, to Dr. Tensel Brown.

Dr. Brown, you might not be aware of the way in which your scientific endeavors support the long-range vision held by the founders of our great corp. We feel that the time is right to acquaint you with our true vision, which is not a modest one: the Wolf Corp exists to enable humanity's departure from our solar system, and to determine ways to arrest the human aging process.

Traditional cryogenic technology ("deep sleep") has been useful for journeys within our solar system, but the potential to combine deep sleep with anti-aging technology is more limited than we had hoped. With your help, we are exploring a new avenue of research, one that can create a future in which humanity isn't obliged to die with its home planet or star system; a future in which individuals are not limited by the ephemerality of the physical body or confined to our solar neighborhood.

As one aspect of our multifarious effort to achieve this vision, we will establish a human colony on Wolf 1061 Patience, a planet in the Wolf 1061 system that has been undergoing terraforming since we sent our beta fleet of ships over 200 years ago. This colonization effort holds tremendous potential for commercial and scientific advancement; for example, we hope to gain access to a wellspring of potential solutions for Earth's biomedical industry, and to make important advances in the field of terraforming.

Also, in keeping with our core vision, the colonization effort will enable us to test our emerging technologies in ways we are prevented, by regrettable bureaucracy, from doing here on Earth.

Full tests on natural-born humans. Tests where the original hosts would die the way Trixie had, their macro quantum patterns transplanted into clones. This was what he'd wanted, right? But now, reading the idea as Ark meant to realize it, he felt a tremor pass through his body. Zoë stopped treading and locked eyes with him.

The door clicked and Jessica walked in, and the reading slate went blank.

"What are you doing?" she said. "You look guilty."

"Memo from work. It's nothing."

Jessica changed into her soccer clothes and left, and as the front door shut, the slate lit up again. Tensel continued to read.

Colonists will be stored in a soul-only format—

"It's not a fucking soul, God damn it!" He closed his eyes and put a hand over Zoë's head, covering her ears. "Oh wow, sorry," he said to her. "You wouldn't stress about it, would you. The idiots can call it whatever they want." He looked back at his slate.

Colonists will be stored in a soul-only format aboard the spaceship *Svalbard* for the 88-year duration of the trip. Near landfall, shipboard artificial intelligence will grow clones of the humans represented by these souls, then reunite each soul with a clone of its original body in time for the colonists to disembark on their new home, the planet Wolf 1061 Patience.

As you no doubt perceive, this trip is not without risk for those who will venture forth upon it. Our now-patented soul detachment and reattachment process, hereafter referred to as Merge®, will place mild strain on the human body and soul even in ideal conditions.

Merge? He never called it that, and he hadn't patented his idea yet. His detachment and reattachment methodology was still in Phase I of development — maybe there were referring to something else. He returned to the memo.

We plan to mitigate the risks of Merge in various ways: some of your colleagues have been applying their skills to the task of developing criteria that will allow us to select colonists most likely to survive the rigors of Merge. This meticulously selected group of colonists will make up most of the complement and provide us with most of our test data.

Secondly, to ensure the continuation of the revenue stream that supports this vital project, we are reserving spaces among the complement for those citizens who are willing to remunerate us for our efforts. We are given to understand that there exist wealthy people for whom the risks of staying on Earth outweigh the risks of leaving, or for whom the benefits of colonizing Wolf 1061 Patience outweigh any benefits they might expect from life on Earth. To some, the opportunity will be worth the necessarily high fee that we will charge.

As you can imagine, non-scientists are incapable of appreciating the nature of our long-term vision. For this reason, we will market our colony expedition as one involving traditional deep-sleep technology enhanced with newly developed youth-regeneration technology. This is not misleading: colonists will arrive on Patience in bodies that are approximately 18 years of age; the particulars of how their bodies are made young are a matter of technical implementation, irrelevant to all but those most closely involved in the project.

Detailed specifications of our colonization plan are now unlocked to you. Peruse them at your leisure, and we remind you that your contract binds you to secrecy about this and all

Tensel stopped reading and let the slate drop onto his lap. He fell back against the couch and shut his eyes, and Zoë pressed herself up against the bottom of his chin. He reached up to stroke her fur to help himself calm down. A colony trip? Macro quantum patterns stored for 88 years? The longest non-fatal rat test had lasted 68 *days*.

A wave a shame and self-hatred swept over him. He knew he'd throw up soon, and he got ready to run for the bathroom. He thought about the Wolf 1061 star system, one of his favorites when he'd received his first telescope as a boy. The Wolf Corp? Post-Earth Arks? How could he have been so stupid. A colony expedition to the Wolf system had been their intention from the start, and they were grasping at any technology that seemed likely to make it work.

He glanced at the final paragraph.

conditions and restrictions described in the attached legal holodocs. DNA-level signature assent is required.

*
**

Sam, Arjuna, and Tensel were spread out around the table in the corner conference room. Zoë was the table's centerpiece, snoring quietly on the throne of her padded cat bed, surrounded by used coffee mugs, an empty box of pastries, crumbs old and new, and six or seven tangled cables.

"So," said Sam, fidgeting with his mug, "we all know."

"Yep," said Arjuna.

Tensel was silent, his arms crossed and his gaze unfocused.

"I don't know how they think they can keep this secret, something this big," said Sam. His brow was furrowed, and he was drumming his fingers on the table, his rings clinking against the metallic table edge now and then. "Why should we have to hide what we do from our friends and loved ones? They'll think we're doing something wrong. And calling it 'enhanced' deep-sleep tech when it's really soul transfer? That's crazy! How can we keep people from knowing what we're actually working on?"

"That's easy," said Arjuna. "Do you usually go into detail about our work with friends and loved ones? No. A vague answer is all they want. Just say we're working on tech that'll make the colonists young on arrival, and that the details are confidential because Wolf has competitors. All true, as far as it goes. And about containing the press, Wolf's supremely capable of creating spin if someone gets footage of the equipment prep, or whatever. Corps do this kind of thing all the time."

"No they *don't*."

"They're already doing it," said Arjuna. "Clearly this project is almost complete, and each of us has been working on it without even knowing it. Even you, Sam. Your long-distance communication will be a boon to the Patience expedition, don't you think?"

"Whoa. I hadn't thought of that." Sam felt a moment of satisfaction, then returned to what worried him. "It seems wrong that we'll lie to the colonists."

"Telling them about Merge would scare the shit out of 'em," said Arjuna, "but this way they get the benefits without the extra anxiety."

Sam turned to Tensel. "What do you think?"

Tensel shrugged, then stood to face one of the room's whiteboard walls. He picked up an eraser and a marker, cleaned off a section of smudged mathematical symbols and doodles, and started writing an equation. "Now that this thing is out of our hands, all we can do is make sure it works," he said. "So here's a detail I was thinking about this morning, and I'd like your input."

Embodiment

soul *noun* \sōl\
: human being
—Merriam-Webster Unabridged

In the sixth grade, a teacher asked Miriam what she wanted to be when she grew up. "A mother," she'd said. But when motherhood was upon her 10 years later, it wasn't as much fun as she'd imagined. Now here she was at this stupid birthday party for Eliza. It was a sunny day with a pretty good air-quality rating, so her mom's friends set up food and games for the older kids in the yard and on the sidewalk.

The party only lasted a few hours, but for Miriam it was an eternity of kids screaming and middle-aged strangers wanting to talk about babies and the weather. One lady seemed to think Miriam had gotten her piercings for the sole purpose of helping people start conversations with her. *Awkward* conversations.

She glanced at her watch to check her reflection, tucking a stray lock of hair back into the scarlet tower atop her head. These frumps from St. Malcolm's were probably jealous. They were mom's friends, not hers. She didn't believe in God, didn't go to church, and didn't see why Rachel had to invite these people to Eliza's party.

But Sam showed up. Phew.

"Finally," she said, hurrying over to him at the food table.

"Hey, Mira. I can only stay a minute." He scooped a huge portion of popcorn into a cup and started tossing pieces into his mouth one at a time. "You seem to be handling things just fine on your own here."

"Gah!" She punched him on the arm and tried to get him to stay, but all too soon, he was gone. At last the neighbors and church friends left and it was only Rachel, cleaning up, and Eliza asleep on a blanket on the lawn.

Miriam hurried into the house.

In her section of Room 3, she lay down on her bed and slipped her body into her new VR harness — a gift from Sam. VR was the smart way to interact with people, she reflected as she buckled the straps and adjusted the headset around her hair and over her face and ears. You could get to know people at your own pace.

She logged into the VR software by way of the house's cloud bridge, and her mind shifted, adjusting to the input. Her body relaxed, then went limp.

Thank God for that hack from her boyfriend Exscalibur: a few lines of code hidden inside the VR software opened a backdoor into her neural implant and prompted it to release dopamine into the nucleus accumbens area of her brain. Technically illegal, but it made VR so much more fun.

She walked into an eighteenth-century British pub and Ex waved her to a barstool.

"Took you long enough, wench," he said. "Welcome to Annwn! Barkeep, a pint for my Gwendolen!" He turned back to Miriam. "We're watching the match."

"Well I'm not," she said. "I'll be in Dirty Linen if you want me." She blinked an adjustment to her settings, and the pub disappeared. She was on a sofa with Becca and Dominique, small voluptuous dragons like herself. A sensation of well-being entered her head and spread down through her body. Silverback, the gorilla who hosted "Dirty Linen, the Net's Best Gossip!" sat across from the couch in a recliner.

"Welcome, Gwen," said Silverback. "Apes alive, do I have a story for you. We were right in the middle of it, but I'll catch you up!" He clambered up to stand on his chair, gave an ear-splitting hoot, beat his chest with his fists a few times, then sat back down. Miriam and her friends shook with laughter.

Silverback put on a pair of pink-lensed glasses that had been hanging around his neck, pulled a piece of paper from thin air, and began to read. "The Wolf Corp has been dumping billions — no, bananazillions! — into their previously fledgling Ark Project." He tilted his head down and looked at Miriam over his glasses. "Hey, isn't that where your brother works? Oooh!"

Miriam's friends and an invisible crowd echoed, "Oooh!"

"Okay, lemme see," he said, returning to his notes. "The Ark Project says it hires only the smartest, and The Work-Fun Times rated Ark the most stimulating workplace in the solar system, yada yada. Well, my own brother-in-law Virunga would know. Ark hired him. And what do you think he did? He quit!"

"Oooh!" said the invisible crowd.

"And gadzooks, do I have a surprise you'll adore," the gorilla continued. "It's Virunga! Ladies and lollipops, give a big Dirty Linen welcome to our very own Ark expert: Virunga!" An enormous gorilla appeared from thin air and crouched to sit. A recliner appeared just in time to catch him, sending Miriam and her friends into new spasms of laughter.

"Well Virunga, what was it like to work at Ark?" said the host. "We want facts."

Virunga leaned forward and moved his gaze from Miriam to each of her friends as if about to impart ancient wisdom. "It . . . it . . . it SUCKED!" he said, then jumped on his chair to hoot and scream.

The dragons screamed too, and the one on Miriam's left fell off the couch in a seizure of laughter. Everything felt so damn good here.

Virunga sat back down and crossed his huge hairy legs. "But seriously. I sailed on Ark Lake. I tanned my hide on Ark Beach." (He leapt up and spun around to show them his brawny gorilla hide.) "And of course work was involved, not that I could do any of it, because they blocked my access to the files I needed. I couldn't make any progress, and so I told those pretentious assholes, 'I've had it. Take this job and shove it where the sun don't shine. I'll take my talents elsewhere.'" He lowered his huge brow ridge into a frown, and two deep lines appeared between his eyes.

"Ah Virunga, you did the right thing," said his brother-in-law. "So tell us. What's the Ark Project up to? They say they're planning an extra-solar expedition with enhanced deep-sleep tech, but we know there's more to it, don't we? What's the big secret?"

"My buddy Dave thinks they don't want anyone to find out they're only sending *undesirables* on this expedition."

"Ha ha! That's a good one." Silverback turned his head toward the dragons on the couch and rolled his eyes. "And how many of these undesirables are we talking about?"

"Dave overheard a meeting where someone said it'll be at least a thousand. Ark's testing something crazy, so they only want to test it on people they have a problem with. Makes sense to me, and I have a complementary theory."

Silverback nodded sagely, waiting for more.

"I saw a memo. Well, part of a memo. It made me think Ark's protecting a really great discovery. They don't want people to know they have this magical thing almost finished, whatever it is. They'll make people pay to go on the expedition, or they'll select only artists and great thinkers. Something like that, but it'll be a privilege. An honor. They don't want people to find out how awesome this expedition is going to be, or there'll be a stampede to get aboard that spaceship."

Miriam giggled with delight at Virunga's illogic — the colony expedition was both genocide and a golden opportunity. The last time Virunga was on the show he said Ark was blasting holes in Saturn's uninhabited moons to test its new atomizer. He was a flake, but he was fun.

"That's quite the smorgasbord of possibilities," said Silverback. "If it weren't rude, I'd roll my eyes again . . . ah, what the hell." Moving slowly for effect, he took off his glasses, plucked his eyeballs out of his head, and rolled them across the floor to bump against Miriam's dragon tail. She was in heaven — this was hilarious!

"Okay, serious now," he continued, putting his pink glasses back on over his empty eye sockets. "Let's talk about the journey itself. Has Ark developed deep-sleep tech that doesn't kill people? Or maybe they don't mind if everyone dies en route? Or maybe they've solved faster-than-light travel? Last anyone told me, the closest habitable system was . . . ." He moved his lips and counted on his fingers, then on his toes. More laughter. "Er, almost 14 light years away."

"And that's why they're designing something new," said Virunga. "No one knows what it is, but Crystal in receiving told me they've been getting shipments of weird stuff. Literally tons of soul fabric, plus a shitload of class 4 lasers and protective gear. And they've installed cloning crèches big enough for gorillas." Gorillas were something of a theme this week on Dirty Linen.

"That's crazy."

"Yep, and there's more. They've placed bulk orders for cremation retorts and urns. As in, you know . . . *urns*."

Silverback turned to look at Miriam and her friends, his eye sockets huge and round. "Whoa. New tech, interstellar travel, colossal risk with breathtaking potential payback. Is it death, or is it fame and fortune in a distant star system? The facts—"

and here he arched an eyebrow at Virunga — "are somewhat fuzzy, but we know for sure that Ark's planning a trip outside the solar system." He leaned toward the dragons. "Dragon girls, you want to go, don't you? Deep down inside? Hm? Hm?"

Miriam felt a delicious thrill of horror and knew that her friends were feeling it too.

A vintage display screen came down behind Virunga with a map of the solar system, and the image zoomed out until several galaxies were in view. The image then flew to the Ophiuchus constellation, stopping at a small, powerful star with tens of planets and hundreds of moons.

"And there it is," said Silverback, "Wolf 1061."

Miriam stared at the map. Sam must know all about this. If she could get a few juicy details out of him, maybe *she'd* be interviewed on Dirty Linen.

*
**

Sam was on the train, heading for Ark. He was thinking about Miriam. "Don't be a stranger!" she'd said in the short video she'd transmitted during the night. "681 East Elm, Thursday dark, haptic rage with Ex's friends. Seriously, don't miss it. Ex works at The Womb, and you won't *believe* the full-body VR he borrowed from the store." She paused to smooth her hair with her hands, and Sam noticed a few weeks' worth of black roots showing above her forehead. It wasn't like her to let herself go. "Oh, and I want to talk to you about something."

He looped the message three times in the center of his field of view. Miriam was wearing a dirty cowboy shirt with snaps on the front pockets. She was talking fast, and Sam wondered if she was high.

He checked his calendar and the map. "Reply," he said under his breath. "I'll be there. Send."

One problem: he'd promised to help Tensel mine data on Thursday night. Well, he'd just tell Tensel he had to visit a sick relative. Wouldn't be far from the truth.

*
* *

Sam shoved his way onto a full ferry that was heading across the lake to Ark Island. He leapt ashore before the ferry docked, ran through the front doors of the central Ark building and up two flights of steps to the lab, and slid into his chair. It was almost 10.

"Hey you," he said to Arjuna, who looked like he'd been there since the night before, "My sister invited me to one of her boyfriend's parties. They get into some amazing stuff with their VR gear. You and Ezra wanna come along?"

"You're late," said Arjuna. "You said you'd help me get ready for my presentation. It starts in three minutes."

"Oh, dude, sorry about that. You'll do great! You didn't need my help, I knew that. Hey, you might want to use two of those minutes for a quick visit to the grooming bots down the hall, they can give you a quick shave . . . or not," he added, seeing Arjuna's scowl.

*
* *

The presentation went perfectly: Arjuna was cleared to access 9 percent of the anonymized data he asked for. It didn't sound like much, but he took the execs' meaningful looks and two-handed handshakes as the go-ahead to do whatever needed doing. As he saw it, the execs were covering their asses by giving him access only to data that couldn't be abused. They expected him to overstep, and if he got caught they'd act shocked, point to the official agreement, and send him to jail.

But he wouldn't get caught. He was excited to dive in, so when he got back to his cubicle he darkened his face screen and lit his privacy icon before Sam could ask any questions.

Arjuna's task obsessed him. He knew he would find the exact right answer, but it was frustrating to think that the execs would see it as no more than an educated guess. He hated that it might be more than a hundred years before anyone knew that he'd found the right pool of candidates for the trip, before anyone knew just how smart and intuitive he was.

Current physical illness or disability on Earth was irrelevant; it was the colonists' clones who would bear the children. The group had to be genetically diverse, but selecting for diversity was easy. What worried Arjuna were the characteristics that no one could quantify — characteristics of the heart and mind. If too few of the re-embodied souls were able to function once they arrived at the planet, or if one of the newly Merged colonists went crazy and sabotaged the others, the colony would fail. The candidates needed to be psychologically and emotionally robust, and able to maintain that robustness through Merge and out the other side. So he wondered: was a person who volunteered to have his "soul" removed unstable by definition?

It would take the *Svalbard* 88 years to reach the Wolf system. What kind of soul would be stable after 88 years of storage? Their longest success with rats was 68 days, and research into the differences between rat and primate souls was nascent. No one knew how to correlate the two, thanks to the bureaucracy that surrounded primate trials. Getting clearance for these kinds of tests on rats was hard enough.

What kind of human, coming awake in a new body after an 88-year lapse, would accept and grip tightly to their original (but long disembodied) soul, and stay sane? How could you know who was such a person and who wasn't, this far in advance?

Could a person's chances of survival be related to the quality of the person's soul itself?

Arjuna ran a hand across the stubble on his cheek, then tugged on his mustache as he thought. Everyone acted as if the people stepping onto the *Svalbard* would step back off of it when they reached their lovely new home, but Arjuna understood that the colony would begin with the second generation, the children born and raised on the planet. If the second generation was soul-healthy, the colony might survive. The real goal had to be a long-term fix that didn't rely on the first generation's survival . . . beyond the time it would take for each female to produce two or three viable babies. If they were able to do a little bonding and help raise the kids, great, but the colony's AI bots could do all that if necessary.

The only predictable way to get a soul to attach to a human body was also the oldest, simplest way: fertilize an egg and let it grow. Therefore, the second-generation colonists would be conceived and birthed using the traditional human method of sexual intercourse and in utero gestation. While nobody could prove that this would promote soul health in the babies, nobody could prove that it wouldn't, and it seemed unlikely to do harm. Or not to the babies, anyway.

Who knows, thought Arjuna, maybe the first-generation colonists themselves would be happy and healthy on Patience, but whether they were or weren't didn't matter to the mission's success, so it didn't matter to him. He needed to find a group of people whose souls could survive being separated from their bodies, stored in a database for the better part of a century, "Merged" into a cloned human, and then bred like animals. Sam was too emotional to think it through in such dispassionate terms, but someone had to be clear-eyed about the reality.

He had a hunch that the data he'd lifted from certain companies would point him in the right direction . . . .

An urgent beacon from Sam interrupted his thoughts, and Arjuna disabled his privacy icon and cleared his face screen. "Hey!" said Sam, arching back luxuriously in his chair, "It's time for lunch. It's almost two o'clock. Are you stuck? Let's go feed the seagulls. It'll help."

"I'm not stuck, lame-ass," said Arjuna. But now that his focus was broken, he noticed that he was hungry. Ravenous, actually, and a walk would do him good. He peeled off his work gloves and focused his eyes on the Pause button that floated in the lower left of his peripheral vision. His work space disappeared from his line of sight. He took off his headset and followed Sam out of their cubicle, out of the building, and into the fresh winter air.

As usual, they set out for the food court on the island's eastern shore. "So I have this idea about workers whose jobs involve soul verification," said Arjuna, extending his arms over his head as they walked. "That's the data I was begging for this morning in the preso, though I've already accessed most of it to be sure it was worth the trouble. Most of the workers whose data I looked at would be disqualified in a heartbeat — mental illness and all that. But those who make it to the testing round come with one huge benefit, from my point of view: their employers have terabytes of data about their souls. It's unbelievable. Sure, Wolf will have to slip someone a favor to get the *legal* rights to the data, but that's not my problem, is it?"

"Wait, seriously?"

"Absolutely. The tests we plan to give the candidates can only give us crap data at best. We're only guessing what tests to run and what sorts of results would come back from a viable candidate. A viable candidate is one whose soul will survive the most horrific sort of craziness, let's face it—"

Sam stopped walking." You know my mom's a voice worker at Human Converse, right? She's routinely verified."

"I know you're squeamish about this," said Arjuna, "and of *course* I know what your mom does; you talk about her all the time. I almost feel like I've met her. But what are the odds she'll come up in my sample? There are tens of thousands of workers in the Bay Area alone whose jobs are soul-related. And on the off chance my software pegs her, participation will be voluntary."

They were moving again and had almost reached the taqueria near the end of the boardwalk. "Well," Arjuna continued, "a good candidate is one with a robust soul. That's another way of looking at it. The best way to get data about a person's soul is to expose it to soul fabric hundreds or thousands of times, in all sorts of stressful circumstances. But that's time-consuming, expensive, unethical, etcetera. The miracle about the data I'm looking at is that these people's jobs have already exposed them to hours and hours of contact with soul-fabric technology. Sometimes they happen to be stressed when the readings are taken, so there's information about their stress responses. It's in the data."

"How can that data even help you?" asked Sam. "Soul fabric gives a yes-no result. What's so interesting?"

"It's the data companies shouldn't keep, but keep anyway. In some cases I'm not sure they even know they have it. They buy expensive soul-verification gadgets so they can produce an audit trail, and the gadgets have bells and whistles that not everyone bothers to turn off. So when they check a worker for a basic soul-fabric response, they're also checking emotional, psychological, and spiritual functionality, plus blood pressure and other physical stats.

"For a lot of these workers the data spans decades, and I can correlate it to the types of work they were doing when the readings were taken, rated according to stressfulness and intellectual difficulty."

"No," said Sam. "No. They have to delete data like that."

"Well, it's there," said Arjuna. "I can pull it out, and it's a gold mine. It's going to make my career."

Sam was silent, and Arjuna went on as if he were alone. "I suppose, if they've been exposed to unsafe fabric levels, they could be soul-damaged . . . ."

"Shut up now, okay? I don't like you today," said Sam, nervously twisting his rings. Today it was a silver one in the shape of a dragon, an iridescent metal one that looked like an antique etched silicon chip, and a couple of plain titanium bands.

Arjuna kept talking. "The truly damaged folks would fail the first round of tests," he said. "Not a problem; they're out. We're only after the best. My guess is that I'll find a couple hundred soul adepts, max. No higher than the percentage I'd find in the normal population, but the difference is that with all this employer data, I can find them."

"Mariana's waiting for you." They'd reached the front of the line, and Sam indicated the wrinkled woman leaning over the counter toward Arjuna.

They ate on a bench facing the water. "So there's a chance these colonists might die, right?" said Sam between bites. "And they'll need to leave Earth, their families, everything they have. Isn't that a lot to ask? Do we have that right?"

"C'mon, you're taking all this way too seriously. Odds are low that we'll end up knowing *anyone* who goes on the expedition. And like I said, it's voluntary."

"What if none of these adepts want to come in for testing? What if they see right through it and refuse, 'soul healthy' as they are?"

"That's yet another problem that belongs to someone else, isn't it?" answered Arjuna. They ate in silence for a while, and then he added, "Strange to think that anybody could be a soul adept. How about Mariana, who makes our burritos? How could we tell?"

"Yeah. Anybody."

Aptitude

soul *noun* \sōl\
: a seat of real life, vitality, or action
—Merriam-Webster Unabridged

Sam put up his face screen, lit his privacy icon, and phoned his mother. He knew she'd be at home, so she'd accept the call audio-only. That was fine — he didn't particularly want her to see the beads he'd added to his hair that week anyway.

Rachel picked up the phone with her usual, "Peace."

"Mom!" he said. "What's up?"

"Oh, this and that. How are you, honey? How's your job?"

"Mother, I asked you first. I demand to know what's up."

"Well, let's see. We're still having trouble getting Eliza the tests and therapies she needs, but we're making progress. Sister Elsinore's pulling strings downtown — you remember she's a social worker? — and I have my covenant group and all of St. Malcolm's praying."

"Great," said Sam. "But how are you?"

"Oh, I'm fine," she said. "A little trouble with my back, nothing serious."

"Mom, Mira told me you missed three days of work last week and spent most of that time lying on the floor."

"Well, we all have our aches and pains," she said. "Are you still sleeping under your desk at the Ark Project?"

"I shouldn't have told you that. Work's good. It's great!"

"So . . . you're busy and happy?"

"About my work . . . ." He wished he could tell her exactly what the Ark Project paid him so much to work on, and why he'd been willing to put off finishing his degree when school had been so important to him. "It's been a bit overwhelming

lately," he said. "But yes, I'm happy, and I'm definitely busy."
He told her a few specifics she hadn't heard yet about working
on the Island, and how much she'd like Arjuna if she ever met
him.

Meanwhile, Rachel was thinking. Of course she'd heard
about the research the Wolf people had been doing through
the Ark Project, which they called the "charitable" arm of their
organization. She watched the news, she talked with people at
work and church and at the childcare center. She knew they'd
hired cloning experts, and there was crazy talk of moving souls
from body to body, "soul tampering," to use her pastor's term
for it. But honestly, the whole thing was farfetched. Why
would anyone do that kind of experimentation? And was it
even possible?

"You're not working on anything creepy, are you?" she said,
"Like soul tampering?"

"No!" he said, a little too quickly.

Silence.

"I'm not involved with soul tampering with people, okay
mom? My project, the communication thing I told you about
before, does involve animal testing, implanting some particles
in them . . . but I don't think it affects their souls at all. It's like
any other animal experiment."

"I know. But even if you're not tampering with their souls,
it's a bit sad that you have to use animals for your tests.
Doesn't it bother you?"

"Sometimes. But the animals help us learn what we need to
learn, so they're doing important work, and in exchange we
take care of them. Everyone has to work."

"Okay, well, I'm proud of you, sweetheart. You know I'm
always proud of you, whatever you do, and I love you."

Arjuna was probably right—there was almost no chance his
mom would come up as a potential colony candidate, but it

couldn't hurt to plant a seed about pushing back, just in case. "You know mom, one thing I admire about you is your boundaries. You've worked hard on them, and you're better than you used to be at saying no to things that aren't yours to do. Or things that violate your beliefs, like some kinds of tech. I appreciate that about you. Don't ever change."

Rachel laughed. "Well thanks, hon'. I try."

*
**

Late Thursday night, Miriam was splayed out in Exscalibur's loft sipping a fizzy vodka drink that Dominique had given her, looking down at the party from under her lion's head AR helmet. When Sam arrived she watched him make his way through the crowd in the semi-darkness, muttering apologies as he brushed past people who could barely see him under the pulsing colored lights, flashing that magnetic smile of his. What was there to smile about all the time, anyway?

She watched as Becca eyed him flirtatiously and saw him nod, accepting the invitation to exchange profiles. Miriam snorted. Her little brother was such a prude — he'd never follow up on this lead, even though Becca was the naughtiest, most fun-loving bitch a guy like Sam could ever hope for. And why did her friends think Sam was so cute, anyway? Sheesh. They'd never seen him pick his nose and wipe it on the table.

Sam picked up a beer and a mild enhancement hack at the bar, and Miriam smiled with satisfaction as he downloaded the hack into his in-eye display. Good. Now everything at this party, including Miriam's idea, would take on a tiny bit more sparkle for him.

Just as he spotted Miriam in the loft and headed her way, Dominique shouted that it was Miriam's turn to go into the Hellion, the VR body bag Ex had borrowed from his workplace. What shitty luck.

"You take my turn, Domi," she shouted back, hating the sacrifice she was making. But it was worth it if she could talk Sam into this favor.

Sam climbed into the loft and sat cross-legged facing his sister. "I found you!" he said cheerfully. "I'd recognize you anywhere. Your shoes gave you away."

Miriam glanced at her tattered five-year-old high tops and felt a moment of self-consciousness, which turned her angry and mean.

"You're such a prick," she said. "And I see that you're wearing some serious tech on *your* feet, Mr. Nerdy. Why even come to a party like this one when you're such a dork? Good women like Becca are wasted on you."

Sam's forehead folded into that worried look Miriam hated so much. "Well," he said, "I'm at this party because you invited me. And I *like* these." He lifted up one of his thermo-molded shoes for her to look at. "They power my personal-tech batteries 13 percent more efficiently than my old shoes, and they cue me toward interpersonal entrainment."

Miriam loved tech, she loved expensive, and these shoes were both. "Interpersonal entrainment?" she said, examining the shoes. "So you're the master of *all* social situations now, I can see that." Making fun of Sam was always entertaining. She relaxed and reminded herself what she was after. "So tell me about your job," she said.

"Since when do you care about my job? Do you even know where I work?"

"*Everyone* knows where you work. *You* are the subject of most sentences that come out of mom's mouth. Apparently our lives went to hell the day you moved out."

Sam slid over to sit next to her with his back against the wall of the loft and sipped his beer, leaning to look down at the party below. "Sorry," he muttered. Her baby brother, usually afflicted with verbal incontinence, was now a bit stopped up.

"Oh come on, let me help you," she said. She took the beer out of his hand and yelled for someone to hand up a cup of Dominique's concoction, which she gave to Sam. "Drink. You're at Ark, everyone knows that. What're you working on?"

Sam took a deep breath and slouched further down the wall, letting his legs flop out in front of him. "Oh why not," he said, taking a large sip of his drink, and pretty soon he was on a roll, not knowing quite what he was saying or why, but enjoying the comfortable feeling of being next to this person he'd adored his whole life, no matter how mean or crazy she got once in a while. He told her about his entanglement experiments, and how he hoped to create a high-bandwidth instantaneous communication channel that would use semi-organic brains to transmit, receive, and process data. As he chewed the ice from his second fizzy drink he told her about Arjuna's habit of chewing ice every afternoon after lunch, and how Tensel always looked like his best friend just died. Still, he was careful not to mention Merge or anything else confidential. Miriam listened, showing nothing through her lion's head face.

"Tensel's Jessica's boyfriend, right?"

"Yeah," said Sam, looking away.

"Ah. You and Jess have been friends for a long time, haven't you?"

"Since third grade is all."

"Do you like Tensel?"

"Of course, I like everyone, you know that. Tensel's brilliant, and his work is the reason Ark's investing so heavily in everything that might relate to it, including *my* idea."

"But you don't think he's good for Jessica."

"I didn't say that."

"Well, whatever." She threw her empty cup down into the party below and shouted for someone to get her another drink. "What's Ark doing with all this tech?"

"Why do you care? You're drunk," said Sam, who was drunk.

"I'm not even close to drunk," said Miriam. "Here, have another drink and help me get there. Tell me what Ark's doing with the tech."

Sam accepted the fresh drink that she pressed into his hand and leaned closer. "You have to promise not to tell anyone," he whispered. "This is confidential."

"Pinky promise."

But Sam leaned back and waved his hand dismissively. "No, no. I can't tell you. Sorry, no, not you."

Miriam was angry again. "Why *not* me? Why do *you* get told all the secrets? Everything's easy for you."

"No Mira, it isn't."

"Everything is *easy* for you." She pouted into her drink, grateful that between the darkness in the room and her lion helmet, her mood was invisible. Not so Sam, whose countenance lay open to her like a book. He looked sorry and guilty and drunk; now was the time to make her ask. "The least you can do for me is invite me to see where you work," she said. "God knows I can't actually *work* anyplace that fancy, but at least you could let me see it . . . ."

He nodded and looked like he might be feeling a bit sick. "Okay," he said.

She took the drink out of his hand. "Good, and I'm finishing this for you, Mr. Lightweight. It's not good for you."

"And it's good for you?" said Sam.

"Sure, I know what I'm doing. You don't."

*
**

Tensel stood in the mist of hot water, blinking up at the ceiling as cleansing enzymes warmed his shoulders and trickled down his back. Zoë sat on the bathroom sink, waiting for him. Today she'd decided to stay dry, though some days she'd stand in the mist next to him, then spend half an hour licking the enzymes out of her fur.

Jessica put her head in the bathroom door and yelled over the shower noise. "Hey you two, it's 7:30. If you care." Tensel grimaced. "Do we care?" he mumbled.

A blue star pulsed in his peripheral vision—an urgent message from Wolf. Probably Dr. Kendel complaining about his latest no-show with the marketing team. Couldn't they leave him alone? Do it without him? He flicked his right index finger to signal an override, and the star faded from view.

Wolf wanted the idea of youth-regenerating deep sleep, the tech they would supposedly use to transport colonists to Wolf 1061 Patience, to slide uneventfully into the public's consciousness, to go down slick and fast, like an oyster: unpalatable, but worse if chewed or thought about in too much detail. Bad press wouldn't stop the Patience colony trip, but it would make it more expensive.

Tensel sighed.

His job now was to be the project's human face, the expert who would reassure the public that Ark's "augmented" deep sleep was safe. He had no aptitude for sales or marketing, but there wasn't a need for aptitude — the young men on the Patience project's marketing team would take care of everything. "They're gonna 'touch me up,'" he said to Zoë. "What do you think about that?"

The voice of the Channel Wow! newscaster droned somewhere toward the back of his head. He stepped out of the shower and started to dry off, tuning his attention to the end of a vacuous report about the Patience expedition. He blinked to shut off the feed. The brilliant Doctor Tensel Brown, he thought with bitterness. The genius with the idea for youth-regenerating deep sleep, though he'd invented no such thing and knew little about cryogenics. His whole life felt like a lie. And Merge, the actual technology that would take colonists to Patience—would it save them, or kill them?

He'd have to spend time with marketing at some point, so he might as well get it over with. The blue star pulsed again. "I'll be there," he replied.

*
**

Dr. Kendel presented Tensel to the marketing team the next morning. Three hipsters introduced themselves as Tensel's brand manager, personal touch-up coder, and stylist. Mr. Brand Manager quickly identified the key selling points: boy-wonder credentials, shy smile, solemn face that could be made handsome, empathic bond with attractive pet. They scheduled the first 3D shoot for the next day and told Tensel to get a good night's sleep and wash his hair in the morning.

It took an hour to shoot the first set of baseline images. He had to stand naked in various poses, then walk around and talk, with Zoë far enough away to be out of the cameras' lines of sight—not a comfortable hour for either of them. After they left, the marketing coder used the images to generate the first set of touch-up algorithms, then spent the rest of the day hand-coding a few special touches of his own.

The next day they did another shoot, this time in light summer clothing chosen by the stylist. While fussing with Tensel's hair and makeup, the stylist noticed Zoë's face subtly mirroring Tensel's every grimace and look of resignation. Their bond was charming. Maybe it would be useful to create touch-up algorithms for Zoë too? That way they could make her face mirror Tensel's touched-up face, and even make her expression contrast his once in a while for humorous effect.

From then on, she was included.

When the team was finished, they'd created a mix-and-match toolkit of clothes, poses, and moods for Tensel and Zoë. The result was software that could autocorrect any photo or vid of Tensel and Zoë on the fly, as the images were streamed to the public. The correction algorithms replaced what was missing along Tensel's hairline, fleshed out the skull-like hollows of his cheeks, added a healthy shine to his hair and a livelier tone to his sometimes ghoulish skin, and adjusted his facial muscles to emote as needed — with Zoë in sync, of course.

If a hologram of the touched-up Tensel Brown appeared in your in-eye display or beamed into your living room and told you that the colony expedition to Patience was safe, you'd believe him. That was the plan, anyway. You'd think well, why *couldn't* scientists like Dr. Brown adjust deep-sleep tech so it could keep people alive and healthy for 88 years? And the colonization project had so much potential for good. Life extension, a cure for Mercurial flu, clean star systems where humans could start new lives and breathe clean air . . . so many possibilities. How could such a brilliant man be wrong? Such a healthy, handsome man. And that darling transgen of his! How could a man who loves an animal so much tell us anything false? And isn't saving the human race worth taking risks?

It was hard to pinpoint what was so appealing about him, but the angle of his cheekbones, the quirky tilt of his smile, made you optimistic and filled you with a vague sense of well-being. Watching him was *pleasant*.

The introductory hologram in the lobby of Wolf's VR site was filmed on Ark Island's boardwalk. The sky was a vibrant blue. Sunlight glittered on the water. He wore a plain gray shirt, a gray blazer, and jeans, and a faceted green crystal hung from a silver and leather cord around his neck. He gestured with his right hand but kept his left behind him on the railing, near Zoë. Like him, she looked calm and content. Her head bobbed as she watched him gesture, and when he was finished with his explanation, he turned and scooped her off the railing, held her to his face, and murmured something inaudible.

Everyone loved it.

Outside the VR lobby, you could visit sitting rooms that immersed you in stories about Tensel's private life and his work. Rooms that featured Zoë were often at capacity. The Wolf team posted new material each week, revealing pieces of Tensel's private life bit by bit. The fourth episode included a short squabble between him and Jessica, and people liked it, so she became a regular. Sam was introduced in the tenth episode, sitting close to Jessica on the couch and exchanging knowing glances with her as they discussed Tensel and his work.

Miners on Titan, Saturn's largest moon, sent Tensel a prayer wreath when his mother got the flu in the fifteenth episode. Kids named their pets Zoë. A group of girl scouts in the Io colony orbiting Jupiter adopted Zoë as their mascot, etching a portrait of her into the rock of an abandoned sulfur plain so it was visible to telescopes on Earth.

But no matter how famous he became, strangers didn't recognize him on the street. The famous version of Tensel was no more than an avatar, but "it" was being marketed as if it were the real him. Something about this stretched his sense of self to the breaking point. As his public persona grew larger, his already small circle of intimates became even smaller. He stopped visiting his parents and turned down invitations from his brother and his few friends, preferring to stay home when he wasn't at work. He dropped out of the soccer league he'd been in with Jessica. For a while he kept running, getting up before dawn to avoid being seen, but one morning a group of fans was waiting at the water tower at 5 a.m. Even though they didn't know it was him running past, he heard them chattering about some *other* guy with some *other* transgenic cat peeking out of his backpack, who they were expecting to appear at any moment. The experience made him anxious for the rest of the day, so he stopped running.

*
**

"Tensel's out today, or I'd introduce you to him. You know who he is, right?" Sam was leading Miriam around the visitor-approved areas of Ark, stopping to point through observation windows at deep-sleep chambers, and showing her the equipment that he used in his own entanglement research.

"How could anyone not? He's adorable. Too bad he's taken." She gave her brother a significant look, which he ignored as he continued his spiel.

"Tensel's the public face of the project, as you've noticed. Ark's using him in a marketing campaign to make sure people know that what we're working on is safe."

"And it might not be safe because . . . ."

Sam stopped walking and looked at her. "It's safe."

She glanced again at the red pulsing light in her peripheral vision that told her she was still recording. Sam wasn't taking her bait, and this "insider" visit to Ark wasn't going as planned. Still, maybe Dirty Linen would be interested in this personal tour of the facilities, which wasn't available to just anyone. And the response he'd just given to the safety question was a bit odd.

Two Ark executives stepped out of the elevator as Sam and Miriam were going into it. The taller, older one paused with his hand on the elevator door to take in Miriam's spiked hair, pierced face, and visitor badge; then Sam's locs and his employee badge. "Why hello, young man," he said, now smiling.

"We're proud to have employees like you. So glad to have you here at Ark."

When Sam and Miriam were alone in the elevator, she reached up to pat him on the head, pursing her lips and raising her eyebrows as if she were talking to a dog, or a baby. "Good boy."

"C'mon, it's not a big deal," said Sam, brushing her arm away. "How do you know they weren't awed by my reputation and truly proud to have me at Ark?"

Miriam scoffed.

"Yeah, I get it," said Sam, "those guys are senior VPs. They probably assume I'm a lab tech or a plant-waterer or something. It's not a big deal. Forget it."

But Miriam knew what it meant when her brother's jaw clenched like that and his eyes hardened, and those guys had acted like pricks a meter away from her, center screen in her retinal recorder — perfect footage. Maybe this wasn't a wasted visit after all.

She fingered the used scrap of soul fabric that she'd slipped into her pocket while Sam chatted with a tech. Maybe Dirty Linen would find the presence of soul fabric in the lab's trash can interesting, though she couldn't think why. But they'd come up with something.

"So how do I get myself aboard the *Svalbard*?" she said as Sam escorted her out the front door of the building. "How does a person sign up to be a colonist?"

"It's not like that; they're selecting people. Special people."

"People like me! I'm young and enthusiastic, I'm an early adopter by nature, and—"

"No, Mira." Sam was suddenly serious. "Not you. Definitely not you."

She smiled. That was another moment they'd have fun picking apart on Dirty Linen.

Confusion

Most dangerous
Is that temptation that doth goad us on
To sin in loving virtue.
—Shakespeare, *Measure for Measure,* 2.2

Bernadine asked Rachel to stop by her office before her next shift. "Someone from Wolf Corp did a background check on you," she said. "They called to verify your employment, find out if you've ever been under company discipline, hear my impression of you, things like that. I'm not supposed to tell you, but I thought you should know."

Rachel's mouth hung open in perplexed surprise as Bernadine went on. "I asked what it was about, but he wouldn't tell me. He said you'll hear from them soon."

Talking with her first caller, Rachel turned the episode over in her mind. Why would someone from Wolf check into her background? Was it about Sam?

*
**

During the walk from the streetcar stop to her house, Rachel skimmed the messages she'd received during the day. Mostly bulk-mail ads and scams, plus one from Human Converse marked "Please print to read." She blinked on "Print" and closed the message, knowing the printout would be waiting for her by the time she reached her room. Probably a new way to handle medical claims, or an updated employee handbook. Something like that.

Nothing from Sam, but she'd see him later this evening. She wanted to ask him if he knew why Wolf was checking on her. Her tendency to worry hooked up with her imagination and she found herself spinning stories in her head about Sam in various kinds of trouble — was he going to be fired? Had he made a mistake at work?

She pushed open the front gate and leaned down to pet the squeaking, bouncing Springy, dodging his tongue as he tried to lick her face. "Believe it or not," she said to the tiny dog, "all I want to hear right now is you." She reached behind her right ear and flipped off auto-receive and auto-send. "Get out of my head," she whispered.

Most people never shut off their implants, but Rachel loved knowing that for a few hours, with auto-receive turned off, no sight or sound would appear in her head beyond what she conjured up on her own. If there was a shooting or a fire, she might not know until the drama was wrapped up. If someone left her a message, she wouldn't know until she went back online.

With auto-*send* turned off, she wasn't having her blood pressure monitored, sending tweets to a ladies' salon, adding prayers to a pray-a-thon, having her food-intake data transmitted to a weight loss challenge, whispering her thoughts to a confessional priest robot, or sending data to any of the other lifestyle apps that a woman like her might be expected to use while puttering around the house.

Today Sam had agreed to bring Eliza home from childcare, because he was coming over anyway to drop off a sweater that needed mending. They wouldn't arrive for another hour, and Miriam would be later than that. She breathed a sigh of relief to be alone, though she immediately felt a bit guilty about her relief. "Well, what's wrong with enjoying a little empty space once in a while?" she said out loud as she sank into her rocker.

The message from Human Converse was on the table in front of her, fresh from the printer. She picked it up and read it the way she'd read the back of a cereal box — she was tired and felt like running her eyes across words, any words. But she was hardly through the first sentence before she sat up and inhaled sharply. The message had been routed via her employer, but it used the letterhead of the Wolf Corp's Center for the Study of Post-Earth Arks. Sam's employer.

"Dear Ms. Deimos," the message began. Bad news? "As you know, our company upholds the highest standards of experimental fortitude and the loftiest ideals of how to conduct ethical research projects with the utmost emphasis on . . . ." She closed her eyes for a moment in frustration, then opened them and skipped ahead to the second paragraph. "We are pleased to inform you that our research has identified you as a potential candidate for our colonist-selection trials, during which we will screen candidates for our proposed colony expedition to the planet Wolf 1061 Patience . . . ."

She sat back in her chair, still holding the paper in her hand. Had Sam put her name on a list so she'd get this letter as a joke? If so, it wasn't hilarious. And if it wasn't a joke, why would she care about these trials and candidates and whatnot?

She threw the letter onto the pile of things to worry about later. She needed to prep dinner, and before she headed back to work, she hoped to find a few hours to embroider those three quilt squares she'd promised Sister Elsinore. When she said yes, she hadn't realized she'd be taking extra shifts at Human Converse. But Sister Elsinore had promised the food bank that people from St. Malcolm's would do three squares for the fund-raising quilt, and no one had volunteered, and Sister Elsinore was terrible at embroidery. Maybe Rachel should've said no, but it seemed too late to back out now. To her way of thinking, she had no choice.

When Sam came in carrying Eliza, a pot of stew simmered on the small stove under the window. Rachel dozed in the rocker with her hands folded across a half-embroidered square of fabric, but woke when she heard the sound of Eliza's delighted squeal. "Nana!" Eliza said as she struggled out of Sam's arms and onto Rachel's lap, launching into an incoherent tale about her nose.

After they ate and Sam left, Miriam arrived. She disappeared without comment into her corner of the room, and it was 20 minutes before she came out, now wearing sweats and a threadbare flannel shirt. She served herself a bowl of stew and sat at the table, idly picking up the sheet of paper at the top of the message pile. Eliza was her daughter, but this evening she acted as if the girl in Rachel's lap was a stranger. Eliza, for her part, didn't bother trying to get her mom's attention when Nana was at hand.

"What's this, mom?" Miriam asked when she saw the Ark letterhead. "Something about Sam?"

"I don't know, hon," said Rachel, looking up from Eliza's face. "I meant to ask Sam about it, but I forgot. Anyway, I'm too tired to figure it out right now. Who knows."

Miriam sliced herself a piece of bread and chewed on it while she read the letter. "Hey! Mom, did you read this? Do you know what this means?"

"You tell me," said Rachel.

"They think you might qualify for the colony trip."

"Why would I want to?"

"Oh, *mom*. I'm so jealous. They have tech that'll let you sleep through the trip, and you'll wake up on a new planet, but younger, much younger in *your* case. And you'll never need money again."

"Well, what I've heard so far is ridiculous. How could I wake up younger?"

"It's simple. Haven't you been paying attention to the feeds? Ark is augmenting deep-sleep tech so that — well here, lemme show you —"

Rachel glared at her, and Miriam froze with a holovid harness partway out of her backpack. "Fine," Miriam said, tucking the harness back where it came from. "Watch it later, however you want to. But you really might be interested."

"I don't want more details about this. Forget it."

Eliza had dozed off, and the two women were silent until Miriam noticed the quilt squares. "Why can't you just say no to things like that? Make Sister Elsinore sew the damn quilt?"

"Hush," said Rachel.

Soon Miriam took Eliza to bed with her, and Rachel embroidered for another half hour. Then she showered in the bathroom down the hall, dressed for work, and gathered up her purse and keys. With her hand on the door she looked back at the stack of papers. She was thoughtful for a moment, then walked briskly to the table and dropped the letter from Ark into the recycling slot.

*
**

The next day was filled with sleep and work and embroidery and child care; the day after was more of the same. Thursday afternoon, the message from the Center for the Study of Post-Earth Arks was redelivered. Once again, Rachel printed it. Miriam and Eliza were gone, the quilt squares were complete, and she had 45 minutes of solitude before her scheduled phone call with her friend Josephine, who was ill. She carried the message into her section of the room, threw both her down pillows onto the floor, and wearily lowered herself onto them, crossing her legs with some effort. It wasn't her normal time to pray, but this wasn't a normal piece of reading. She had a strange feeling about this message from the Ark Project. A strange, bad feeling. The conversation she'd had with Sam, when he'd complimented her on her boundaries, came into her mind. She slid the corner of the letter under the Virgin Mary, letting most of the page hang down in front of the nightstand. "Here it is, Mother," she said. "What do you think?"

Mary was as quiet as ever. Rachel turned up the wick of the oil lamp, flicked the lighter that she kept nearby, and held the flame to the wick. The flame waved gently in the draft that came through the small window, which was open a crack.

She settled back onto the pillows, put her hands on her knees, and closed her eyes to let her thoughts settle down to the ground along with her body. She took time to notice the lingering pain in her back . . . the quiet downbeat of music from Room 5 . . . the laughter and talk from the kids smoking on the front porch.

She let her awareness wander deeper, into her own emotions. She noticed anxiety about Sam. Would he ever take the time to develop a relationship with a nice young woman? Was he working so hard he'd never get married? Should she be doing something about it? How could she fix it? She let it go. Then she relived a flash of anger toward that lady who'd phoned from Eliza's childcare—that lady was always a bitch—how dare she imply that Eliza wasn't bright? Eliza was shy around strangers, and her hearing problem could explain everything that the lady was complaining about. Eliza seemed brighter than Miriam or Sam were at her age, and plenty social. "It's that lady who has a problem, not my grandbaby," she caught herself thinking. "She's judging us."

Ah, irony—judging someone for judging. She reined herself back in and reminded herself that at the moment, she couldn't do anything about that lady. She reminded herself that that lady was precious and unique, just like Eliza. Beloved. She breathed quietly for a few minutes, then let her self-awareness sink a little deeper. She noticed a vague, deep sadness. A tiredness, like how the soles of your feet feel after a long, long walk.

"God," she whispered. "Please give me wisdom. I need your wisdom."

She prayed this prayer knowing it would be answered. Once in a while, rarely, God answered by giving her an "Aha!" moment; a flash of insight. But most often the answers came generally and through many means — people, circumstances, good sense. Sometimes God's direction, the better path, the road toward life and health, took years to emerge from the fog. Even decades.

For some answers, she was still waiting.

She pulled the piece of paper out from under Mary and began to read where she'd left off.

We are pleased to inform you that our research has identified you as a potential candidate for our colonist-selection trials, during which we will screen candidates for our proposed colony expedition to the planet Wolf 1061 Patience, which circles the star named Wolf 1061. Wolf 1061 is visible from Earth in the Ophiuchus constellation.

We would like to invite you to immerse yourself in a holovideo that we have prepared especially for high-value potential expedition candidates such as yourself. This holovid should answer most of your questions and give you a rich sense of what the project means for humankind, and how much you could contribute by allowing us to test you for possible participation.

You are no doubt aware of the global challenges that the human race faces today. Modest outposts established within our solar system have relieved some of Earth's overcrowding, but because of their proximity to Earth, these colonies are plagued by the same bureaucratic and social ills that plague us here. Also, although miners on Titan and on the asteroid 62 Ursilia have discovered a few metals unavailable on Earth, this is nothing like the useful and life-giving minerals, metals, flora, and fauna that we hope to discover and develop further afield, outside our own solar neighborhood.

In short, we need a new star system. As a species we must start over, and we need altruistic humans such as yourself to help us do it. We need an ultimate solution in which you, Ms. Deimos, are uniquely qualified to participate. *You* could help us take meaningful steps forward toward real solutions to our global challenges.

We realize that traveling to our office and immersing yourself in the two-hour holovid would take time out of your schedule, and so we would like to offer you a payment of 2,500 credits—

Rachel gasped and looked up at Mary. That much money would cover Eliza's next round of tests, childcare for a month, or a new stove for the community center at St. Malcolm's. She turned back to the letter.

. . . . we would like to offer you a payment of 2,500 credits for your time. If you are interested, we will transfer the money to you as soon as we receive your response, and you can schedule the immersion session at your convenience. And of course, immersing yourself in the holovid does not oblige you to come in for subsequent testing. Likewise, if you do ultimately choose to be tested, it will not oblige you to join the expedition.

The choice, in short, will always be yours.

The next time Jax phoned, Rachel told him about the background check, the letter from Ark, and the invitation to come in for the holovid. She heard his rich, warm voice saying "Uh-huh, hmm, wow," as she talked. His video feed showed Jasper in a turquoise satin pet bed, his white and gray fur fluffed up as if freshly washed and dried. His ears were pricked up and slightly forward, and his black-rimmed eyes were wide as he studied Rachel.

"I won't go on the colony trip itself, of course," Rachel was saying, "but what can it hurt to immerse myself in an ad for a couple of hours? For 2,500 credits? And they promise I won't be under any obligation. Do you think I'm crazy?"

"Not at all," said Jax. "I'd do it in a flash. "I'd go in for the holovid, the testing, the works, and they wouldn't even have to pay me."

"Really? Why?"

"Because I'm curious. Aren't you? Maybe you'll learn something that'll surprise you."

"I know as much as I need to know," she said. "The whole idea of an 88-year deep sleep makes my skin crawl. It's a bad idea, plain and simple."

"What makes you so sure? Brilliant, well-intentioned people are doing the best they can to make it safe. And your son works at Ark, right? To tell the truth, I'd go on the trip myself if I had the chance. It's one of my dreams. To start over."

This got Jasper's attention. The animal turned away from Rachel, staring somberly at something to his left, and a scarecrow of a hand appeared in the camera frame and gently stroked his head. "Don't worry darling," said Jax in a soothing voice, "I'm right here."

Suddenly he brought his volume back up. "Ah!" he said. "I just had a thought: maybe we could *both* go on the trip?"

Rachel laughed. He couldn't be serious. Or could he? "Hey, look at this!" he said. "Apparently anyone can sign up for the special holovid if they pay a fee. And if I pay an even *bigger* fee, they'll send bots to my house and set it up right here so I don't have to fire up the ol' outside-the-house wheelchair. How wonderful! I'm signing up . . . okay, done. They're coming tomorrow, and I'll tell you all about it when it's over. Maybe me going first will make it easier for you?"

Startled, Rachel didn't have much to say. After they hung up, she noticed that she felt off, less grounded and sure of herself. Something was strange about all of this.

*
**

Rachel paused at the red front steps of St. Malcolm's, tilting her head to look at the cracked stained glass and the chipped paint on the bell towers. Maybe money would fall from the sky so they could repaint the stucco and preserve the stained glass windows before they collapsed into the sanctuary. Maybe money would fall from the sky so they could replace the clanking, clattering furnace that heated the community center on winter nights when they opened it as a homeless shelter.

Maybe a bit of money *was* falling from the sky, by way of the Ark Project.

She climbed the steps and went in, padding across the soft carpet in the narthex to dip her fingers in the bowl of holy water affixed to the wall. "Help me," she whispered as she touched her wet fingers to her forehead and entered the sanctuary to find a seat.

The sermon was about Jesus and his willingness to take loving action, even when he had to suffer for it. "Show me how to love," she said under her breath during the time set aside for silent prayer. "Teach me what it means to lay down my life for others."

She could hardly imagine doing more for others than she already did. Maybe God wasn't asking her to give more, but to give differently? Rachel knew that sacrifice wasn't always love, but the trick was in figuring out the difference.

112

Those quilt squares came to mind. Why had she not only said yes, but offered to do more than what was asked? She enjoyed embroidery when she had time, but she didn't have time. Embroidering the squares, feeling resentful when she had to rush, then spending energy trying not to feel resentful, had sapped her for days.

It was okay when other people said no or "not now" to requests like that. What was so special about her that she required herself to say yes? Was *everything* hers to care about?

"Show me how to love strongly," she whispered, amending her prayer. "Help me discern between what's mine to do and what isn't. Help me let go of things that aren't mine, so I can focus with all my heart on things that are."

Eternity

Rachel never expected to enjoy anything she was paid to do, but she enjoyed the holovid immersion. It was lightly augmented reality, just sound and visuals. As unobtrusive as they'd promised.

The vid began with a tour of a typical colony ship, rows of deep-sleep beds in a chamber rimmed with cheerfully lit monitors. "Ark is part of the Wolf Corp, and as everyone knows, Wolf knows space-travel," the narrator explained. "Our conservative values mean we test, test, test before we launch, and we pay attention to details. Thanks to our meticulous research and development, your deep-sleep bed will keep you safe, healthy, and one more thing that we know will delight you." The scene shifted, and Rachel watched a group of young people emerge from a ship into a lush meadow bordered by an evergreen forest that stretched to the horizon. "Our technology heals disease and reverses the aging process! You might've thought this part was too good to be true, but believe us, it's real. Yes, over the course of your 88 years in space, your body will become a perfectly healthy version of what it was when you were 18 years old. Given enough time, enough rest in the deep-sleep bed, and a boost from the right technology, you'll be young and healthy again. Imagine that!"

Apparently it would happen by some means too complex for non-specialists to grasp, but the narrator explained that it was based on "centuries-old scientific principles, and tech much like the tech you already rely on every day. Our scientists know what they're doing, and your body is safe with us."

But what about my soul, thought Rachel?

As if on cue, the narrator said, "The process will require your soul to exert some effort, like any mild trial or temptation here on Earth. During your deep sleep your soul will grow and change, because after all, isn't deep sleep the prayer of the body?"

With a start, Rachel recalled words from the ancient Wendell Berry poem she'd read earlier that week: "Sleep is the prayer the body prays."

One of the women in the holographic meadow was taller than the others, and the big twists of her hair bounced as she ran toward the forest and then stopped, looking off in the distance. "So imagine this," the narrator continued, "and think of the consequences: your soul, your mind, and your hard-won wisdom remain as they are. Safe with us, housed in a body renewed and refreshed, full of all the vigor and promise of a young person, after 88 years of prayer."

Prayer?

Before she could process that idea any further, she realized that the woman she was watching was her, at 18. Startled, she took a deep breath and rubbed her right hand up and down on her left arm to ground herself, then switched to rub her left hand up and down her right arm.

"I'm nearly 50 years old, and I'm right here on Earth," she whispered. "And I'm watching a holovid." Apparently some components of this vid were personalized. The woman she saw, though realistic, wasn't her. How could tech reverse the aging process and make you wiser in the bargain? It was hard to imagine how such a thing could be done, or that such a thing *should* be done.

On the other hand, deep-sleep tech had been around a long time, maybe long enough for scientists to add refinements like anti-aging. Sam could help her sort this out later; he knew a lot about what tech could and couldn't do.

The vid moved on to show other aspects of the expedition — the need for plant-lovers and farmers among the colonists, and the tech that would allow the colonists to stay in touch with Earth. Rachel smiled when they mentioned Sam and his invention of Infinite Distance Loosely Entangled Communication, which the vid referred to as IDLE-COM. Sam was an important part of the project, and Rachel's heart swelled with pride. Ark experimented on animals, and that was troubling, but the tech used for the colony expedition didn't sound to Rachel like it crossed the line into soul tampering. And Sam wouldn't work on anything that was flat our *wrong*, she felt sure of it.

The scene shifted to a comfortable living room in a house on Patience, and Rachel in her present middle-aged form was part of the scene. A woman about her own age entered the scene in a wheelchair and pulled up next to the couch where she sat. The woman's expression was flat, and her arm moved stiffly as she raised it a few centimeters in greeting. Speaking slowly and without affect, she introduced herself as Maggie. "As you might guess, I have Parkinson's disease," Maggie said with effort. "I've been through so many treatments—drugs and their side effects, physical therapy, deep-brain stimulation. I even had surgery to replace my brain's lost dopaminergic neurons with new ones grown from stem cells. But none of it cured me, as you can see." Rachel wished she could reach out and put her hand over Maggie's own, but Maggie was just a hologram. "To be honest," Maggie continued, "my hope now is to die a good death. And of course I hope my children, and their children, never have to go through what I've gone through."

Maggie paused, and both women sat quietly for a minute while she gathered strength to continue. "The researchers I've talked to believe that terraformed planets are the biopharmaceutical frontier, and ecologists on the terraforming team are adding genetic 'hints' to the flora that'll grow on Patience.

Maybe someone will find a cure for my disease on Patience? Maybe a cure will come from one of the technologies that the colonists test?"

Rachel felt tears slide down her cheeks and thought of her friend Josephine, who'd be in Maggie's condition soon enough.

The vid faded as Rachel's real physical setting came back into focus, and a woman named Yolanda gave her some tissues and asked whether she had questions. She said she couldn't think of any — it was a lot to take in. Eight other potential colonists were also in the room, and Yolanda set out coffee and snacks and left them to talk with one another.

Rachel liked all of them right away. One woman knew Sister Elsinore from a previous church, and another lived in the projects on Jalquin St. between Rachel's house and St. Malcolm's. Like her, these people were uncomfortable with the idea of too much tech, but they'd come in for the holovid because they needed the money, and because it seemed that a loved one wanted them to, and because there was no risk, so why not? One man was working two jobs to support his sister's family; another had been diagnosed with bone cancer just that month.

As she talked with these kind and needy people, Rachel was coming to the conclusion that a person like herself would be the ideal colonist: likely to withstand the soul-storm of a long stay in deep sleep, able to live with and support the other colonists, motivated to do good for the people back home. She remembered her conversation with Jax that morning. "Don't you ever wish something in your life was all about you?" he'd said. "When do you do anything for fun, or just for you?" But what he didn't understand was that she *enjoyed* doing things for others. It gave her meaning and purpose. She was a helper —shouldn't she help?

It seemed Ark understood something about her that even her friends didn't get.

Maybe Miriam could take care of Eliza without constant intervention, and it might be good for her to learn how. Rachel's covenant group, Sam, and even Jax had dropped hints to this effect, and maybe they were right: her children on Earth were grown. Maybe they shouldn't need her so much anymore.

The idea of starting a new family intrigued her, and a few more tears slid down her cheek. Her third child hadn't even made it out of the womb. Wouldn't it be amazing to be pregnant again? To have an infant again? How would it feel to raise kids with abundant resources, and maybe even with a dad?

What kind of men were going on this trip, anyway?

The man on her left, his shirt damp with sweat, introduced himself. "I'm Bob," he said, offering her a warm hand to shake. "The holovid was *amazing*, wasn't it?"

Rachel nodded.

"*Everyone* knows my mom passed away, after such a long, long illness," Bob continued. He ran a hand back and forth over his glowing bald head, as if remembering the feel of hair up there. "I shouldn't be surprised that Ark knew it too. It's a fact, public information, no secret. But how did they know how much I needed to *play* — how long it's been since I had fun, or laughed for real? I didn't know it myself until I was in the vid with my *mother* watching, smiling, yelling crossword puzzle clues at me while I practiced my swing on the putting green out back. Which I haven't used since before she got sick . . . ." He stared into space, patting his hand against his leg. "Maybe they made a lucky guess."

Rachel was distracted, but Bob was willing and able to maintain both sides of this conversation himself. No matter how flashy Ark was, he said, they all needed to keep level heads. Would he take the next step and come in for testing?

He'd never been one to turn down free money, especially since that last layoff, sweet Jesus! And it would only take a day. But surely this was some kind of bait-and-switch scheme? Ark wouldn't pay them so much if this was on the up-and-up.

On the *other* hand, as Bob sagely pointed out to himself, it was obvious why the Ark Project needed to find special people for this expedition. Maybe it was worth it for Ark to spend millions to find the right folks. And he and Rachel and the others were under no obligation to actually *go* on the trip, right?

She nodded, thinking. She liked Bob, but he was a stranger. What did he, or any of these people, know about her and what mattered to her?

She was relieved when it was noon, and she made sure to be first out the door so she could be alone on her way to the train station. She walked fast, and her thoughts cleared. Of *course* she wouldn't go on the colony trip. Still, it was flattering to think that because of her strong soul and deep empathy, she might be uniquely suited to help. If people like her didn't take their courage in hand and go on the trip, could the colony survive?

The idea felt true, though the vanity of it embarrassed her.

*
**

She spent the afternoon playing with Eliza. She caught a tune going through her head, the Patience expedition jingle. "Your body is safe with us, safe with us . . . ."

Catchy.

Eliza wanted to cook and serve meal after imaginary meal, so Rachel knelt on the floor helping to measure pretend ingredients, sipping from an empty cup, eating imaginary banana flambé with a tiny blunted fork and knife, complimenting the genius of the chef. She reflected on her morning at Ark, rehearsing in her mind the new ideas and stories she'd heard, viewing them from different angles, noticing how it felt to let these new thoughts wander among her accustomed thoughts.

Jax's holovid had emphasized how healthy and vital the colonists would be when they arrived on Patience, which was perfect for him, given the current state of his body. Evidently each person's holovid experience was customized. What did it mean?

"We'll be right as rain by the time we get to the planet, all problems fixed," Jax had said to her the last time they'd talked. "Wouldn't you give up everything to be 18 again?"

"I can't tell you how grateful I am not to be 18 anymore," she'd said. "Are your memories of being 18 happy ones?"

"Some."

"Yes, some of mine too, but there are some I'd erase in a flash if I had the chance. And I'd never give up what I've learned since then. I'm content to be myself."

"But that's the beauty of it, you don't have to give up anything. They say you'll keep all that you've learned, all that you remember, all that you are, but in a young body. If youth is wasted on the young, then step aside and let us older folks have a shot at it!"

"What you're saying makes me wonder if I should just drop the whole thing right now, 2,500 credits or not," said Rachel. "I have faith in God, and you don't, so certain things are important to me that you might not . . . well . . . it's personal."

"What does God have to do with this?"

She was quiet. "I just . . . my body belongs to me and God. My body, which includes my soul. It's not a machine, it's not public property, it's not for playing around with. It's my eternal self."

Jax snorted. "Eternal?"

"You're making fun of me now?"

"No, of course not. I'm sorry. But I don't think God would have any problem with you doing this. You belong to you and God, and you're eternal. Nothing needs to change about that part if your eternal body and soul are moved from one planet to another, maybe even made young again along the way. Don't worry, God won't get confused."

"Now you *are* making fun of me," she said, feeling the awkwardness of being seen by Jax without being able to see him. She blinked the command to turn off her camera. "Bodies have a natural lifespan," she said, more free now to say what she meant. "We die to make space for the young. God made us, and our mortality helps us remember who and what we are, which is dependent creatures. Created, and that's the way it is, whether you believe it or not. So drop it."

"Okay, but . . . I still don't see the problem," said Jax's voice. "What if your heart went bad? They'd replace it with a new one, grown from your stem cells."

"They'd replace yours, maybe," said Rachel. "I could never afford that."

"Well, maybe *I'd* pay for yours. The point is, you'd still be yourself, right?"

"Yes, but . . . ."

"So this is the same thing, except instead of just your heart it's your whole body being rejuvenated, made younger by the miracle of tech."

"You're confusing me. This is totally different than a heart problem. You're not hearing what I'm saying. What I'm saying is that I do not want to do it."

"Okay, but you're going in for testing, right? As you've said, what harm can it do? And they'll pay you more money, which I know you need. Please, try to keep an open mind?"

And she was trying to do just that. She'd made it through the holovid in one piece, and although none of her doubts were resolved, she felt invited forward in a way that had nothing to do with Jax, money, or anything else.

Although she didn't plan to try to explain this to Jax, an invisible hand beckoned her forward, urging her to keep exploring the possibilities for reasons she couldn't articulate, even to herself.

*
* *

The day became overcast. Pixel by pixel the colors in the room changed into grays, until finally Rachel and Eliza could no longer see their culinary playthings. Rachel hoisted herself off the floor, turned on the lights, and started preparing real food for supper.

Eliza colored while Rachel talked to her and puttered around the house. She paused and exchanged a long look with her granddaughter. "Will you be okay without me if I leave?" she whispered.

*
* *

By the time Miriam came back from wherever she'd been, Eliza had settled down to sleep, and Rachel was in her rocker doing a word puzzle. Before Miriam could speak, Rachel put a finger to her lips and pointed toward Eliza's small bed. Miriam rolled her eyes and sat down with a thump, then flipped noisily through a catalog.

"I went in for the holovid," Rachel whispered, "and I'm thinking of going in for testing. For the colony expedition."

Miriam nearly jumped out of her chair. "Oh *mom*! I'm so jealous."

"Shh!"

"I knew you'd change your mind," said Miriam in a loud whisper.

"I haven't changed my mind. But they're offering more money, and all I have to do is go in for testing."

"Becca will love this," said Miriam, now speaking at a normal volume. "I can't wait to tell everyone. I wish I could see what they're gonna do to you. Hell, I wish *I* could go. And my voice is *not* waking her *up*, mom."

"All I said is that I *might* go for testing," said Rachel, a bit vexed. "And I'm not letting anyone *do anything* to me."

"You know," said Miriam, "if you don't like it, you can get up and walk out. That's what I'd do. They have to give you the money anyway, right?"

"No, hon, they wouldn't give me the money."

But the idea stuck: yes, she could always just get up and walk out if she wasn't comfortable. And if they kept the money and didn't pay her, that would be okay. She hadn't lost anything.

Testing

O God, test my heart and mind
for your unfailing love guides me,
and I live in reliance on your faithfulness.
—Psalm 26:2–3

The morning of the test, Rachel was awake before dawn. The confirmation message from Ark said nothing about what the testing involved, and every possibility made her nervous. Was it a physical test? Aptitude? Knowledge? She tried to meditate, but it was hopeless. "Have mercy on me," she prayed over and over as she fried her breakfast eggs and rice.

Maybe Miriam could just get up and walk out without a word if a situation bothered her, but that kind of thing was harder for Rachel, so she prepared herself. She thought up a line she could use if she needed to leave, vague enough to work in any situation. She would shake her head for a moment as if trying to hear a spotty transmission and say, "I'm so sorry, but something's come up. I need to leave."

She stood on the crowded train as it pulled her toward the Wolf Corp campus, and then she transferred to a ferry that took her across the lake to Ark Island. Would Sam be at work today? She'd forgotten to ask when she told him about her testing appointment. He'd been strangely quiet during that conversation, so she called him again.

"Are you in the office today, honey? I'm on my way in for testing."

"I'm here, but I won't get to see you. I don't know much about that aspect of the Ark Project. The testing, I mean . . . ."

"I'm already nervous enough, and you being mysterious isn't helping, Sam."

"I'm sorry mom, I don't mean to be mysterious. I'm sorry you're nervous. Hang in there, it'll be fine." He paused. "Look, I've gotta go—call me tonight."

Had he said it would be fine because there was no turning back now, and he just didn't want her to be nervous? No, that was a crazy thought. But he'd been using his extra-cheery voice, the one he used when he was faking it. Or exaggerating. Or both.

Oh stop it, she told herself. He's right, it's going to be fine. What's the big deal?

But as she stepped off the ferry and made her way toward Ark building 19, a shining edifice nestled among exotic trees in the Testing neighborhood of the island, her nervousness came rushing back. She practiced her exit line as she walked the last 10 meters to the building. "I'm so sorry," she whispered, "but something's come up. I'm so sorry . . . ."

A young man in a red polyester suit was by the door, pointing a scanner toward her. By the time she reached him he was ready to greet her by name, and probably knew tidbits about her that she didn't even know herself. "Good morning, Ms. Deimos," he said. "We're so glad you came. Please come right in and join us."

As he spoke he put his hand around her elbow, and she noticed that his short fingernails were manicured. Handing her a card with the number 402 on it, he steered her toward a seat in the waiting room with hundreds of people, some chatting and laughing nervously. To her surprise, she recognized Anya from Human Converse, and she gave a little wave in Anya's direction. Anya, in her tube top, poncho, mini skirt, and green thigh-high boots, seemed even younger than she usually did—especially among all these elderly folks. She gripped the hand of the bearded man next to her, and Rachel recognized him from the last Human Converse holiday party. Ollie? Oscar?

Something like that. Maybe Anya and her man were hoping to travel to Patience together.

An ancient woman wearing a wrinkled denim dress sat to Rachel's left. The woman's hands, lying relaxed in her lap, were shriveled and knobby. "I'm Serenity," she said as if to no one. Rachel wasn't sure whether Serenity was offering her name or her condition, but the man on Rachel's other side leaned over Rachel and took Serenity's hand between both his own, pumping it up and down. "How do you do, Serenity," he said with a friendly grin. "And hello again, Rachel," he said to Rachel, now shaking her hand. "I'm Bob. Remember? We met when we did the holovid." Rachel nodded and arranged her face in a polite smile.

"Don't know about *you*," said Bob, settling back into his seat, "but *I* keep thinking about the experience I had in the holovid." He folded the magazine he'd been reading and lay it across his belly. "Seeing my mom again like that, it was . . . well, it made me realize I wasn't 100 percent done *griev*ing. Know what I mean?"

Normally a topic this charged with emotion would bring Rachel to attention, but she was only half listening. "Uh-huh," she said.

Why was she even here? The money would help, she reminded herself. Yes, the money. The Ark Project must be made of solid money. She planned to put today's payment into a savings account—her first deposit in five years.

She started to sweat, and she was getting a bit light-headed. She probably hadn't had enough breakfast. "I'm so sorry, but something's come up," she whispered, practicing.

She turned her attention to one of the displays that hung from the ceiling. It showed a horizon with a lovely blue-green globe suspended above it. "The view from Tetheus," the label said, "Wolf 1061 Patience's larger moon." The scene shifted to an animated diagram of a ship circling the blue marble of planet Earth and slingshotting into space. A buttery voice described the massive terraformers and other support ships that left for Patience more than 200 years ago. The ships had traveled for 88 years, just as the colonists would. "Now they orbit Patience like benevolent, celestial patrons," the voice continued, "mechanical visitors from Earth, carefully, steadily transforming the blank surface and poisonous atmosphere of Patience into a blue-green haven for life. What a gift we're offering the entire Wolf 1061 system, building this jewel in its midst."

Rachel pretended to be engrossed in the scene, which now showed two soft-looking moons suspended over a warmly lit desert. She noticed an augmented reality headset resting on a hook on the side of her chair. The usher had told her it would be at least 15 minutes before her number was called, so she unhooked the headset and held it, hesitating. Less AR was better, that was her rule. But what would 15 minutes hurt? And besides, she was curious, and she felt guilty about not being fully present to Bob. As she seemed unable to make herself listen to him right now, she might as well put on the headset as a signal that he shouldn't *expect* her to be listening.

She activated the headset's face screen, and the docudrama came to life. She was standing in a mauve desert landscape. She turned her head to look at the succulents and blue wild-flowers that covered the ground around her. Reassuringly, she could still see the waiting room and Bob's knee in faded colors behind the scene, so she felt grounded and oriented to where she was in physical space.

The buttery voice was closer now. "Imagine that this Eden is filled with people who've become your dearest friends," said the voice. "People who've journeyed with you through the most important transition of your life. Your body is strong.

Young. Your life is ahead of you. Imagine all this, but in a society where people are equal, where all have meaningful work, where all are cared for from birth to death. And now imagine this: you helped make it happen."

The voice changed to a plainer voice, one Rachel had heard in reality just a few minutes earlier: the girl who was making announcements over the loudspeaker. "Attention, future heroes of Earth. If your number is 341 through 425, it's your turn. Within the next two minutes, please bring your AR experience to a close and return your consciousness to the room. Thank you."

That was polite — they gave a bit of warning instead of just cutting you off. She removed the headset, smoothed her hair, and got up to join the other 84 chattering, excited people whose numbers were up. The usher with the manicured nails herded them toward a small door.

At the door, she stopped.

The room was filled with gurney-like cots, and she'd seen photos of cots like these in Miriam's VR catalogs. They were haptic full-body immersion VR technology table harnesses, or as Miriam and her friends called them, full-body bags.

*
* *

She backed up and bumped into Bob. "I'm so sorry," she muttered, "but something has . . . something . . . ."

She felt a hand grip her forearm, and it was that usher boy, asking if she was okay. She stared at his hand on her arm, and at his wrist, a skinny wrist with a few dark hairs sprouting out of it. The red polyester sleeve was too short, and it showed a lot of wrist, a lot of arm. She suddenly wondered how this boy cleaned his red suit. Did he send it out? Could he wash it at home? Did Ark pay for cleaning?

"Now don't worry," he intoned quietly, his mouth close to Rachel's ear, "I know that you in particular, Ms. Deimos, aren't crazy about VR." He pushed her toward a chair outside the gurney room, turning the chair so it faced away from the open door. "The thing is," he continued as he guided her gently into the chair, "it's tough for us to deliver information to this many people all at once. So we ask that you participate in the VR segment of our day, which lasts only 20 minutes. Only 20 minutes." He was on one knee by her side, handing her a glass of water — where had that come from? "We have privacy curtains around the tables; we're extremely respectful of folks who value their privacy. No part of the experience will violate your personal beliefs," he said. "While you're in harness, you won't be asked to accept any programming. If you'd like to view our privacy policy, I can transmit it to you in a jiffy, here, it'll just take a moment. And here's Angelica, she'll help you into your VR harness, and she'll help you afterwards too . . . ."

His voice was rhythmic and soft, his face close to Rachel's, and now a young woman was next to him, bending to look into Rachel's eyes. Angelica's eyes were a deep brown, and widely set, she noticed. Like Sam's.

A long document appeared in Rachel's peripheral vision, but she dismissed it, and the red-suited usher's words pattered on like rain. "It's only 20 minutes, but we're limited to these 85 tables. As you can imagine we've processed more than 85 people today, so obviously you won't spend all day on that table. We need you to get into the harness for just 20 minutes, and then your group will move on to the next phase of our testing so the next 85 people can use the harnesses. And that's it, that's all there is to it. It's about sharing, not so complicated, really. You're in Angelica's hands now, she'll take you in . . . ."

Angelica helped Rachel to her feet, then propelled her through the door and toward a table marked 28. She recognized Bob's face peeking out of a glutinous sack of VR gel on table 29, and he smiled up at her. Angelica whisked a privacy curtain into place around table 28, but not before Rachel noticed naked people on other tables, wriggling into their sacks, squeezing their fingers into the fitted gloves.

"I'm sorry," Rachel said, "but something's come up." Her volume trailed off. "I need to . . . ."

Were those tears welling up in Angelica's eyes? It seemed as if she knew what Rachel wanted to say, and that she just might cry if Rachel said it. "I'm sorry," Rachel began again, and social shame washed over her, a sense of being out of step with everyone around her. No one else was trying to leave, so what was wrong with her? "I'm so sorry, oh . . . you're waiting for me, aren't you? I'm slowing you down. I'm so sorry."

The gear was awkward, and getting into it took a few minutes after she got undressed. "You're in," Angelica said, smiling.

Terror washed through Rachel as the bag tightened around her, pressing her gloved hands against her sides. Angelica held a mask against her face, and it sealed against her skin. "God help me," she tried to whisper, but she could no longer move her lips. Her body twitched with panic as the machine sucked the air out from around her face and body. She tried to draw a breath, but couldn't.

Suddenly the machine took over her respiration with a jerk. Her panic stopped as if someone had toggled it off. She couldn't breathe, but she didn't need to, and she was oddly calm about this fact.

*
**

She'd expected to fade out of regular reality and into VR, but the change was abrupt. Without an in-between, she found herself standing barefoot on warm sand, wriggling her toes to enjoy the gentle softness. She looked up and saw, on the horizon, the two moons that had captured her attention before —

only now she felt as if she could reach up and touch them. Inexplicably, she knew many facts about these moons. The big one, Tetheus, looked much larger than Earth's moon, and it seemed dangerously close to Callista, the smaller moon, but their orbits were thousands of kilometers apart; they never intersected. She wondered what it would look like to see Tetheus eclipse Callista. It happened every 412 days, of course. Of course! A gentle wind blew a fishy, ocean smell past her. Remembering that Patience had a sun, she looked to her left and saw it rising, warm and strong.

People stood around her — young people, without a stitch of clothing. The man next to her patted himself on the chest, looking down at his hairy body. "I can't believe it!" he said in a familiar voice.

"Uh, Bob?"

He grinned.

"Weren't you, aren't you, right there in the bed next to mine?" said Rachel.

"Yes! Can you believe it?" He laughed, then let out an ear-splitting whoop. Everyone around them was carrying on as Bob was, and not one of them had gray hair or a spare tire. She looked down and gasped. It was as if her head were now on a stranger's body, a young woman's naked body. And yet . . . this body was something like the one she'd had 25 years earlier.

She remembered the red-suited usher and his promise of respect and privacy, and the privacy curtain around her table when she took off her clothes, but these memories left her mind as quickly as they arrived. Instead of indignation she felt a giddy elation, but she forced herself to be calm. Bringing herself back down was a habit borne of decades of the disappointing grit of real life. This is simulated, she reminded herself. Not real. Not true. She brought to mind the disorienting experiences she'd had in VR when she was young. This isn't fun for me, she told herself.

The people around her obviously didn't agree. The beach they were on was wide, inviting, and scattered with beach toys. A few people started a volleyball game, and a few others batted at a large, colorful ball. Five or six ran straight for the water and started splashing each other.

"Is this what the planet actually looks like? And is this what they think we actually *want*?" said Rachel, grabbing a towel to cover herself as she gestured at the volleyball game. Bob guffawed at the ridiculousness of the question. "Who cares!" he said.

A perky young lady appeared, seemingly out of nowhere, with a tray of drinks.

"No thank you," said Rachel, holding up her hand.

"Oh, come *off* it!" said Bob, with mock horror on his face. He took two pink umbrella drinks off the tray and held one out to Rachel. "Just have a sip. Or eat the cherry! It looks *delicious*, doesn't it?"

She smiled. "Okay. Yes." As she offered this verbal consent, she reached out and took the drink from Bob's hand, then sipped the icy pink liquid. A sweet flavor filled her mouth, and she felt a painful jolt of panic as clear insight reached her, too late.

She blacked out.

*
**

Rachel came to herself only a moment later, it seemed. Contentment washed through her body and mind. This wasn't the effect of drugs or innerbots or anything strange or dangerous — she felt sure of it. It was all so natural, a gentle and glorious sensation, like waking up in the world's most comfortable bed after a 14-hour sleep. She opened her eyes and discovered that she was sitting upright on a soft maroon couch in a dim, warm room. Someone had cleaned the VR gel off her body and re-dressed her in the clothes she'd been wearing when she arrived. This should trouble her, she knew, but it was hard to push her thoughts any further than that.

Bob and others relaxed near her, people she was beginning to recognize. They looked as they'd looked that morning — mostly over 60, most with a few extra kilos, and all fully clothed.

Angelica was on an ottoman by Rachel's feet.

"Well," said Angelica, leaning toward her, "you're back."

Her mouth felt cottony. "Strange," she managed to say.

"Do you feel okay?"

"Okay? I'm . . . happy. Comfortable."

"Good," said Angelica. "When you're up to it, you can go home. No rush. But when you do go, we'll make sure a few items are waiting for you online — links and access codes for research that you can do, if you still have questions about the expedition."

"When does the testing begin?"

Angelica laughed. "You passed our tests with flying colors. And we hope you enjoyed your taste of what life on Wolf 1061 Patience might be like for you after your body spends 88 years being rejuvenated in one of our patented deep-sleep beds aboard the *Svalbard*. That's what you experienced on the beach in the VR world."

"Oh."

"A simulation of what your new life might be like for you. Easy, wasn't it?"

Rachel's face was blank.

"And now you know what it'll feel like when you make your greatest contribution to the well-being of humankind. If you're worried about the effects of the journey itself, we can assure you that your long rest aboard the *Svalbard* will leave you feeling how you just said you're feeling right now. Happy. Comfortable."

Rachel blinked, and her eyes felt sticky. A numb fuzziness had lowered around her intellect like a curtain. "It's late," she said, checking her in-eye clock. "I feel like I've only been here an hour. What happened during the rest of the day?"

"You were resting."

"But, drugs? Or . . . did you . . . ."

"Please don't worry," said Angelica, putting her hand on Rachel's knee. "We did nothing that wasn't spelled out clearly in the release form you signed. You remember that, don't you?"

Her smile was kind.

For reasons she couldn't explain, Rachel knew now that she wanted to go on this expedition. Why had she doubted? She couldn't remember. As she made her way home by ferry, train, and streetcar, the Ark jingle circled in her head. "Your body is safe with us, safe with us, your body is safe with us . . . ."

Guilt

> But now, as the soul plainly appears to be immortal, there
> is no release or salvation from evil except the attainment of
> the highest virtue and wisdom.
> —Socrates, speaking in Plato's *Phaedo*

Dirty Linen was Arjuna's guilty pleasure. Sam made fun of him
for hanging out in tawdry pop VR like that, but it helped him
relax.

It was Sea Monster Day, and he was a shiny violet hippo-
camp. Without a straight dopamine feed he was less entertained than the krakens and grindylows around him, but he
still found himself giggling like a little girl during Triton's
opening monolog. He stopped giggling, though, when Triton
introduced the day's featured guest. It was a striped sea-
wyvern named Toryu who was, Arjuna quickly figured out,
Sam's sister Miriam. He was not at all amused when Toryu
produced a recording of Sam Deimos, a significant contributor
to the Ark Project, being paternalized by an Ark executive.

"And there's more!" Toryu roared with her dragon mouth.
"I found this in the trash can in the lab at Ark!" She used a
wing claw to dig a small item out from behind her ear, and
Arjuna recognized a used strip of soul fabric, printed royal blue
in the Ark style.

Triton and Toryu, with shouted hints and advice from the
other sea creatures, decided Ark must be doing some kind of
soul tampering. How could they create anti-aging deep sleep
any other way? It made sense, right? Or maybe they weren't
planning to get the colonists to Patience by means of deep-
sleep tech at all. Maybe something else was going on. Triton
promised to get a soulistics expert on the show as soon as he
could possibly spear one with his trident.

Arjuna disengaged his VR and returned to the reality of the pillow and blanket under his workstation at Ark. He messaged Sam. That idiot needed to get a handle on his sister, and fast.

*
**

Tensel was slumped in his workstation chair at home. His reading slate was perched on Zoë's back as she slept, curled in a circle, on his lap. He'd had it open to the same page of Dr. Su Fordyce's paper for 45 minutes, but his reverie broke when Zoë stood up to stretch and lie back down. Although his fans wouldn't recognize him, bedraggled as he was, they'd know Zoë. Her expression was as sullen as Tensel's, but she was sleek and well fed, and there was no mistaking her vivid green eyes, her long neck, and the black spots that patterned her brown-orange fur.

When she resettled herself, Tensel rested the slate against her side, then flipped back a few pages to reread the part about why Dr. Fordyce and her team at Ark chose the name "Temenos" for the database. A temenos was a holy place, a sanctuary. A place to rest, a place of safety.

Safety? Was Su high? Or maybe trying to be ironic?

Ark's Temenos was a massive cyborg holding tank—a storage facility for the colonists' macro quantum patterns during their trip to Wolf 1061. The concept was Tensel's, but the technology had moved light years since his first experiments.

In her paper, Su theorized that the colonists' patterns wouldn't be able to interact with each other at all during their years of confinement together. But she argued that if they *could* interact, their communication would consist only of "honest signals"—signals containing only truth; signals such as the ones nonverbal animals send and receive.

So-called souls, living together without bodies, for decades. Near each other, but unable to touch, speak, or hear. As he thought about this, Tensel felt his mind and heart tilt downward. He hoped the colonists would be unconscious during the trip, but what if they weren't? What if they *could* communicate, unable to send or receive anything but truth? That seemed more frightening than 88 years of blank unconsciousness. Truth, the commodity no one seemed eager to share with the colonists while they were still on Earth, might be the only thing they could share with one another during the enigma of their journey.

His interior weather was changing, and the clouds inside him were pulling together to block out the sun. "It's my fault," he thought. "A disaster no one has yet imagined will happen — something terrible. And it's my fault."

Panic came closer. He tossed the slate aside and picked up Zoë as he stood, trying not to wake her, but she jumped down and ran to the balcony door. He let her out and sat at his writing desk, a plain wooden antique with no tech input or output.

"Slow down," he told himself. "Calm down."

He opened a drawer and pulled out a real ink pen and his journal, then turned to a fresh page and took it between his thumb and index finger. "Slow down." He focused his mind on the feel of the crinkly, tough cellulose against his fingers, the glint of light on the shiny barrel of the pen, and the scratch of the pen's nib as he began to push and pull it across the fibers of the paper. His breathing slowed as he wrote.

Learning about the Temenos. So strange. Last night I dreamed that my legs were numb and heavy. In the dream I'm trying to make my way through a jam-packed casino, but I can hardly walk. I struggle to move one leg and then the other, pushing people out of my way in slow motion. Up ahead, I see a kid I knew in grammar school. I try with all my strength to catch him, but I can't. I never will. I'm terrified and frustrated.

The scene changes. I'm inside a warm, dark room, asleep, but I'm not dead. I'm thinking nothing. No thoughts. Relief, but I haven't killed myself, not exactly, because I *can't* kill myself.

I woke up thinking about my new obsession: I want to go on the colony trip.

It was just past dawn. Did Zoë want back in? He opened the balcony door and gazed at her, perched on the railing in the pale light, eyes half shut. Well, *one* of them might as well take a bit of joy from the morning. He shut the door and sat back down at his writing desk.

I don't know why, but going on this cursed voyage, which I helped create, seems a fitting end for me — better than a quick death here on Earth. But how will I pull it off? They've made the final selection, and they're prepping the Temenos to receive a particular set of macro patterns, not including mine or Z's. I need to find out how they plan to compensate for en-route fluctuations in the density and comp. of the patterns; that'll tell me how to recalibrate. Hmm.

I'll keep thinking, but the important thing is to *go*. It comes into my mind a hundred times a day.

If I asked Jess, Sam, Dr. K, they'd tell me I need to eat more superfoods, take more pills, talk more, run more, the list goes on. But wouldn't their lives be easier without me? I hate my work. I'm not doing my share. Su, Sam, all of them must be tired of holding me up.

And I cling to Jess — that's how it must feel to her. She has so much life, so much to explore, while my circle just winds tighter and tighter, smaller and smaller. Without me she'd be free, and she could keep growing. She probably wishes I weren't holding her back.

He heard the front door click open. Feeling guilty, he folded his journal and locked it with his thumb print.

"Oh good, you've been writing in your journal," said Jessica as she came in and bent to kiss him on the forehead. "The doctor said it might help."

*
**

A few days later, Jessica was waiting in the hall when Tensel and Sam left their weekly status meeting at Ark. Her hair was down, softly framing her face, and she was wearing makeup, something that didn't happen often. Tensel's face hardened when he saw her. "Jess!" he said, pulling her aside and turning his back on Sam. He spoke quietly. "I told you this morning that you can leave me be, because I'm fine."

Zoë was riding in a black courier bag that hung against his left hip. She put her paws over the edge of the bag and stared hard at Jessica.

"I'm not here to see you. Either of you," Jessica answered, glancing at Zoë. "Sam and I are having lunch."

". . . Sam?"

They looked at Sam, who was pretending to look for something in the bottom of his backpack.

Jessica held out a lunch bag to Tensel. "I brought a sandwich for you and Zoë, if you want it."

Tensel took the bag, then turned and walked toward his office as Jessica stared after him.

"See what I mean?" said Jessica to Sam as they set out for the food court. "Inscrutable."

She asked about Miriam's feature on Dirty Linen, which it seemed everyone had heard about. "Is it true, what they're digging up about Ark? Are you treated fairly here?"

Sam just smiled.

"And the part about that soul fabric Miriam found, wow," Jessica continued. "You'd think Tensel would tell me if you people were using soul tech, but the way he's been lately, who knows?"

"Mira's way off base, about everything," said Sam, careful not to look at Jessica while he said it. She could read him pretty well, and he hated lying to her. "She's off the rails, and I've only just now forgiven her. But no harm done."

In truth, Sam wasn't sure he *had* forgiven her, and he was furious with himself for letting his sister visit him at work. He should've known better. Miriam's lack of discretion had created a PR nightmare about the undercurrent of racism at Ark, which Sam preferred to ignore (Ark was easy, compared to some environments he'd been in as a black man). And thanks to that scrap of soul fabric Miriam had found, plus the footage she got of him seeming to express doubt about the trip's safety, Ark had moved up the launch timeline by three months. No one wanted to deal with what would happen if the busybodies at Dirty Linen, or anyplace else, put together the truth about Merge before the launch.

Three months was an eternity in a complex, tightly scheduled project like the Patience expedition, so this already stressful project was beginning to feel panicked and maybe even sloppy.

"I'd rather not talk about all that right now," he said to Jessica. "I just want to enjoy being with you. How about Thai? They have an awesomely spicy papaya salad, and I know you like that." He kept chatting until they got their food and found a window seat overlooking a projection of Mt. Everest.

"Was that harsh, not inviting Tensel to eat with us?" said Jessica as they ate.

"What was harsh about it? It's been ages since you and I spent time together without him."

"Exactly. I wanted to do this because I'm *happy* to spend time without him. I feel guilty about that."

"What's going on with you two, anyway?"

"He never smiles, he hardly sleeps. Did you see his face just now? He looks like he just came home from a war. We haven't had sex for a month."

"T's a serious guy."

"This is beyond serious. You need to make him promise not to do anything crazy."

"Me?" said Sam, raising his eyebrows and smiling.

She didn't return his smile. "Okay fine. Then tell him you're worried, you want him to get more help. Maybe he'll listen to you."

"Hoo boy, Tensel is *everyone's* project these days."

"Meaning?"

"It's not just you and me worrying about him. Ark noticed too, and they're trying to help him, in their own way. Between all of us, I truly believe he'll be okay."

"I hope so."

Sam handed her a napkin from the dispenser on their table, and she blew her nose and dabbed at her eyes. "So how's *your* life?" he said. "How are *you*?"

"Fine, I guess. It's hard to concentrate on my thesis when Tensel's like this. And it's hard to get a good night's sleep next to him. He has nightmares, and what goes on inside him reaches me."

Sam's warm eyes were earnest, and he was listening attentively. "I can see that," he said. He put his hand next to Jessica's on the table so that his little finger, with its black onyx pinky ring, was touching her thumb. A few of her nails were bitten down to the quick. "I'm worried about you," he said. "And Tensel. I'm worried about you both."

She smiled. "I'm glad you and Tensel are friends. You and I have known each other for so long, and I'd hate it if you didn't get along with my boyfriend. It's nice the way things've turned out."

"Yes, *nice*," said Sam. His eyes were fixed on their hands next to each another, his dark one next to her slender pale one. He couldn't help but notice how, well, *nice* they looked together.

*
**

Tensel was lying on the couch with Zoë. "I had another dream about sleeping inside the *Svalbard*," he said.

Jessica's hair was back in its usual tight ponytail, and she had her acrylic paints and a canvas set up in front of the window that looked out toward Ark headquarters. Her plan was to paint a group of pink and yellow tulips she'd photographed at the biopreserve, but she hadn't made it past the outline, which she sketched with a pencil, then erased. Her penciled flowers looked to her like strange, angry faces.

"Well, you can't go. And even if you could, Zoë can't go with you."

"I know," he said. "I'm just saying I had that dream again."

"It doesn't mean anything. Dreams are your mind trying to make sense out of the flotsam of life's events. Making a story. It's what we do."

"My mind could make any story out of the flotsam. Why this story?"

Jessica set her pencil down, slapped her hands onto her knees, and turned toward Tensel.

"I'll tell you why. It's because you feel guilty. Guilty about sending those colonists off to Patience with their lives depending on half-baked technology, lying there in deep-sleep beds that are a whole lot like coffins. And even though it's not your fault, you believe it's your fault. The only way to not feel guilty would be to suffer along with them. Your psyche is offering you a way to be free of your debilitating guilt."

"Oh, thank you Dr. Jung," said Tensel. He turned onto his side to face the back of the couch, and Zoë scrambled onto his hip to stare at Jessica.

"Well, I think it's pretty obvious," she said. Her flower outline would never be good enough, so she needed to call it done and start painting, but she couldn't begin. She put her brush down, picked it up, held it, bit the end of it, put it down, picked it up.

Ten minutes passed, and Tensel rolled to face Jessica again. "You're wrong when you say it's not my fault. You want to make everything fine, you want everyone to just carry on. But the truth is, it's my fault."

"No." Jessica lay her paintbrush on the table a little harder than she meant to. "That's not truth — this project was taken out of your hands. They're using deep-sleep tech, which isn't even your area of expertise. You don't *own* this anymore. You need to let it go."

He was quiet for a long time. "There are things you don't know," he said. "Can you simply believe me when I say that bad events are unfolding, and that I'm to blame? And about me going on this trip, yes I'm depressed, I'm sad, but those feelings don't control my thoughts. I'm not irrational. It might actually make sense for me to go."

"Okay. Why?"

"When they reach the planet they might need a human with a nuanced understanding of the technology."

She sighed. "I want to hear you on this, but once they reach the Wolf 1061 system and slow down, the bots will reestablish communication with scientists on Earth. Those scientists will know more then than you know now. You have to admit it."

"Yes, but . . . the colony tech is part mystery, part art. It's not all about knowledge. I don't usually talk like this, I know, but they might need a human scientist to be physically present with them, for reasons we can't foresee."

"And you might die."

"If I stay here, I'll be dead long before they arrive. What's the difference?"

"You know they've already made the final selection, right? You going isn't part of the plan. You know all of this. Just tell me that you'll talk to Dr. Kendel and see what he thinks about the idea before you do anything on your own to make it happen, okay? I'm worried about you. Please? Tell me?"

He stood up and pushed Zoë off his lap onto the floor. "I don't want to talk about it anymore." He went in the bedroom, Zoë scooting behind him through the bedroom door just as it shut.

*
* *

Tensel had a few promising ideas about how the emergence of macro quantum patterns could be more effectively suppressed within clones, and he was supposed to flesh out his notes and develop experiments. Dr. Kendel scheduled a one-on-one to see how it was going, and he'd barely settled into his chair when Tensel, who was standing, started to talk.

"Dr. Kendel, I think, I think, I should be one of the colonists. Zoë should go too."

"You're not on the selection list, Dr. Brown."

"There's no reason I can't be. A few people are paying to go. Why can't I?"

"We need you here."

"They might need me there."

"Look, you know they'll be fine without you on the other end."

Tensel sat down facing Dr. Kendel's desk, lay his long hands on his knees, and closed his eyes for a moment, willing himself to settle down. "I've given this careful thought," he said, "and I have my reasons. It wouldn't just benefit me, it would benefit you too, and Ark, because I'm famous. If I go, it'll prove that the trip is safe, and you'll get good press. Sending Zoë could open up whole new areas of research."

"Ah." Dr. Kendel spoke more slowly. "Alright Dr. Brown, here it is. I'm disappointed for you, really I am, but we aren't sending people like you and me. You get it?"

"Like you and me?" Tensel said, raising his eyebrows. "Like you and me. Like you, like me . . . ."

"Please, take your time. Would you like a glass of resveratrol water? A cup of herb tea?" Tensel shook his head, looking perplexed, and Dr. Kendel continued. "I don't know what your imagination's cooking up about the dangers of this trip, or some kind of conspiracy theory — maybe you've been visiting Dirty Laundry? Oh my!" He chuckled. "But as you well know, the trip *does* involve uncontrollable factors. Of course there are risks, and our colonists have agreed to take those risks in exchange for the chance to win life's jackpot. A fresh start! A young body! A planet to explore!"

"They agreed? Your so-called soul adepts? Give me a break." Tensel stood up, suddenly animated. "They hardly had time to see the legal docs you flashed past them, let alone read them or think about what they were agreeing to. And they didn't just sign papers, they affixed their biological assent. They can't think rationally about the trip anymore. They can't even wonder whether they might be making a mistake, because their bodies have said such a deep yes."

"Oh come on, let's be real." Dr. Kendel leaned back in his chair with his hands clasped behind his head, smiling up at Tensel where he stood. "Even though we disagree now and then, we're friends here, aren't we? You and I? Now. We both know that those people wouldn't have read those legal documents if we'd given them a year to do it, let alone a couple of days. Hmm? They're being given a unique and complex opportunity! It's a good deal for them—we know that, you and I can see that, and we're the ones who've thought it through."

Tensel stared hard at a spot on the front of Dr. Kendel's desk. The irony galled him: if they were the ones able to think it through to the point that they saw the danger, then they were the ones who should pull the emergency brake and stop this catastrophe.

". . . and as you're aware," Dr. Kendel was saying, "a few of these people aren't qualified but are paying us a king's ransom to go, which means they *want* this, risks be damned. As for our selected colonists, Arjuna's precious soul adepts, this is the best thing that ever happened to them. They're famous, and their families will have heaps of money after they depart. Sure, some might not survive, but some might. Be happy for their good fortune, let them go, and be grateful for the excellent experimental data they'll provide."

He paused, fixing Tensel with an evaluative stare. "Have I clarified things for you?"

"Perfectly," said Tensel, turning to leave.

Loosening

We look for the resurrection of the dead,
and the life of the world to come.
—Nicene Creed

Sam went for a bike ride along the path that rimmed Ark Island, turning his face to catch the mild breeze and the warmth of the sun, trying to clear his thoughts. He understood Merge technology, he trusted the expertise of Tensel and the other scientists who'd developed it, and he understood why Ark was lying to the colonists. To him it felt like an unpleasant but necessary lie, one designed to keep people from panicking. He knew Tensel had doubts about Merge tech, but Tensel was depressed and pessimistic. Sam's earnest belief was that in the end, all would be well. He believed that Merge would produce the same end result as the imaginary anti-aging deep-sleep tech that Ark had sold to the public.

But it bothered him that his mom didn't know what would happen to her. She'd care if she knew her body was going to die in its current form. No doubt she'd have something to say to God about it. She'd probably want a ritual or a prayer service, or even a whole funeral.

Or maybe if she knew what was really going to happen, the shock would snap her out of the control that Ark had over her mind and body.

No, Ark had probably made it impossible for her to doubt them. But who knew?

For the millionth time, he went over his decision not to tell her. Should he? Probably not. But maybe . . . ?

No. He should've paid more attention, he should've intervened before she went in for that first holovid immersion, but now it was too late. To try and talk her out of it now that she'd given full biological consent would do no more than create painful cognitive dissonance within her. He'd be asking her to hold two incompatible beliefs at the same time: I believe Sam when he tells me not to go; I believe Ark when they tell me to go.

No, the kindest thing he could do for his mom was to help her accept Ark's version of the truth, help her walk forward into a future that was already scary enough without him adding extra stress and pain.

He pedaled faster, trying to think about other things. He dreaded saying goodbye, and he wanted to be distracted — that's probably why he'd gotten so involved in Tensel and Jessica's drama, he realized, smiling faintly. He wanted life to stay just as it was, his mom safe on Earth where she belonged, helping to raise Eliza, going to church, working at Human Converse, only a phone call away if he needed her.

Ugh, his mind flashed on the image of bone chips and teeth in the prototype scanner, left over from tests on rats. That would be his mom, soon enough. But her soul would re-emerge on Patience in a new body. That was good, right? And she had a strong soul, a fantastic soul. If anyone would make it, she would.

But believing that his mom would be okay on the other side didn't fix the pain that welled up more insistently within him every day. "Keep it together, you," he told himself. "You can grieve like crazy when the trip is underway, after she's gone." He wanted to be upbeat when he said goodbye, and he wanted to be there for Miriam and Eliza. He knew that his part in Eliza's life would be bigger than ever once her Nana was gone.

The ceremony would be in the Ark auditorium, which seated 2,000 — nearly 500 colonists, plus their closest friends and family. The audience would hear speeches, watch vids, sing, applaud, cry. They'd be told that the colonists were on the threshold of life's greatest adventure. Each colonist would be called by name, walk or be carried to the podium, shake the hand of some gas-bag Ark exec, and disappear offstage to be sedated. Kind of like a graduation and the after-party.

But no one in the audience would see what happened after the sedation, what had already come next for plenty of rats.

Sam couldn't suppress a shudder as he parked his bike and went back inside.

*
* *

Spring was a glory of cold, sunny days. Rachel paused on her way up the front walk to touch the stems of the first yellow daffodils, just opening. She meant to take note of every blossom this year. As she ran her fingers up one green stem, an aching nostalgia filled her. Plants on Patience would be for food, not beauty — or so she assumed. The ships that carried the terraforming machines had had a long head start, and by the time the *Svalbard* arrived on Patience, the planet would have a life-sustaining atmosphere and biosphere. It made her sad that she'd never see her new home in its original state. If those scientists were so smart, couldn't they think of ways to use what was already in the Wolf 1061 star system instead of engineering something new? She would never experience Patience the way God had created it.

And here came that question again, the one she kept trying not to ask: was this trip God's plan for her? God's hope, God's dream for her? Her hand froze on the daffodil stem, and her thoughts stopped short. A familiar numb confusion entered her mind, which happened when she entertained doubts about the trip. To make it go away, she turned her thoughts around and marched them back toward sadness and nostalgia. "It's grief," she muttered to herself. "Grief. You know grief." She remembered the words from the latest memo from Ark: "We expect you to feel grief. It's an acceptable and healthy emotion for you to experience at this time." And the fact that she had to be ready to leave three months earlier than she expected wasn't helping.

Sam was swinging by tonight, and he'd probably want dinner on his way through. She turned away from the blossoms and went in the house. She had an uneasy feeling she was forgetting something, but that feeling was common now. It passed out of her mind entirely as she went inside and found Sam chopping vegetables.

"I didn't see you get here!" said Rachel, hanging her keys by the door. "What're you doing? *I* was going to make dinner for *you!*"

Sam turned to her sadly. "Mom, let me do something for you once in a while, will you? I have time to eat with you before the show tonight." He turned back to his task. "Hey, you know what they're calling the departure date now? The 'Day of Heroes.' Can you believe it? You're a hero, mom."

"You're not smiling, sweetie," said Rachel as she gave Sam a one-armed hug, pulling off her earrings with her other hand and dropping them in her pocket. "These days I can't tell if you're joking."

"Am I ever not joking?" he said, still not smiling.

"Sam, I don't want to go on the trip."

He stopped chopping and turned to face her, seeing her own surprise at what she'd just said. "I'm sorry," she said. "I don't know why I said that. It just came out . . . ."

Sam put down the knife and guided his mother to her rocker, pushing her down into it. He sat facing her. "Mom," he said, taking her hands in his, "the trip is safe, and I'm glad you're going. It's possible that Ark's not telling you everything, but trust me when I say that I'm familiar with the tech that'll be used on this trip, and I have confidence in it."

"I know, sweetheart," said Rachel, brushing away a tear.

"We're rushing the schedule to make our date, but Ark scientists are the best in the world. And . . . even if you want to back out, it's too late, and I think you understand that. I know you hate hearing about this kind of thing, but they might've implanted powerful suggestions in your psyche, and maybe helper nanobots in your brain. You wouldn't be able to tell them no, even if you tried."

Rachel looked confused. "But the choice is mine. They say the choice is mine."

"Let's give it a try, shall we?" said Sam, his voice soft. "What happens when you think about backing out? Try it right now: think about the details. How would you tell them? What would you say?"

"I . . . I . . . oh Sam, I can't concentrate. Let's finish making dinner. What was I thinking?" She smiled at him uncertainly, then stood up, put on an apron, and looked for a knife.

"That's what I thought," said Sam. "At this point, you might as well let go of your doubts and go with the flow. You're headed for Patience."

*
**

Three days before the Day of Heroes, Rachel spent the afternoon alone at home. She sat cross-legged next to her bed, a small metal memory box open on the altar in front of her. In this 4,000 cubic centimeter box, she was supposed to put everything that meant anything to her. How was that possible? She glanced again at the instructions. "Fill this box with anything you imagine might ease your transition into your younger body." Rachel could imagine no such thing. She felt a chill pass through her as she thought about the young version of herself who would emerge on Patience, a stranger to her, the one who would open the box on Patience. Why would she need this box of stuff to help her remember who she was now? Wouldn't she be able to remember on her own?

She pushed the thought aside. She had to fill the box, seal it with her fingerprint and iris scan, and submit it to her Ark representative no later than tomorrow morning. She'd already filled the bottom with printed photos: Eliza, Sam, Miriam, her mother and father, Josephine and other friends, and her favorite sights on Earth—the flowers in her own front yard, a sunset as seen from her window, the inside of Room 3 and the outside of the house. One of her favorites was a picture of Sam and Jessica that she'd taken when they thought they were alone in the front yard. Sam's arm was around Jessica and his mouth was up against her ear. Who knows what Sam's future might hold?

She held one more photo in her hand, an old one that she hadn't looked at for years: Jackson sitting on the front step smoking a blunt, decades ago. His smirk probably meant he'd just made a joke about the post-pregnancy weight Rachel was carrying, or maybe about her "career" as a voice worker.

Why would she take a photo of this man with her to another planet?

She dangled the photo over her lamp, holding it by a corner as the image melted and shriveled. The heat scorched her fingers, and the curling plastic smelled toxic. She dropped it onto the wood of her altar, then burst into tears when she saw the burn mark she'd made. In three days she'd leave her altar behind and never see it again. How would she know who she was? And what if God wasn't there for her, with her, on the other side? What if God didn't want her to go on this crazy trip after all?

Now she sobbed, plucking tissue after tissue from the box until a wet, soggy pile lay next to her on the floor. When she couldn't cry any more, she looked at the memory box again, her eyes red and stinging. Crying wouldn't make this thing fill up, damn it.

She still hadn't finished the letter she was writing to her future self. What about that? It was one of Ark's many suggestions. She smoothed one of her precious sheets of real paper out on her burned altar and thought about what she might write. Should she write about Miriam and Sam when they were babies? Her own childhood? Her job? The whole thing seemed hopeless. How could she possibly know now what might help her adjust on the other side? On a whim, she shoved her half-filled journal into the box instead of a letter. The journal filled most of the rest of the box, and its blank pages pleased her — they signified days ahead. She was sending the unfinished story of her life into the future as her blessing to her future self, leaving room for what was coming. Yes, it felt right.

She was almost there. What else? She toyed with the question: how can I remind myself of who I am? All my body parts, all my organs, my skin, my hair—they'll be *younger*. She pulled a pair of scissors out of a drawer in her altar and cut off a lock of her steel gray hair, wrapped it in a tissue, and lay it on top of her journal in the box.

She fingered the small gold cross around her neck. Would they let her wear it into deep sleep? What if they wouldn't? She took it from around her neck and held it up close to her face, turning it from side to side to let the light shine off of the emerald. "Thank you," she whispered as she dropped it into the box, not sure whether she was thanking God, Sam, or herself.

Done. She closed the lid, looked into the eye scanner, and pressed her hand into the fingerprint reader. The lock clicked, and only she could open it now. Somehow the thought was comforting: opening the box would reassure her that she was still herself, even if the deep-sleep tech did make her body younger.

Young or old, she'd still be herself.

*
**

Tensel spent the morning absorbed in Zoë's every move. He fed her, talked to her, played with her, and stroked her fur until she fell asleep on his lap. After she was asleep, he opened his journal to a fresh page and screwed his pen together with a new ink cartridge. His hands were shaking as he began to write.

> My mind terrifies me. I might get lost in here — forever. No one can protect me from the inside of my mind. If it slips and falls over the edge of this cliff, who or what can save me? If terror starts to travel with me, inside my head, then terror will be everywhere.

> So much inside me wishes this could all end. In a way, it's already over: my future is one long string of bad days, dead days, big black X's on my calendar. I want to disappear into the Temenos and experience whatever awaits our test subjects. I don't just want to do it, I *need* to do it, I *must*, but figuring out *how* takes so much energy. If only I could just push a button and be gone.

> I have to find the energy. I have to do it.

> I'm growing the stem cells that'll hold my soul and Zoë's. At the end I'll have to put Zoë through the machine. God, I don't know how I'm going to do it — my heart just might break. But I have to do it myself. I deserve that fate. And who knows, if all this crazy tech actually holds up, we might make it to Patience. And I'll see her there.

But the details, the details. A lot of things can't happen until *after* my soul's out of my body. Who can I ask? Who can I trust? Sam. Yes, Sam . . . .

*
**

Sam was late the next morning, not that anyone cared, least of all Tensel, his nominal supervisor. Tensel sat bolt upright at his workstation, but not hooked in. Just staring.

"Are you okay?" asked Sam.

Tensel turned toward Sam. "Yes. Absolutely." He looked calm, as if he'd slept, and he had color in his cheeks. Sam had the idea he'd decided something. "I haven't felt this good for a long time. I was thinking about this equipment, is all. Just . . . wondering."

"Huh. Okay. Well, you do look a little better."

Sam sat down and hooked into his gear. Something was off. "You're sure you're okay? Has something changed?"

"Don't worry, I'm fine. I've been getting outside, taking long walks. I'm doing everything my doctor told me to do, and I think it's working."

"Wow, that's terrific."

And it *was* terrific, but Jessica had texted him a couple of times that day, telling him Tensel was acting strange. Sam decided to be more direct.

"I'm glad you're feeling better, but even so, I'm worried about you, and Jessica is too. We're worried that you might do something to hurt yourself. I know you just told me you're on track with your doctor's advice, but still — I worry. We worry. And we care about you."

"I'll be fine, Sam. I feel peaceful."

"So can you promise me you're not going to hurt yourself? Promise you'll contact me right away if you're thinking about anything like that?"

Tensel paused. "Yes," he said quietly, "I'll let you know."

This was Rachel's last day on Earth, and every moment of it felt precious. When Jax called, she almost let it go to voicemail. She wouldn't mind a break from him, given that they would have plenty of time to talk on Patience. He'd decided to go, and he was paying a huge sum for the privilege.

But he was going through some hard things, so she picked up.

"I decided what to do with Jasper," said Jax's disembodied voice. Rachel had heard a lot about this decision: Jax could euthanize Jasper, but that would break Jax's heart, and it didn't match what Jasper seemed to want. He could let Jasper loose in the woods or send him to a transgenic sanctuary, but this was a fantasy — Jasper was civilized and needy, and he didn't get along with other animals, even transgenic ones.

Last Rachel heard, he was devising a way to sneak Jasper along on the trip, maybe by bribing someone.

"We've settled it," he said now. "Bringing Jasper to Patience with us would be hideously expensive, and the person I'd have to bribe says he's not sure he could pull it off anyway, which I take to mean something could go horribly wrong. So I'm leaving him with my niece Agatha, and I think it'll be good for both of them. Agatha's my niece by blood, so she and Jasper share a little bit of genetic material. Once they develop the routines of their new life together, I think they'll be okay. Agatha's thrilled, of course, but Jasper whines and looks bereft when the subject comes up. As you can see, that's how he looks right now."

"You sound sad too," said Rachel. "Look, I'm sorry to cut this short, but I have lots to finish up. I'll see you tomorrow, and on Patience we'll have all the time in the world to talk about it."

Jax paused. "Yes," he said, "all the time in the world." A withered hand reached into camera range and came to rest on Jasper's head.

*
* *

Tonight was Rachel's last chance to babysit her granddaughter. Ever. She tried not to think about it as she chopped Eliza's dinner into small bites and filled a sippy cup with emulsion.

Eliza followed her around the kitchen, chatting and clutching the afghan that Rachel's own grandmother had crocheted so long ago. Sure, she'd probably turn it into a snot-covered mess within a day or two, but it comforted Rachel to think that her granddaughter would handle this heirloom as an everyday object after she was gone. Eliza's great-great-grandmother Rose had breathed the same air that Eliza breathed, and she'd rubbed this same yarn between her fingers. Their earthliness and blood connected them — Rachel's mother and grandmother and foremothers long dead, and her daughter and granddaughter and daughters to come — all of them connected, stitched and looped together in some mysterious way that only God could fathom.

A soft mop of toddler curls swirled across Eliza's forehead as she waved her free arm and sang about trains, dragging the bottom of the afghan back and forth across the floor. What would Eliza say if she knew the details of what was happening in her Nana's life, if she knew what her Nana was about to do? Maybe she'd say, "Don't do it! I need you! Who'll watch out for me if not you?"

But Sam would be here, and the women from church. And Miriam of course. Maybe Eliza would sing her encouragement. Maybe she'd say, "Go, Nana! Because of you, my hearing will be fixed, and I'll have everything I need as I grow up. Because of you, this expedition will thrive, and you'll send back medical miracles, food-production tech, energy sources!" Rachel's mind fuzzed out as she wandered into an ego-pleasing fantasy about how she would give birth to the children who would make these discoveries; she'd serve as the entire group's spiritual mother, supporting and encouraging all the colonists, adults and children alike.

She returned to the present with a jolt. Good grief, this child, this one right here with the shining eyes, was most certainly not thinking about medical miracles, food production technologies, or energy sources — she needed her dinner, and then to be put to bed!

After dinner they settled in the rocking chair, Eliza in the crook of Rachel's right arm, and soon Eliza was fast asleep.

"I want you to know some things," said Rachel as they rocked back and forth. "Where I'm going, you can't follow. But I want you to remember me. I know I'll remember you." Tears began to stream down her cheeks, but she kept on rocking, taking strength and comfort from the warmth of Eliza's relaxed body. "You come from a line of long-lived women, my darling. They say your great-great grandmother on my father's side lived to be 103. But who knows. Anyway, I expect for you to hang on until I make it to Patience. I know it's crazy, and I haven't said this to anyone else. Are you with me?"

Eliza's peaceful face was open, and though she was clearly asleep, it seemed to Rachel that she was absorbing the essence of the message in its purest form, so she kept talking.

"Maybe someday you'll have a brother or sister, or a cousin. If that's going to happen, I won't be here to see it. But *you're* here, and that's what's important now."

Rachel paused to blow her nose and wipe some of the tears off her face.

"You'll hardly be in your nineties when they wake me up on Patience. I've been thinking lately that during all those years in limbo, in deep sleep, my soul might . . . well . . . what if I lose my bearings? What if I can't remember who I am? That's why I plan to take the memory of you with me into deep sleep. If you're the last thought in my mind when they sedate me, if I think of nothing but you as I go under, then you'll be my guiding star. You'll anchor me. You'll remind me who I am."

Eliza lapsed into a quiet snore, her arms loose and relaxed on Rachel's arms. Utterly trusting.

Forgetting

Is the truth about yourself a river that seems too cold to swim in? Your soul will ask you to put your toes in anyway.
—Julia Proxima

Tensel thought about the promise he'd made to Sam and felt a moment of guilt. Was sneaking aboard the Temenos the same thing as hurting himself? Maybe.

But to be precise, what he'd promised was to let Sam know. No matter how this plan came together, Sam would be the first to know about it, if only *after* it was too late to stop it from happening. He opened his journal and smoothed it down. Zoë, asleep on his lap, lifted her head to watch his pen jump across the page.

> The meds have given me a little more energy, and I went for a long walk this morning, halfway to the aqueduct. It wasn't a run, but it was something, and it got Jess off my back.
>
> But everything still hurts me. Small sadnesses hit me like tragedies. I got a card in the mail from my grandmother, and it struck me that she's lonely. The idea of grandma being lonely just about killed me — I can't stand it. I can hardly function.

Zoë stretched and butted her head against Tensel's writing hand, forcing him to pay attention to her. He stroked the top of her head, studying her face, then returned to his journal.

> But I can pretend to function. Thank you, meds. And now I can do what I need to do to get out of the pain.

Zoë was asleep again and he couldn't bring himself to disturb her, so he closed his journal and sat motionless, his hands cupped around her relaxed body, staring out the window at El Capitan in a fake Yosemite vista.

When Jessica got home from the gym he was still sitting there, staring. He looked like a scarecrow — gaunt, sad, and saggy. The high Jessica felt from her workout faded, and a weary irritation took its place.

"Hey," she said, more gently than she felt. "How're you feeling?"

"I'm thinking about the trip. I want to go."

Jessica collapsed into the recliner next to the desk.

"This isn't the time to make big decisions. One day at a time, remember? You're getting a little better every day. Maybe if you hang in there and keep stepping in the right direction, we'll get through this."

"No," he said, "you'll get through this, but I won't. I don't deserve to."

"Deserve!" Jessica's voice was sharp. "This again. What've you done that's so terrible?"

"It's more what I should've done. I should've stopped Ark from using my idea like this, for this terrible purpose. I should've paid attention to what was actually going on instead of burying my head in my work—"

"Ark's purpose is not *terrible*," said Jessica. "You're catastrophizing. And it's not your job to decide what to do with tech, it's your job to *create* tech. Yes, your head was buried in your work, and that's right where it belongs."

"You have no sense of social responsibility, Jess."

"That's not fair. I just trust others to do their jobs, that's all. And I don't catastrophize." She stood abruptly and walked into the kitchen to get a glass of water.

Tensel stood up and followed her, shifting Zoë so her stomach was against his chest and her paws were draped over his shoulder. "The other thing is," he said, "I'm not sure I can handle waiting. Sending them off tomorrow, living the rest of my life, continuing my research. Hearing nothing from them except status reports from the ship and the AI's robot agents. I want to be *with* them."

He paused, thinking. "I have no choice. You mentioned truth. Well, here's the truth: the people, the human beings we're sending on this trip, are being experimented on, and they're just boxes. That's it. They're complex packing crates, and within them lie the seeds of the real colonists: their children and their children's children. The crates might or might not survive — their purpose is to protect what they carry so the experiment can go forward. So data can be collected. That's how Ark sees it."

Jessica had tears in her eyes now. "What are you talking about? Deep-sleep tech is safe, and the age-reversal tech sounds harmless, noninvasive. I've read about it. Sam told me about it. You're getting paranoid, Tensel."

"Deep sleep?" Tensel laughed, a cruel, short sound. "Oh right, of course. Deep sleep. That doesn't change what I said."

"That they're all packing crates, a big experiment. Right. So this is an argument for why you should go, so you can be a packing crate too?"

"Yes, it's exactly why I should go. If these people never reach Patience, if they die on the trip, it's only right that I'd die too. And if they make it, maybe some horror could be prevented by having a live human scientist with them when they arrive. Ark's not sending any scientists, Jess! They want complete control of these people, don't you see? I created this tech, which as you said is my job. And now that it exists, it's my burden. My obligation."

"But you *didn't* create regenerative deep-sleep!" said Jessica. "You created soul transfer, which they're not using. You sound crazy, and I can't listen to any more of it. Stop talking about it. I've *had* it."

Tensel's eyes went cold, and his jaw hardened. "Then I won't talk about it anymore."

Jessica froze. "Where are you going?"

"To the lab. There's something I need to take care of."

*
* *

Rachel was getting ready for her last sleep in her own bed. She could hear Eliza breathing — slow, relaxed, unafraid. She couldn't think of anything else she needed to do, and nothing would go with her on the journey except that memory box. Wistfully, she touched the table that had been her altar. Now the table held nothing but a plain lamp, and Room 3 belonged to Miriam, along with this table and this bed and everything Rachel hadn't given away or put in the memory box.

She put her hands across her heart and felt it beating, her chest rising and falling as she breathed. She'd soon entrust all of this, every cell of her body, into Ark's care.

Miriam wouldn't be home for a few more hours, if at all that night. She was making the most of her last day and night of no-fuss babysitting from Nana, no doubt.

Convinced that sleep would never come, Rachel got into bed and turned out the light, ready to spend the next few hours praying in the darkness. She reached out to God, whispering a prayer—"O God, O God."

Nothing.

She lay calm and still, setting her mind on gentle, joyful things that had happened lately. Eliza crawling through the tunnel at the playground for the first time, Sam agonizing over what to wear to the ceremony.

Then the memory of the trip grabbed her like a hand around her throat. Just a few more hours, and Ark would put her into a long, deep, abnormal sleep. What if she died? Suddenly she felt sure of it: when they closed her into that deep-sleep box, she would die.

A wave of panic rushed into and through her torso. She felt the panic clench around her heart, delivering a short, small burst of adrenaline. The horrible feeling passed, and her thoughts were calm for a few minutes. And then another wave hit. Bigger. Nearly irresistible — she felt as if she were falling over backwards, the room spinning around her, the bed tilting to drop her into a dark void of space. Vertigo. She couldn't see a way to move herself from these feelings into calm thoughts about the safety and sanity of the trip. She whispered the name of Jesus, then stretched out her exhale for as long as she could. "One . . . ." She inhaled, then began another long exhale. "Two . . . ." A pause, an inhale. "Three . . . ."

She fell asleep for a short time and woke up calmer. It didn't really matter whether she slept that night or not, so she decided to lie awake and be present to the darkness, keeping vigil with her anxious thoughts. After all, these were the last hours she'd spend on Earth, the planet that had always been her home.

*
**

Tensel was grinding his teeth, but what did it matter? No need to stop any bad habits at this point. He and his teeth would all be gone soon enough.

Techs and scientists on the other side of Ark Island were buzzing around the production scanners and target chambers, working through the night to prepare for the Day of Heroes. But in Ark's research buildings, all was quiet.

Still, better safe than sorry: he opened every door in the lab and poked his head inside every office to make sure they were empty. After the *Svalbard* was underway, Ark scientists would notice an anomaly when they sent the first ping to the Teme-nos, and they'd begin to speculate about what was inside the database along with the expected macro quantum patterns. At that point it wouldn't matter, but for now he needed complete secrecy.

He would be asking a lot of Sam. He wondered how Sam would feel about it, then forced that question out of his head. Sam was a rational person, and a good friend. He'd understand.

He ran diagnostics on the batches of cloned stem cells from himself and Zoë. The bioengineering team had advanced their techniques to the point that Tensel hadn't needed to grow his and Zoë's weight in stem cells; only about a hundredth of that. The cells were healthy, and they'd multiplied fast. He had enough to carry out his plan — no more procrastinating. He was leaving Sam all the necessary technical information, and he had nothing more to say to Jessica.

Remembering their argument, he felt a flash of anger and searing pain, the kind of pain he needed to put an end to. He was leaving Jessica. He was leaving his parents, his brother, his grandparents, and everyone else he cared about. It was too much, so he banished the thought from his mind.

And he wasn't leaving *everyone* he cared about. He turned to look at Zoë watching him from her bed on top of the hard-drive rack. He stood to face her, reaching up to put a hand on her head. "Are you ready? Do you trust me?"

It seemed to Tensel that love and understanding passed between them as they gazed at one another.

"Yes, I can feel it, dear one," he said, using his private nickname for Zoë. "You're ready. You trust me."

He sat back down and returned to his ablutions, which took most of the night. Recording the cover letter for Sam was the hardest part, and he had to restart four times, but at last he was satisfied. The message would be delivered when the scanner and incubator indicated their success.

He lifted Zoë out of her bed. Cradling her in him arms, he carried her down the hall and into a room marked "Prototype Chambers."

"Dear one, dear one," he whispered as he bent over to tuck her into one of the chambers, "there are two possible outcomes, both of which mean that you and I will be together forever." She relaxed onto the chamber's black metal floor and looked at him, her face cupped in his hand. "We're ready," he told her, "and we trust one another."

He closed the door, then crawled into a nearby chamber and closed himself into it from the inside. He took a deep breath and shut his eyes tightly. *"Security override Tensel Brown 59142-X!"* he shouted, loudly enough for the security software to hear him and verify his voice pattern from inside the crematory. *"Start procedure 372!"*

*
**

After midnight, Jessica fell into a restless sleep on the couch. Some time later she sat up as if she'd heard a gunshot or a slamming door. "What was that?" she said out loud, forgetting that Tensel wasn't there. She was never prone to hunches or intuition, but she couldn't shake a sense of wrongness. She was shivering. After all, something *was* wrong — Tensel wasn't okay, and he hadn't been okay for months. She'd had a fight with him, and now he wasn't here.

She called Sam, ungodly as the hour was. He was probably awake anyway, fretting about saying goodbye to his mom at the Day of Heroes, which would start in a few hours.

She told him about her strange, bad feeling, and about her fight with Tensel. "He was telling me about a conspiracy, saying crazy things, and I told him that I've had it, that I can't listen to him anymore. Why did I say that? Why couldn't I hold my tongue, wait for a better time to talk?"

Sam could see tears forming in her eyes, and in between sentences she was biting one of her nails — a habit she'd just broken. He kept her talking while he put on his jacket and left his apartment. "It's okay, Jess," he said. "You have excellent reasons for being frustrated."

"He said he won't talk about it anymore. And that's when he and Zoë left. That stupid cat sure looked pleased with herself." She tore harder at her fingernail. "Well, she can *have* him!"

"Have you tried his beacon?"

"No answer."

"He's not answering for me either. I just got off the ferry and I'm close to your building. I'll be there in five minutes."

He was heading up in the penthouse elevator when a call came in from Tensel. "It's Tensel," he said to Jessica. "Just a sec —"

He switched to the incoming channel and saw Tensel's face. "Hey there buddy," he said, then realized it was a recording. Tensel's voice, reedy and tense, spoke directly into the auditory nerve in his brain. "Sam," he began, "by the time you get this—"

"Pause!" Sam shouted, switching back to Jessica. "Jess, he left me a note. We should watch it together — I'm almost there." By the time he finished this sentence he was out of the elevator, and Jessica was dragging him by the hand into the living room and over to the couch. "Okay," she said, gripping his arm with both her hands as they sat side by side, "show me."

Sam signaled the message to play in an external hologram, and an image of Tensel Brown appeared in front of them. He was in his Ark lab surrounded by stem-cell flasks and scattered cords and cables, a feral look in his eyes. Zoë was behind his shoulder, watching the camera.

"Sam," he began, speaking slowly, "by the time you get this, Zoë and I will have completed the first part of our journey. I encrypted our genomes and hid them inside the shipboard AI, so don't worry about that part. What I need from you is help with our . . . *souls*." He paused to smile ever so slightly.

"He called them *souls*," Sam whispered to Jessica, as if Tensel might hear.

"Zoë and I need you to put our souls in the Temenos," he continued. "Check the beta scanners right away, the two on the left. I secured them to open for your imprint, and yours alone. Zoë's stem cells were healthy last I checked, and mine too. You know what I'm asking you to do. Goodbye, friend."

That was it. Jessica and Sam turned to look at each other, confusion on her face and dawning horror on his. "Replay," said Sam, and they watched the message again.

There was a pause like the vacuum that follows behind a blast wave.

"So . . . ," said Jessica, "you can open the scanner with your imprint and let him out. Right? And we'll get him to a doctor. We should check him straight into the hospital, he needs inpatient care . . . ."

Sam was silent, letting Jessica talk her way back around to what she was trying not to see: Tensel had ended the conversation. The scanners were only used for one thing, and no one could undo what he'd done to himself, or bring him back. He was gone.

Or was he?

It hit Sam that if he was going to follow Tensel's instructions, he needed to act fast. "Jess," he said, jumping up off the couch and pulling her up with him, "there are only two options now. We get to T's lab in time to make sure that his soul and Zoë's are transferred into the Temenos, or we don't. If we get there in time, they have a chance, a small chance, of living again on Patience. If we stay here, they both stay as dead as they are right now."

"What the hell are you talking about? What's the Temenos? The colonists will go into deep sleep. How can Tensel go into deep sleep if he's . . . if he's . . . ."

"Jess, listen. What Tensel said when you two fought isn't as crazy as you think. Ark's been lying to everyone. For good reasons, but lying. They're not using deep-sleep tech, they're using Tensel's soul-transfer tech. Do you understand what I'm saying? If I finish the procedure that Tensel started on himself, his soul can live again. The AI will clone him on Patience and reunite him with his soul. That's what's happening to the colonists, to my mom, to all of them. The tech isn't perfected yet, but it will be by the time they arrive."

This was one crazy thing too many, and Jessica had reached her limit. "No goodbye?" she said quietly, her eyes taking on a thousand-yard stare. "He left without even telling me good-bye? Maybe he left me my own note?" She looked around the room, bewildered, as if her note might be sitting on a counter somewhere.

"C'mon, you'll be okay," said Sam, coaxing her out of the penthouse with him, down the elevator, and across the dark-ened street to Ark's main research facility.

Sam rushed them past Tensel's lab and straight to the pro-totype room, where he looked at the readings for the first scanner on the left. It had been up to 590 degrees Celsius in the last hour, but now it was cool enough to open, so he put his thumb on the lock plate and looked into the iris reader. The scanner door unlocked and opened, exhaling a blast of warm air.

Inside was a tiny amount of gravelly material that the ma-chine had scraped into a neat pile. Jessica gasped, shook her head back and forth, then snapped out of her fugue. "This isn't enough to be Tensel. This has got to be Zoë. Open the other one."

Sam did, and in this scanner the pile was much larger, several kilos, with whitish chips of bone and what looked like a few teeth. Small metal widgets were stacked neatly to one side —all that was left of Tensel's neural and spinal implants, ready for recycling.

Sam felt a wave of nausea and an urge to leave the room, leave Ark, leave the city, and never look back. Instead he closed his eyes and took a breath. If the equipment had worked as planned, his friend's macro quantum pattern was now resonating in a batch of stem cells in an incubator behind this scanner, and he needed to take the next step. He also needed to help Jessica. "Well hmm," he said, stalling as he looked for words, "I guess we're looking at Merge tech's first human test subject. Tensel was always the innovator. Let's hope it worked."

Jessica too was collecting herself. "We have to take care of this right now," she said. "We have to make sure these remains are treated respectfully and returned to T's parents and brother. We can't have those dickheads from Ark processing this scene."

"I'm sorry, Jess, I can't help with that now. His body's gone, but his soul's probably in the incubator, and I need to take care of it."

Jessica set her jaw and turned back to the chamber and its grisly contents. "I'll do it," she said. "I can't help you with the soul-transfer tasks anyway."

Sam touched her shoulder gently before he left the room.

*
**

Sam knew what Tensel wanted him to do. He plugged himself into a workstation in the lab, pulled a headset over his face, and accessed the confidential trip data. Yes, there it was:

Tensel had adjusted the Temenos to compensate for his own soul matter. Zoë would be a challenge, because the Temenos was calibrated for humans. But a trail of clues led Sam to a custom configuration for uploading a soul that matched Zoë's specifications.

He examined the cloning instructions that the AI bots would follow when the ship reached the Wolf system. Buried within the exabytes of colonist data, he found Tensel's and Zoë's genomes, along with epigenetic details about both of them.

Sam marveled at the intricacy of Tensel's plan. Ark scientists might discover anomalies when they did their first in-flight ping of the Temenos after its departure aboard the *Svalbard*, but at that point, what could they do?

He disconnected from the workstation and went into the incubator room. Diagnostics showed Zoë's and Tensel's stem cells positive for macro quantum patterns of the expected length and amplitude. "You're in there, I see you," he said to the incubator, stroking his thumb across its smooth casing.

The only thing left to do was to implant these patterns into the Temenos, and then all the fragments of Tensel and Zoë would be ready for reassembly on the other side. He imagined Tensel and Zoë, reunited on Patience.

And Rachel. They'd meet Rachel on Patience, too.

"I can't think about mom right now!" he said out loud. He set to work, talking to his memory of Tensel as he made his way through the procedure. "T, you have my full attention. Show me the next clue, bud . . . ."

*
**

An hour later, two souls were acclimating to life in the Temenos. Sam patted the machine's shiny grey hatch, hoping he hadn't disturbed the machine's delicate biological functions when he opened and resealed it. "Have a restful sojourn, you two. When you see my mom on the other side, tell her I love her. Actually, I need to tell her that myself before she leaves. Gotta run!" The Day of Heroes ceremony would begin in less than an hour.

He reconnected with Jessica and found her sitting on the floor, whispering to a plain aluminum urn cradled in her arms. She looked up. "I thought about what you said, and I get it. I understand what's going to happen to the Heroes today."

Sam sat next to her on the floor and put his hand on the urn.

"So I looked around," she continued, "and they've got boxes of these in the big scanner room on the north side of campus. Knowing Ark, they have plenty of extras and they won't miss this one. I mixed Zoë in with him — I think he'd want that. We're hiding this in your locker, and we'll come back for it later, when the press isn't here." She looked down at the urn. "And I need time to figure out how to explain all of this to T's family."

"About that," said Sam. He stood up slowly, then held the urn while Jessica got to her feet. "I think there's only one way to play it: we need to tell everyone, including Ark and T's family and the whole world, that he's aboard the *Svalbard* with the colonists. But we need to wait until *after* the ship launches — *after* it's too late for anyone at Ark to remove his pattern from the Temenos. Can you do that for me? Can you wait?"

Jessica, overwhelmed, just nodded.

"And when we talk to T's family and the press, we have to keep Ark's secret about what's really happening to the colonists, which means we have to say he put himself into deep sleep aboard the *Svalbard*, which means we're going to have to take care of his remains together, just you and me. Privately." He put his hand on her arm and moved her toward the door, still talking. "I'll help you. We can do it. It'll be okay. We can talk it through later, but right now we have to get out of here."

* *
*

Ticket-holders milled around outside the amphitheater, waiting for the doors to open. Inside, the Heroes were finding their seats, talking nervously.

A familiar, comforting tune started up in Rachel's private neural feed. "Your body is safe with us, safe with us . . . ." It was coming over the loudspeakers too, and her mind turned to the transition that lay ahead.

All would be well, she knew it. Her body, Jax's body, Bob's body, all their bodies would be safe with Ark. Sure, some details about what would happen after the ceremony puzzled her, but what didn't make sense to her, made sense to Ark.

* *
*

Fizzing with adrenaline, Sam cut to the front of the line of people filing into the amphitheater, and an Ark employee waved him inside. He spotted his friend Anya and her partner Oscar at the back of the Hero section, both of them dressed in black leather as if ready for their own biker funerals. "Anya!" he cried, then folded her into a bear hug when she turned around. "You two are going to be so happy, this is marvelous, so gorgeous—I have to find my mom," he babbled as he kissed her on both cheeks, shook Oscar's hand, and kept moving without waiting for them to respond. He had to find Rachel.

Walking on tiptoes to better scan the crowd, he collided with Dr. Kendel, who stood at the edge of the Hero section gazing with imperial satisfaction over the sea of colonists. "Ah, Sam," he said, clapping Sam on the back, "or should I say Dr. Deimos? Heh. Congratulations. This whole project looks to be one *hell* of a victory for us—screw you, Linda, ha ha!—but anyway, I've been meaning to talk to you about a little something. Do you have a minute?"

Without waiting for an answer, he gripped Sam's arm and steered him irresistibly toward the edge of the crowd. "So," he said as Sam craned his neck to look for his mother, "I've been testing the waters, and I think I can guarantee you a quick promotion. How'd you like to be a Director? Ark's new Head of Soulistics? Or whatever you want. We're moving into a whole new phase of theoretical investigation, and you're gonna have a big chair at the table, my friend . . . ."

His words flowed on, background noise as Sam spotted Rachel among the colonists. She was leaning over a man in a mind-controlled wheelchair, her hand on the man's shoulder. Must be Jax. Nearby, a young woman in librarian glasses was trying to hold onto a white and gray transgenic as it strained toward Jax.

"You're usually such a cool cucumber, son, pull it together," Dr. Kendel was saying, jostling Sam's shoulders and exhaling boozy breath into his face. "This promotion'll take the sting out of saying goodbye to your mom. You two were close, but you'll be fine! She'll be alive long after you're dead, just think about that! Heh. Anyway, just between you and me, Dr. Brown's not thriving at Ark. Such a waste, really a shame, but an opportunity for *you*. I imagine he'll be leaving the company soon."

This got Sam's attention, and his mind leapt to the two macro quantum patterns in the Temenos, and his mom's pattern joining them soon—

Wrenching himself out of Dr. Kendel's grasp, he pushed through the crowd and over to his mom.

"Oh Sammie," she said, enfolding him in a hug. He felt tears begin to stream down his face. She was calm, more settled than she'd been for months. She seemed ready to go, and he felt her strength.

Pulling back, he realized who was missing, guilty that it had taken him so long to notice. "Mom, where's Mira? She said she'd be here early with you, she promised—"

"It's okay, sweetie," said Rachel, running her hand across Sam's wet cheek. "She's doing the best she can. She doesn't feel well today, and she left me a note. And this way Eliza can be with her mother today instead of a babysitter."

"Oh mom, you know she's probably hung over, or in VR, or God knows what. Why couldn't she come through, today of all days?" He was too exhausted and overwhelmed to care what he might sound or look like. Everything in his heart came pouring out in his tears and in his words, lots and lots of them. He forgot about Miriam, Tensel, and everyone in the room as he and Rachel told each other how much they'd miss each other, and how much they loved each other.

Too soon, a voice over the loudspeaker said it was the final call; observers needed to take their seats.

"Goodbye, sweet child," said Rachel, looking into his eyes and holding his face in her hands. "Tell Miriam I love her. May our gracious God bless and keep you and your sister and Eliza."

*
**

Sam took his seat in the front row of the observer section, still weeping. He blew his nose and drenched the last of the tissues that he'd remembered to grab from the box at the end of the aisle. He put his hand on the empty reserved seat next to him, Miriam's seat, and imagined he was holding his sister's hand.

The pomposities began, the music blatted, the congratulations rolled forth.

Sam willed the speeches to slow down, the names to be read more slowly, but nothing could prevent the moment from arriving. He tried to keep a neutral expression on his face when he heard his mother's name, but he let out a loud sob.

"Rachel Anna Deimos."

And then she disappeared behind the curtain.

He hardly noticed as the other colonists' names were called. His mind and heart were with Rachel now. He knew that she was being sedated and placed in a scanning chamber. She'd lose consciousness soon. He hoped she already had.

Merge has to work, he thought. It *has* to. Dr. Kendel had seemed to be offering him a promotion — well, he'd take it. He would spend the rest of his career making sure Merge worked without a glitch when the *Svalbard* reached Patience. He'd make sure his mother went on living, just as she expected to. And Tensel, and all the trusting people who'd just gone behind the curtain.

Rachel's quantum teleportation procedure was happening. He knew it, he felt it. His mother's soul was traveling from her body into a batch of stem cells, and he felt his own soul wrench in a flood of empathy.

He blinked and roughly wiped the tears out of his eyes as he checked the time. The process took 83 seconds, and it had been nearly two minutes. Long enough.

He'd been unable to get a waiver to dispose of his mom's remains himself—he'd just have to believe that Ark would take care of them respectfully, as they promised. At least he'd have a say in what happened to Tensel's.

He felt calmer now, and his tears dried up as he thought of Miriam and patted her empty seat. He thought about Eliza, and Jessica too. They needed him, and he wouldn't let them down.

*
**

Miriam lay across her bed in Room 3, clutching a protesting Eliza in her arms, rocking both of them back and forth. "Mom, mommy!" Miriam sobbed. "I'm so sorry, I'm so sorry, I'm so sorry . . . ."

Suddenly aware of Eliza's fear and discomfort, she sat up on the edge of the bed and wiped her tear-smeared makeup on the bed sheet, then put a hand on her disheveled hair.

"Oh dear God, I'm a shambles. I'm sorry, baby girl, I didn't mean to scare you. You'll be okay. We'll be okay. I thought this would be a time to celebrate — it's a win-win, right? Nana's doing what she wants to do, and we get money to help us through the tough times ahead. All good, right? I thought all I'd want to do right now is party, relax, shout for joy, but . . . I just don't know anymore. I just don't know . . . ."

*
* *

Rachel found herself in a sterile room on a gurney between two strangers, colonists she hadn't met. A sedative was taking hold, and she noticed with vague interest that she was being lifted and placed in a small, warm chamber with black walls. "I'm being put into the oven to bake," she thought, her mind fuzzy.

With painful suddenness, the fuzziness disappeared and clarity retook her mind. She had a sense of the Spirit's presence with her, and herself as God's beloved creation. A precious child, seen and known. How could she have forgotten?

Her sense of self rushed back to her, along with who and whose she was. All thoughts of her future on Patience were gone. "O God," she said softly, "Take care of my little girl, take care of Miriam, help her to get well."

An old prayer came into her head, one she'd learned as a child. "Hail Mary, full of grace," she whispered, "Holy Mary, Mother of God, pray for us sinners now and at the hour of our —"

Her mind went dark and she lost consciousness, her body relaxing into oblivion and whatever lay beyond it.

Part 2: Between

The Temenos

If you want to live and work in the cloud of unknowing
that's above you and between you and God, you'll need a
cloud of forgetting to drop all your thoughts into.
—From *The Cloud of Unknowing* (5)

Inside Temenos

Oblivion.
A flicker of awareness.
Sound? Too loud!
Agony.
Deafness.

Oblivion.
A flicker of awareness.
Sound? Too loud!
Agony.
Deafness.

Oblivion . . .

Earth

"Uh, Dr. Deimos? Sam?" said Dr. Shandra Wilson, knocking on
the doorframe of Sam's lab.

Sam was perched on a round work stool and doodling in
thin air with a 3D printer pen, connecting the ends of twisted
cylinders and watching the pink and green results drop out of
the printer next to his workstation. Pointless, but he got a kick
out of it. "What is it, Shandra?"

"I had a brain wave: Maybe the macro quantum patterns in
the Temenos are *not* decohering."

Sam stopped doodling and looked up. "Say more."

"Every year, our analysis of the ping data points to active decoherence. But what if the ping itself causes the decoherence? Maybe the decoherence isn't continuous; maybe the patterns reorganize themselves after the ping ends. Maybe we should bring down the wave intensity, or ping less often. After all, we expected the patterns to be affected in some way by the process of observation."

"Hmm." Sam was putting on his headset. "Great point, and the effect might be more significant than we'd thought. What's the lowest intensity wave we can send that'll return data of any kind?"

Temenos

Oblivion.
A flicker of awareness.
Sound? Ah. Hmm.
Incomprehension.

Oblivion.
A flicker of awareness.
Sound? Yes.
Perplexity.

They'd been resting. They stirred when the sound came, but the sound made no sense. None. A vague, shared disappointment rolled across them in the form of a long wave, raising then lowering each soul in a brief moment of affect. The wave passed, and oblivion resumed.

A few years into the journey they shifted, like a sleeper turning over. It was close quarters, and they all had to shift together. From then on, they knew they existed as a group. Nothing beyond that—just a smeared awareness, constant and dim. They existed in the moment, and only in the moment. They'd never been anywhere else, nor would they ever be anywhere else.

No one had any opinion about this. They made no predictions and felt no regret. Ever re-created immediacy: life as nothing other than the experience of springing out of oblivion and into the present.

Earth

"Well, they're not actively decohering," Shandra announced in the status meeting, leading with the good news, ". . . or at least they weren't during the 17 nanoseconds it took for the ping to bounce off of them. Their response to this ping was more nuanced than to previous pings that were longer and more intense, but affairs inside the Temenos are as big a mystery as ever. I'm disappointed to report that the new data doesn't match any of my team's new projections."

"Refactor. Assume fewer patterns," said Arjuna, speaking quickly. "Some patterns might've been lost."

"We tried that."

"Then assume *more* patterns."

"We tried that too," said Shandra, unfazed and unrushed. "We factored in the addition of Dr. Brown and Zoë, of course, but the 'third' pattern for that pairing, the pattern formed by their transgenic bond, is unknown. If only someone had recorded it before the *Svalbard* left, but who knew we'd need information like that? My team tested other transgenic-human pairings and integrated those results into our projections last week. Didn't help. We're open to suggestions."

"Hmm," said Arjuna as an idea came to him. "The Temenos's organic components are well-nourished and thriving, we know that much. Su's team designed those components to act as a generous host environment for macro quantum patterns

—the design spec actually used the word 'generous.' So think about how an entity might behave in a thriving host environment that's generous to it."

This brought a full 20 seconds of silence and furrowed brows, until Shandra spoke. "So if the patterns have grown or shifted into different configurations or even spawned new patterns, we have a whole new set of problems. But is any of this even possible? Sam, your thoughts?"

Sam gazed at his colleagues from behind tented fingers, his elbows resting on the table. "Well," he sighed, "at least there's less evidence of decoherence. And we have no reason to think the patterns are conscious, so they're not experiencing physical or existential suffering, thank God. Our top priority is to keep them coherent, as best we can. And we'll pursue Arjuna's line of thinking, or at least scope it out."

He was quiet again, then continued.

"But also, we might not have a solvable puzzle on our hands. My mom used to say that mysteries can't be measured. She might have had a point."

Temenos

At first, being in the Temenos was like sleeping. Rachel didn't notice this while it was happening, of course . . . because she was asleep. About five years in, when she started to notice herself having her own thoughts (which weren't like thoughts so much as they were like the gentle hallucinations that float in the pauses between deep sleep and deep sleep), she wondered where she'd been. She realized she might've been asleep.

She still slept on and off, and when she was awake she held and sorted impressions from the past. Not exactly memories, as much as the bright afterimages of living, cryptic leftovers from a dream. She held an impression of Miriam, and a fogged view of herself desperately wanting to help and heal, make pain and problems go away. And a glimpse of the gestalt — herself and someone else as a unit, symbiotic. Herself as half of a pair. Always. Who would she be if no one needed her? Who would she be on her own?

As she slept and woke, slept and woke, her perspective shifted and she saw the foundational beliefs that colored her soul. She saw herself: a person who believed she could will happy endings into being for other people. A person who believed that others' struggles and feelings were her fault, her responsibility, hers to adjust. A person who confused herself with God, the creator and sustainer of the universe.

She cringed at her hubris, and she sensed the fabric of the Temenos cringe together around her, crinkling and scrunching itself. She felt her own pain, and then she felt a weaker, similar pain run into her soul, like a racquetball hitting her after bouncing off the wall. What was that?

She sensed someone complaining nearby. "Why dwell on your faults?" the complainer seemed to be asking. "Your painful memories hurt us all." It was Bob. After that he was quiet, but his soul was so close to hers, she could almost feel him feeling. And every year he bled further over the line that divided him from her.

When this first started to bother Rachel, she had an urge to pretend that it didn't. She tried to speak to Bob and say something. Maybe something like, "Oh dear, I'm sorry I'm making it difficult for you to spread out like you want to," or, "Is your space being squeezed on the other side? Are you out of room over there?" But the words refused to leave her mind and travel over to Bob. It was like opening your mouth and forming words to speak but not being able to speak them, standing there with your mouth open. Something within her simply could not speak these words to Bob—it was impossible.

When Bob asked her one year if she was comfortable, she ventured to say "I'm squeezed," and found that she could actually say it, in the incorporeal way they spoke to one another in the Temenos. In her interactions with others too, not just Bob, she found this peculiar phenomenon: she could say certain things, but not others.

About 10 years into the trip she guessed the pattern — she could only say what was true for her. At first it seemed odd, and after a while it was satisfying. Instead of telling a white lie to make someone feel better about having stepped on her toes, she was silent. And whenever a soul spoke to her, she believed what they said. Living with the truth was simple and refreshing, like drinking a glass of cool, crystal-clear water on a hot day.

*
* *

It wasn't just Bob who bled into her space; others did too, especially a certain one whose name she couldn't find in her mind, so she began to think of it as *the Presence*. The Presence lived in a peaceful, comforting rhythm, and as the years passed, most of the souls adapted their own rhythms to match this big, beautiful rhythm:

Rest, Sleep, Rest, Reflect,

    Rest, Sleep, Rest, Reflect,

        Rest, Sleep, Rest, Reflect, ...

Movements in an endlessly repeating symphony, or sets of waves rolling against a wide beach. Consciousness flickering dim then bright, dim then bright, as patient as a star.

Sometimes rest was accompanied by a low rumbling purr that drew every soul into a state of rest, even the ones that resisted the rhythm.

Rachel found the closeness of the Presence comforting, but Bob's closeness was different. Over the years, they fell into a scripted conversation that they repeated each time they were awake and resting. The conversation went something like this:

"Bob, I want you to move back."

"I want to be closer."

"I don't like having you in my space."

"I like to be in your space. It's like my space, but my space is too small. I want to share your space."

"I don't want that. I want you to back off."

"I don't want to."

"I want you to back off."

"I don't want to."

A conversation such as this could last months.

When the Presence lapsed into reflection, Rachel did too, slowly absorbing some of the Presence's ideas. She considered the problem she was having with Bob. She'd been able to say she didn't want what he wanted, which was a big step. As the years passed, she reflected more deeply on the disparity between her true desires and her stated desires. Had there always been such a gap between what she really thought, really felt, and what she said to people about her thoughts and feelings?

Without it seeming like a loss of any kind, some of the pity faded from her leftover impressions about Miriam, and a cool pragmatism seeped in. She began to see that adult Miriam's life wasn't hers to solve, and it had never been hers to solve. She began to experience herself as composed. Stable. "I know where I stand," she thought. She imagined herself as an animal with all four of its feet on the ground.

As her perspective about herself on Earth shifted, the impressions themselves faded. Her parents and her childhood. Jackson, motherhood, divorce. Room 3 and her neighbors. St. Malcolm's and her sisters and brothers in Christ. Human Converse and the colleagues and friends she'd worked with over the decades. One after another, the memories dimmed and became translucent. Her ideas about Sam, Eliza, and even Miriam began to slip out of focus as well, and finally she began to forget about the woman known as Rachel.

She had less and less room for the past, and no room at all for the future. It was the present that held her now, calling her attention into itself, pressing the past and the future out of its way.

Earth

It was eight years since the *Svalbard* had departed from Earth, and Sam hummed a little tune as the elevator sped him toward his office on the 35th floor. What a relief that Channel Wow! had finally done a bit of serious investigative reporting on the Ark Project. Took 'em long enough! Now the relatives and friends of the colonists knew that on the Day of Heroes, their loved ones' bodies had been cremated and stored in an Ark warehouse like so much old paperwork. It was now impossible for Ark to maintain their complicated lie about the Patience colonists being suspended in deep sleep, and they had to tell the truth about Merge.

Sam and Jessica had buried Tensel's and Zoë's remains in a secluded spot in the Oakland hills. They hiked out to visit it once a year on the anniversary of the *Svalbard*'s departure, but now it didn't have to be just the two of them. Now they could show the spot to Tensel's family and other friends. Now they could tell the whole story instead of leaving out the most important part: that Tensel's body didn't get sent to Patience, only his macro quantum pattern and the blueprint for a clone to put it in.

Sam was enjoying the sweet freedom of release after having held a secret for many years, but he also had another reason to be in a good mood: he'd finally moved in with Jessica. She'd asked for lots of elbow room while they dated, while she finished med school and started her neurology residency at UCSF, while she grieved and obsessed about Tensel and his strange departure.

But now Sam had heard her say yes to him with her whole heart. She'd never forget Tensel, and maybe she'd never let him go altogether, but neither would Sam. And isn't it the truth of things that no one really "gets over" anyone, or leaves anything behind? The present metabolizes the past, transforming it into something that travels with you to give life shading and perspective.

A call from Miriam flashed in his peripheral vision and he waved aside his philosophical ramblings, smiling to think what his sister would make of them. Who knows, nowadays, she might even join in.

"Hey bro," she said as her face appeared in Sam's line of sight, "I might get a few pieces installed in a gallery in town — we'll see. Anyway, I need Eliza to stay with ya'll for a while longer. Okay?"

Typical Mira, she got right to the point. They'd talked about Rachel's true fate as a Patience colonist already, and Miriam took it well. In fact, it seemed to help her move forward. She looked good. This commune in the high desert was supposed to be VR-free, and from the sane, grounded look in his sister's eyes, Sam thought maybe she was really on board with the program this time. As if to correspond to the ways she was giving her mind space to return to sanity, she'd given space and respect to her hair, which was natural and big. No gray yet, but no copper wiring or fuchsia either. She hadn't let any of her eyebrow and ear piercings close up, but now she wore colorful hoops with no tech connections or cyber symbols.

"No problem, we're glad to do it," said Sam, and he meant it. Eliza was 10 and had her own room in Jessica's house. Sam moving in wasn't much of a change for any of them, considering how much time he spent there already. He almost thought of himself and Jessica as Eliza's parents and Miriam as the crazy aunt who came into town a few times a year with fantastic stories of farming hydroponic gen-fruit in Maine, waitressing in a haven town in Alaska, meditating at Ghost Ranch. It was an arrangement that worked well for all of them.

"Hey, one other thing," said Miriam. "It's not a done deal, but Hok'ee was a cryogenicist back in the day, and he has a line on some freeze options for me."

Sam's eyebrows went up. It wasn't the topic that surprised him — he and Jessica had talked about going into cryogenic stasis when they retired — but he was surprised Miriam would consider it. "Why?" he asked.

"I've always wanted a chance to say a better goodbye to mom," she said, "in case this Merge thing works and mom really does make it to Patience. I said my goodbye badly. I had so little self and skill and patience and love when she left . . . ." She pursed her lips and looked down, giving her words a moment of respect. "It might not be possible, and it might not be what I expect, but I'm thinking about it, and I'd like you to think about it too. I couldn't do it if you didn't feel good about making your arrangement with Eliza permanent. Or if *she* didn't feel good about it. So talk with them, would you? Eliza? And Jess?"

Sam knew Miriam wouldn't ask something like this is she wasn't dead serious. "Of course," he said. "I'll talk to them, and we'll think about it."

*
**

Eliza and her friend Kate stayed to the soft forest trail until they were close enough to the water to see it through the trees. At this point the trail turned and headed back toward more populated places, so they had to leave it to reach the water.

They stepped over fallen trees as they made their way to the beach. The beach! Only three or four undeveloped beaches existed on the whole planet. At least that's what Eliza was imagining as she unzipped her shoes, stripped off her socks, and buried her toes in the warm sand. In reality there were maybe 20 — few enough to make this visit, which was a gift from Sam, an extraordinary event.

"Let's play human voice worker," said Eliza after they found warm, comfortable places to lie side by side in the sand. "My Nana Rachel was one, you know. I'll be the voice worker, you be the customer."

"I want to be a voice worker too," said Kate. "Let's both be."

"Okay," said Eliza. "Then where's your soul checker? We both need a soul-check machine to check us before each call we take."

The girls jumped up from the sand and ran in different directions on the beach, each absorbed in her own idea of what a soul-check machine might look like and how it might work.

"Here's mine," said Eliza, hunkering down behind a large tree that had fallen into the water from the short cliff near the beach. Its thick, complicated branches had no leaves, but had not yet been worn smooth by the water. Its exposed root structure was a mound on the edge of the cliff above the girls. "I have to touch it with my whole body so it can check my soul. It's checking me now. This is really hard to do." She bent double across one of the largest branches and put her hands on the sand in front of her feet, then edged as close as she could get to the tree's main trunk so that most of her left side was pressed against the tree trunk. "Getting solid contact with the soul checker's important," she said in the voice of one who knows, "but you have to keep your feet on the ground. That completes the circuit."

Kate found a smooth piece of driftwood and put her hands around it. "And here's mine," she said. "Mine's a special one. It works just by touching my hands. I only have to hold onto it for 10 seconds, and then it'll know whether I have a soul or not."

"Mine's beeping" screamed Eliza. "I'm a zombie! It can tell! I have no soul, I have no soul!" and she unfolded her body from the tree limb, found a clear area of beach, and ran in circles with her hands waving above her head and her face contorting.

"Me neither! Arg!!" shouted Kate as she ran at Eliza and tackled her. They rolled away from each other and started throwing handfuls of sand in the air in their best imitation of zombie behavior until Eliza said, "Okay, I need to be checked again — maybe the machine was broken," and the game started again.

An hour later, they ran back to where they'd left their lunch packs, near the base of the cliff. As they ate their faux-cheese and avocado sandwiches, Eliza stared off across the water, her mind wandering to far-away places. "They've been in space for eight years," she said. "Do you think their souls are still alive? My Nana's soul is aboard the *Svalbard*."

"Wow," said Kate. They ate in silence until Eliza said, "I'm going to find a way to be my Nana's sponsor, her Earth sponsor, when she gets out of the Temenos. I'm going to help her. I'll be the one who helps her come back to herself."

"You'll be dead by then, won't you?" asked Kate. "We'll both be dead for sure."

"Not me I won't. I plan to live to be a hundred and one." Eliza was resolute. "I'll meet my Nana, and I'll help her, and you're going to help me."

"What can I do?" asked Kate.

"I'll be her Earth sponsor, and you'll be *my* sponsor. That way I'll have a backup in case anything goes wrong. If I'm unable to perform my duties, let's say if I pass out during one of the VR sessions, you'll step right in and wake me up. When I have to go to the bathroom, you'll fill in for me while I'm gone."

"Okay," said Kate.

And it was decided. Eliza knew it would be true: she'd find a way to be Rachel's Earth sponsor, and she'd save Rachel by helping her come back to herself after her soul was Merged with her fresh clone. Just when the doctors and scientists were about to give up the case as hopeless and let Rachel sink back into the ether, Eliza would save the day by producing an artifact from Rachel's life on Earth. Or maybe it would simply be the sound of her voice that would do the trick — maybe her grandmother would remember her, deep down inside. Rachel would want to die, except for a small nagging thought somewhere in her mind: what about my granddaughter? What about Eliza?

Temenos

About 18 years into the journey, Rachel began to reflect on what it was like for her when other souls in the Temenos set boundaries. She considered that it wasn't so bad. Often it was *helpful* when other people were direct about their limits, because it let her know where they stood. She tried an experiment.

"Bob," she said, "back off."

Bob was silent, then shrank back ever so slightly from her space. They were both silent for the rest of the waking period. They slept, rested, reflected, and when they were awake again, Rachel repeated her request.

Bob backed off a little farther and remained silent.

Soon he was out of Rachel's space completely, and she asked others who were too close to her to back off as well. Finally she had *extra* space around her, room to breathe. She and Bob had nothing further to talk about, and she found herself alone with her own thoughts, and only her own thoughts.

Every year, a directed, intense noise arrived. It rocked everyone and shook some of the souls out of their places. After one such noise, Rachel found herself close to a soul that felt large and familiar, so close that she felt stifled.

"I'm Rachel," she said.

"I'm Jax," said the soul.

She knew that Jax was part of her past, even though she had no memory of him.

He pushed closer. "I want to merge with you," he said.

This was more than Bob had ever asked. Merge with her? Would she still be herself?

"I don't like having you in my space," she said.

"If we merge, I won't be in your space. Your space will be the same as my space, so you'll never feel violated again."

"I feel violated right now."

"I've merged with every soul who was willing to merge. None of us feel violated."

Rachel thought for a while.

"Jax," she said, "back off."

Jax, and all the souls with whom he'd merged, moved away from her. Within a few months she'd forgotten his name, and their encounter.

Earth

Eliza was nearing 30 when her mom went into cryogenic stasis. Sure, she hadn't seen Miriam often as she was growing up, but she'd treasured every visit. She was proud of herself for being the one to talk her mom into waiting this long to go into freeze, long enough to see her put down roots with Phoebe and start her career in Human Converse's executive headquarters, long enough to see her find happiness as an adult.

Sam and Jessica would leave her behind in this same way, she knew, and it wouldn't be long now. Sam regularly pointed out the one or two white hairs on his head and the gentle wrinkles around his eyes, joking that if he didn't go into freeze soon, he'd wake up an old man.

Eliza understood why they were doing it, but it was important to her to meet her commitments, and she couldn't imagine leaving the people she loved simply to prolong her own life and see new sights, or to make sure she lived long enough to see Rachel again. She couldn't imagine leaving Phoebe for those kinds of reasons. Deep freeze for a few decades would help her make her rendezvous with Rachel, but great-great grandma lived to be 103, after all.

Don't worry, Nana Rachel. I'll be there for you when you get out of this hell you're in.

Temenos

Tensel felt a few of his companions go under and merge with the Temenos itself, and the idea tempted him: oblivion in an eternal present. But he couldn't allow himself to weaken and let go of his pain or guilt, because oblivion is similar to absolution, and he didn't deserve absolution. He deserved to be punished.

But for what? The nature of his crime wasn't clear to him, wasn't as real as the pain and guilt themselves, so he gripped these as his two treasures. He clung to them with all the intensity natural to his spirit, until finally they were the closest thing he had to any kind of rational thought. No memories, no words, just pain and a toxic self-hatred that made the souls near him shrink back in self-defense.

Sometimes a supple, warm presence surrounded him, coaxing him toward ease. It wanted him to luxuriate in its own plush, lazy sleepiness. It wanted him to relax and be refilled and absolved, but he pushed it away. For reasons that were lost to him, he couldn't let himself rest. Not here, not yet, no matter who or what beckoned him.

Earth

Dr. Sam Deimos, chief scientist of the Ark Project, sprawled out on his living room couch watching the Channel Extravagant evening entertainment in his head. "For decades, scientists at Ark have struggled to determine the meaning of aberrant readings from their yearly status check of the Temenos database aboard the *Svalbard*," said the giant eyeball who hosted the show. "Ark spokesperson Leila Stanbrook joins us live from Ark Island. Leila, what's the latest?"

"Well Serge, 23 years after *Svalbard's* departure, we can only assume that our initial projections were completely invalid," said spokesperson Stanbrook, raising an eyebrow. "We want to know what's happening inside the soul database that carries the colonists, but we're having trouble finding out."

"Leila, would you go so far as to consider sabotage? Maybe the *Svalbard* ran into a creature in space and it stuck to the ship? Penetrated the hull, then entered the Temenos?"

Leila might've rolled her eyes, though it was hard to tell under her six-centimeter false eyelashes. "Unlikely."

Serge the giant eyeball blinked, then continued. "We know that Zoë's soul is alive and well in the Temenos, and they say that in theory her pattern should be simpler and more diffuse than any human pattern. In a way, then, her pattern should be the strongest one in the database. This presents a chilling possibility: could that cat have taken over the ship?"

Sam chuckled and turned off the feed. He sat up on the couch and stretched, running a hand across his frizzled, graying hair. "What do you think, Jess?" he said loudly in the direction of the kitchen, where Jessica was opening a bottle of wine. "Will they ever just let a mystery be a mystery?"

Temenos

In the third decade of the journey Rachel forgot Bob's name, though he was her closest neighbor. Bob was now focused on a slow interaction with the soul on the other side of his space, whose name, forgotten by everyone aboard the Temenos, had once been Oscar. Soon Rachel had trouble remembering her own name, and then her name was gone. For a while she tried to remember it, but it stopped being important. The richness of the present moment was filling enough; she didn't need even the smallest morsels from the past.

She considered the souls around her. As she lost their names, and even the idea that souls had names, she gained a deeper sense of each soul's distinctness. Some merged with others and became composite selves. Some merged, then separated, a slow, graceful dance of bows and turns and gratitude. Some merged with a few others, and from there dissolved into the Temenos itself. Some merged with no one at all.

And the Presence diffused into everyone so that each human soul was tinted, faintly, by its personality: alternately fickle and habitual, indolent and intense, gentle and ruthless, flexible and rigid.

Rachel could see this tinting in progress—a wet, faint wash of watercolor mist moving joyfully among them at all times. A gentle and eternal rain trying to color each of them with its own balance, self-containment, and free thinking.

Earth

Sam was in his fifties, and it was time.

The more he thought about Miriam's departure and why she'd left, the more he wanted to join her in deep sleep, and not just as a retirement and travel plan with Jessica. He wanted to see his mother again. If the Rachel he remembered actually made it to Patience, there was only one way he'd be able to see her again: he'd need to extend his life long enough so that he could see her after she was alive on Patience, after she'd been there a decade or so and had her bearings. After she'd had a chance to remember who she was. It was a long shot, but why not?

He and Jessica transferred the title of the house to Eliza and Phoebe and threw a huge party. Then they bid each other a temporary farewell and allowed themselves to be sedated and induced into cryogenic suspension, much as the public had believed the colonists did when they left more than 20 years before.

Their journey was underway.

Temenos

Time slowed further. And like scenery outside the window of a slowing train, the time expanded and took on definition as it slowed, bringing the souls ever closer to alignment with the eternity that opens out on the other side of time. The blurry waves of events that make up a usual life had now resolved into a bright multiplicity of infinitely small moments, each a potential foreverness.

Jax, Oscar, and a few other individual selves had disappeared altogether, beyond all sight, lapsing into a deep, silent absence that was as opaque to the others as death. Where did they go? And why? Or did they go anywhere at all? Were they still present, moving along some parallel track, or swimming within some deeper or more shallow rhythm than everyone else, alive but invisible?

The souls who remained sensed a change each time some-one disappeared, but they didn't wonder about it. They lived in each moment, curling right down inside of each one. They wore grooves and patterns into the passing time, settling themselves into routines and favorite spots. Extraverted souls like Bob stayed closer in, now and then exchanging thoughts with each other about resting, reflecting, and sleeping, the way neighbors on Earth might discuss the heat, or a cryobat tour-nament. And in the outer expanse of the Temenos's psychic space, Tensel brooded alone.

Rachel ranged between the inner and the outer reaches, sometimes sending a message to her companions that her old self would've seen as a contradictory. But now she understood its integrity, the oneness of its two parts:

"I love you. Stay out."

Indeterminate

I think I can safely say that nobody understands quantum
mechanics.
—Richard Feynman

Eight years before landfall, the *Svalbard's* AI brought its cloning lab online. Cloning supplies were extracted from their many layers of radiation shielding. Synthetic arms and fingers ran self-diagnostics and whirred to life, creating zygotes to match the genome of each human colonist. Within days the specks were fetuses, and the robots discarded all but the best candidate for each genome. They decanted the survivors into fluid-filled chambers, careful to suppress the macro quantum patterns that would otherwise begin to coalesce within the tiny bodies. The candidate clones needed to stay alive but "blank," each of them ready to receive the soul that belonged to its original host body.

Closer to landfall, the robots cloned bacteria and gut microbes, livestock and pets, bugs and fish. Unlike the cloned humans, these organisms were left to develop souls, or not, according to their nature, and soon the ship's living quarters pulsed with grow rooms, germ tanks, nest rooms, and livestock pens — a bawling, squawking, smelly Noah's Ark of sheep, chickens, cats, birds, and a hundred other types of living things that the colonists might need or want as they settled on Patience.

The only quiet animals on board were the human clones, unconscious in their tanks, each body and brain developing more than twice as fast as a normal child's.

*
**

The *Svalbard* swung into orbit around its new home, joining the huge terraforming ships that monitored and adjusted aspects of the gray-green planet below. The terraformers had begun their tinkering over 300 years before, and now Patience had small seas and rivers, blank fertile fields, half-grown forests, and a nascent weather pattern.

The slower speed of planetary orbit allowed real-time communication between the ship's AI and Earth for the first time in 88 years. On Earth, Dr. Amir pulled off her glasses and cleaned them for a third time, as if a clear view might bring clear thoughts about what was in front of her. As Ark's Director of Soulistics, she got the first live look at them, these floating bodies, each very like an 18-year-old human. They were slightly smaller than their originals, to accommodate the light gravity on Patience. Genetic engineers had added special touches to their lungs, bone marrow, and blood cells so they could breath the mix of chemicals in Patience's atmosphere.

Dr. Amir knew all this, and she'd seen these soul-suppressed clones before, but never in real time. Even 13.8 light years away she could sense a strangeness about the floating bodies, and it wasn't because they'd grown so unnaturally fast. They seemed peaceful but . . . primordial. Or empty. Or maybe *ghostlike*, she thought, reaching for the right word. They were alive and dead, in both states at once, awaiting the reconciling breath of God.

She shivered, blaming the room's air-conditioning, and turned her thoughts in a rational direction. In the generations since the *Svalbard* left Earth, scientists had moved past old ideas about soul transfer. Few of them now believed that the Merge process could restore an original subject's memories or behavior patterns.

But there was no reason to reveal this to the public, and after all, Merge might work as designed. No one knew for sure.

If macro quantum patterns held memories and behavior patterns — and this was a big if — then Merge would mean dropping a mature mind into an 18-year-old brain, a brain with more plasticity and a different enzyme structure than the original. This would be like fitting an optical lens onto a radio telescope: possibly harmless, possibly harmful, but not recommended in any case. No one had solved the problem of how to make the mismatch work, so yes, these "telescopes" might stop functioning.

And if macro quantum patterns held something unexpected, or nothing at all, well . . . Ark would get their money's worth out of this experiment, no matter what the public thought was going on.

*
* *

A group of Ark scientists from around the solar system was anxious to see what Dr. Amir was seeing, and she couldn't put them off any longer. She opened the door and they bustled in, chatting and smiling, specialists in post-quantum soulistics, quantum biophysics, human biology, and psychology.

All of them eager for a live look at the bodies that would serve as test subjects for their important research.

Part 3: Patience

Waking

Invention, it must be humbly admitted, does not consist in
creating out of void, but out of chaos; the materials must,
in the first place, be afforded . . . .
—Mary Shelley

Selex pulled flesh-fiber gloves onto her hand extensions and
opened the lid of the crèche into which the Rachel clone had
been decanted, still aboard the *Svalbard* even though the ship
was now on the planet's surface. Selex was the Rachel clone's
personal attendant, a relationship meant to last for Rachel's
new lifetime.

For 10 hours of each 25, Selex administered mild shocks to
the Rachel clone's muscles to finish their development, and
she stimulated nanoelectrodes in the clone's brain to perfect
the hierarchy of brain spaces in which achieved skills and
knowledge were being stored. She stroked the clone's skin
with flesh-fiber to accustom it to human touch, quoted poetry
to it to give it an aesthetic grounding, played symphonic music
and techno-pop and bird songs to it to nurture its auditory
sensibilities.

Three times during each of the clone's daytime periods,
Selex administered nutrients to its stomach, removed its
waste, and checked its stats. Noting a spike in MQP activity,
she adjusted the mix of chemicals going into the claustrum
and pineal gland within the clone's brain. Keeping the macro
quantum pattern below 1,200 millicogs was ideal at this stage,
according to theory.

Her chores complete for the day, Selex dimmed the lights
and turned off the music. The Rachel clone was alone in the
warm, soft bed to rest, sleep, and dream. For the next 15 hours,
her only companion was the tabby-striped cat that Selex

placed in the crèche before leaving the room. In theory, bonding with a live companion animal would help the Rachel clone stay grounded in her body when she eventually underwent Merge.

The first sight the cat had ever seen was Selex's flesh-fibered hand extensions, but he didn't find his life strange. *Here* was the only place he'd ever been. His MQP resonance hovered near 98,000 millicogs, normal for a healthy mammal.

The cloned human fell into a deeper phase of sleep, and the cloned cat yawned and curled up against the human's side. A few hours later, he pawed at the body as if hoping for conversation. Bored, he hopped out of the crèche to investigate the room, attack his cat tree, and chase a toy that was activated by his presence. Then he hopped back onto the bed and snuggled against the warm body, ready for another nap.

*
**

Down the hall, Selex's colleague Velex checked on the clone of Dr. Tensel Brown. For the third time that month, Velex placed a small, friendly cat on the edge of the open crèche. The newly cloned cat was a female with moss green eyes, tawny orange fur, black spots, and a fresh, spontaneously generated soul all her own. She pressed up against the clone's arm, but the arm twitched as if to push her off, and over the next 10 minutes the clone's blood pressure and stress hormones rose to morbid levels.

Velex removed the cat, and Tensel's cloned body relaxed. "You were wrong," Velex reported to Dr. Amir back on Earth. "You said that the third time would be the 'charm,' but he had a strong negative reaction to this third Zoë clone, just as he did with the first two."

Velex dropped the cat into the recycling chute.

"Should we try again?"

Eliza was summoned to Ark headquarters. The Rachel clone was ready for the Merge process, which meant that Eliza's moment had come — a moment she'd planned her life around since she was 10 years old. She'd been determined to live long enough to be Rachel's Earth sponsor, and by God she'd done it.

In Ark's psychiatry wing, an energetic young doctor named Alyssa Covington greeted Eliza at the door and pointed her to a sleek armchair. "Now that we have real-time communication with the colony," Dr. Covington began, sitting across from Eliza, "we've had a chance to carry out modern diagnostics on the clones. My job is to talk with you about all that you might encounter, and how we'd like you to react, when Rachel's macro quantum pattern is extracted from the Temenos and embedded in her clone. You'll be Rachel's main human contact, a blood relative, the first person she'll see (virtually, of course) when she wakes up. So we need you to be prepared."

Eliza leaned back and tipped the chair onto its hind legs, giving the lie to her feeble appearance. "Honey," she said with a chuckle, "talk to me all you want, but you can't make me any more prepared than I already am. I was preparing for this moment before you were born. Before your parents were born. Hell, probably when your *grand*parents were toddling around in their *diapers*."

Unmoved, Dr. Covington began her presentation of charts and mumbo-jumbo. As she droned on about *required* procedures that Eliza *must* follow when the moment came, it was all Eliza could do to keep from nodding off. These scientists might not believe it would be the same Rachel, but she knew better. It would be Rachel as she remembered her, as she'd built her up to be. The stable, warm, open woman who in Eliza's fantasies had been everything that her own mother, Miriam, never was.

Robots clicked lights into place and set up the projectors and cameras that would allow Eliza to seem physically present with Rachel when she woke up. The VR equipment was the only part of it that Eliza could visually parse, and she wrinkled her forehead as she watched techs set up other, less familiar gear. The delay and all this scientific crap filled her with a wild impatience. If she were 40 years younger she'd storm out of the room to complain again, but age had bestowed her with a modicum of patience. "I've waited this long, I can wait another hour," she told herself. Besides, thanks to her sciatica, standing up gave her a tiny bit of trouble, but the chair where they'd all but ordered her to stay put was nice and comfy.

When the setup was complete, they asked her to stand up and place herself within the field of holographic projection. At last! As she stepped among the projectors and cameras, she was startled to find herself in a greenly metallic, bright room with a fully realized AI bot and a striped cat. The bot, she knew, was Selex. Two of the white-coated techs she'd been complaining to earlier stood near her, holographic projections like herself. The cat walked up to the three of them and sniffed at the warm light that made up their apparitions, then turned around, unimpressed. Selex picked him up and closed him into a roomy cage on the shelf so he could watch without getting in the way, because Dr. Covington had told Eliza that "in theory," that damn cat's physical presence in the room was as important as her own virtual presence. She scoffed as she walked over to the cat cage and put her simulated fingers through the bars, wishing she had five credits for every "in theory" she'd heard this week.

She turned back to the room as Selex lowered the sides of what she'd taken to be a large metal box. She saw now that it was a bed, and in the bed was the body of a young black woman who must be — yes, was — her grandmother. "Rachel!" she said, lurching forward, but one of the techs grabbed her arm. "She hasn't been Merged yet. In theory she's blank. We talked about this, Ms. Deimos! Just hang on."

"Humph!" With that as her final word, Eliza resigned herself to witness in silence, as she'd been instructed.

She witnessed in silence as Selex's flesh-fiber hands pulled a blanket back from the clone's nude body. She witnessed in silence as Selex held and turned the body, checking for small cuts or bruises that might hamper the next stage of Merge. She witnessed in silence as Selex transferred the body into a Merge chamber that had been assembled or brought into the room while she wasn't paying attention. She witnessed in silence as Selex closed the lid of the Merge chamber and hovered over and around it, adjusting controls that Eliza couldn't see.

"What difference could it make to have a witness?" she thought for the thousandth time.

*
**

Rachel's mind was a purple swirl, and she heard a sound. A voice? She saw a pink color and some bluish-green, which is what the voice looked like. The voice, the colors, her thoughts about them—all this was nonsense.

A background noise that had been with her forever was gone, and she missed it, but she couldn't remember what the noise had been. She was trying hard to remember it, but this new noise interrupted again. "Rachel?" the voice said.

It took a moment to recognize that this was language, not just any sound. Language. A voice. A human voice.

"Rachel, you're you again."

That was ridiculous. Of course she was herself. But who was Rachel?

"You're Rachel."

Ridiculous.

"Rachel, Nana, it's me, Eliza. Your granddaughter. I'm real, and so are you. I'm Eliza, and you're Rachel. That's what they told me to tell you. We're both human, you and I. We're human. We're women."

It was just more nonsense. Human. Woman. No, she knew who she was and what she'd been. She was real, she existed, and that's all there was to it. No name, no body, no beginning, and no end. Only the present, unfolding below the surface of time, opening out into the eternal.

Warm? And safe? Her *body* was warm and safe. That thought was foreign — it came from someone else. But who? Who was in there with her?

Yes, warm and safe. She'd always been warm and safe, with Selex and Glass, her only friends. Glass. She named him that, her warm cat. Or maybe he was Selex's cat? Or their cat, together? She'd been lonely.

There were *two* of her, a body and a self. How strange. And this state of affairs had begun moments ago. Just moments ago. What had happened moments ago?

Her body had been resting with Selex and Glass, growing, learning, becoming a someone. She supposed this body might be called Rachel. Why not? She was young, and she didn't yet have any other name that she knew of.

Her self, meanwhile, had been resting with the beloved Presence and the beloved others, inside and with the animal-machine, living in the moment. This aspect of her, her self, might be called Rachel too. Why not?

Wait, listen! More stirring. Were there *three* of her? O God. This was a quieter voice, subtler than her body or her self, but more true and complete. It permeated her, spreading intricately throughout everything.

The outside sound interrupted her thoughts again. It was that pink and bluish-green voice again, from the outside, not inside her.

"You're Rachel!" said that voice, "and I'm Eliza. I'm here to remind you, to help you! I have so much to tell you, wait until you hear all that's been happening on Earth, I—"

Rachel's grip on reality came loose and fell off, and she hurt. The pain increased until it was like a scream in her head (her heads? how could this be? O God?).

She lost consciousness.

*
* *

Easy, sweet darkness. What a relief. She had no way to gauge how long it lasted. Seconds? Millennia? Then that voice again, from the outside.

"You're Rachel. There, I said it. Selex, your friendly neighborhood caretaker bot, told me that's all I should say to you, though I've said it about a thousand times today and I really think you can handle more than that. Don't *you*? I mean, you look *so* much better now, fuller, like you've put on weight. Did that bot finally start feeding you enough? But anyway, I'll say it again, *sigh*. You're Rachel. You are Rachel. You are Rachel."

She was Rachel? This, of all things, made a bit of sense. She'd need a name, and "Rachel" had a nice ring to it. Yes, why not?

"Yes," she heard a croaking human voice say. "Yes. Rachel." It was her voice, the voice of her body, the voice of the body she was in. But she didn't know this voice or recognize its timbre, and its vibration made her chest feel strange. The voice was too young. Or too old? "And who are you?" she said, her voice a bit less hoarse this time.

A torrent of words came back in reply. "You remember! I'm Eliza, your granddaughter. Oh, thank you for speaking, and if it weren't for you, I might not be able to hear you at all, and I mean that literally, because you made sure I got the help I needed for my hearing, and I've always wanted to thank you, but it's amazing we can speak at all, really, isn't it? So many light years away from each other — it's thanks to your son Sam's invention, the IDLE-COM. I have so much to tell you, I'm so much older than when you last saw me, I—oh, oh, oh crap, I can see I'm going too fast. I'm so sorry, I'm just so excited."

The voice paused as if listening to something. "Yes, Selex. Thank you," said the voice more quietly. "I'll keep that in mind. You're quite helpful." Maybe the voice was colored with . . . sarcasm? Irritation? It was louder now, as if definitely addressed to Rachel. "Let's back up a little. You remember that you're Rachel, so far so good. How are you feeling?"

"Tired."

"Okay," said Eliza's voice. "We'll stop for now, and you can sleep. We've made progress, and you and I are going to be friends. We already are friends, or we were, long ago . . . but okay, it's enough for now. I'll talk with you later, Nana. Rachel. My dear Rachel."

The colors went away and darkness returned, and silence, and warmth. Rachel felt her body's mind falling into sleep, and the feeling was delectable. Physical sleep never happened in the Temenos. Only the body could do full justice to sleep . . . what a delicious feeling . . . .

And then she was waking up. Sleep was different from blank unconsciousness, she noticed, because she remembered the dreams she'd been having. Obviously she'd been active and alive, fully alive, while sleeping, or else these dreams wouldn't have been stirring in her. She'd dreamed that she was a child on Earth, visiting a lake, walking on the shore, playing there with a friend. Her cat Glass was there, pleading with her to come back to bed, so she'd followed him away from the water and through the trees.

Here the dream became a nightmare. The forest became an operating room, sterile and cold. Unseen hands strapped her to a bed, a transparent dome came down over her head, and her interior self was sucked out, right out through her chest. She woke with a start, then fell back to sleep.

*
**

Eliza was holding her breath, waiting for Rachel to speak. She let a breath out quietly, and drew in another. Then another. She was determined not to rush her Nana.

It was Rachel who spoke first this time. Phew, Dr. Covington would love that.

"Where's . . . everybody?" said Rachel.

Eliza paused. "Look, hon," she said gently, "You were in that database for a long, long time. Many years, and a lot's happened. It's been almost 90 years. Some people are no longer with us."

The ensuing silence felt like another 90 years to Eliza. Just when she thought she might jump out of her skin with impatience, Rachel spoke. "Ninety years? I thought it was eternity."

Eliza reached out her hand, though she and Rachel couldn't touch. "Mercy, I knew it! Was it that bad? With time just crawling like that, you must've suffered. It felt like it took an eternity. It felt that way to me too! If you ever want to tell me about the details, if you ever feel like that's something you'd want to do, I'm here for you. You can talk to me."

Rachel looked up in surprise. "Crawling? Time?"

More silence. Eliza thought she might explode, but if Dr. Covington had told her once she'd told her a thousand times that she shouldn't rush Rachel's coming-back process, no matter how tempted she was to push things along.

"Look lady, I'm not getting any younger!" Eliza had actually said to Dr. Covington in one of their interminable conversations.

"This is about her, not you," said the doctor with her lips pursed in a priggish frown. "No one can be sure what this will be like for her, not even you."

But Eliza didn't buy that. She knew *exactly* what the Merge process was like for Rachel — she'd been imagining it for most of a century. For Rachel, it was like being awakened from a coma, complete with strange and possibly lengthy, unpleasant dreams. Sure, it would take a little time to pull herself together, get oriented, and remember who she was and what life had been like on Earth. But the waking up process wouldn't take long. Eliza wasn't getting any younger, after all.

*
**

The freshly Merged clone of Dr. Tensel Brown was not thriving, in spite of Velex's expertise and his many consultations with Dr. Amir's team on Earth. Tensel was a special case: in his life on Earth, he hadn't fit the profile of an ideal candidate, and he hadn't been psychologically prepared and pre-suggested the way the other colonists, including the paying colonists, had. His fate was anyone's guess, the subject of many a paper back on Earth.

They'd given up on trying to get him to accept a companion animal, and it was too soon to introduce him to his Earth sponsor. What should they try next?

Then to everyone's astonishment, he muttered words, which wasn't supposed to be possible until after he met his Earth sponsor. He was still in a fugue, unconscious or barely conscious. "Zoë," he said, his voice thick and faint. "Where's Zoë?"

"Ironic," said Velex to Dr. Amir, "but not funny." If he'd had human eyes, he would've rolled them. Thanks to his regular communication with human scientists on Earth, Velex was starting to get the hang of humor.

Selex moved Rachel into a studio apartment in the planet's main settlement site, a village whose name would be selected, in theory, as the colonists' first communal decision. Intelligent machines had constructed the village in a wide, lovely valley, artfully laying it out on either side of a river that meandered down a shallow canyon near the valley's center. An arched stone bridge connected the living area on the east side of the settlement with the barns, silos, sheds, machine shops, and other work buildings on the west side. Each single-story apartment building surrounded a cloistered courtyard filled with immature sagebrush, willow shrubs, small redbud trees, and desert flowers that would bloom when rain came. A large meeting hall doubled as the community's refectory — empty now, but in theory to be in heavy use within a year. Among and around the buildings, small paving robots were creating paths that made graceful curves through the desert scrub.

Though Rachel didn't yet know anything about the world outside her apartment, other cloned humans were being moved into the apartments around hers. Most of them were beginning to wake up to their new lives, though her transition was faster than most.

Every day at what was sunrise in California back on Earth, Selex slowly raised full-spectrum lights around Rachel's bed so she could wake up at roughly the same time her body had woken up for much of her life on Earth. (Eliza found this puzzling, but she was told that soul-reattachment theory was still more art than science, and Merge biophysicists on Earth weren't above trying *any*thing that might help.) Patience completed each rotation in slightly under 26 hours, so her waking time ranged through Patience's day and night. Selex adjusted her clock by a few seconds every day, inching her toward synchronization with her new planet.

Her days, at first, were routine. For breakfast, Selex served her two poached eggs on toast (a favorite of hers on Earth, per the database) and a glass of fruit-flavored nutrients, which she consumed without comment and, after a few days, without help. Then a short medical exam, including a finger prick to collect blood.

After lunch, Rachel would nap or stare into space. Sometimes she ran one hand over the other, marveling at the rich pigmentation of her skin and the difference between the color of her palms and the backs of her hands. She examined her long, strong fingers and her fingernails, which Selex kept short and neat. After Selex gave her a mirror, she spent long stretches of time gazing into her own expressive eyes, unselfconsciously appreciating her beauty. She was intrigued by the neat pattern that Selex had braided into her hair, which the robot washed twice a week. She ran her fingertips across her eyelids and over her nose and her high, wide cheekbones, feeling and looking at her ears, seeing the truth of herself, intricate and miraculous.

At 2:00 p.m. each day, a miniature hologram of Eliza appeared on the coffee table. This was Rachel's standing appointment with her Earth sponsor, and her only connection with a natural human. Mini-Eliza looked like a grouchy, wrinkled doll beaming in from a distant solar system — 15 centimeters high on days when her back didn't hurt, and closer to 13 when she slouched.

As prescribed by Dr. Covington, they talked about whatever interested Rachel, which turned out to be her thoughts about her own body, her sexual feelings, the food she ate, how it felt to eat it, and the view she had of the desert valley now that Selex raised the blinds for a few hours each day. Her past on Earth and her kinship to Eliza held no interest, much to Eliza's consternation, until one day she asked Eliza about Eliza's own life. Did she have a husband? Friends? Children?

"I have friends, of course, though I've outlived most of them," said Eliza. "Humph, old age." She paused, and Rachel, whose words were few and far between, let the silence rest between them until Eliza was ready to continue. "And I had a partner, my beloved Phoebe. But she's gone now. We lived a long and wonderful life together, and she's gone."

"Oh," said Rachel. "I'm sorry."

"Well aren't you going to act even a bit shocked? You know you used to be, er, not particularly understanding about things like two women committing to spend their lives together."

"I don't remember that," said Rachel, "and hearing it makes me sad. I find it hard to believe I'm that person. From what you've said, that Rachel sounds cold and unhelpful, and I don't hear her inside me."

"No no, she wasn't cold or unhelpful at all! She was loving, maybe to a fault. I don't know how to explain. Oh damn, this isn't going how I'd planned, not at all. What terrible first impressions I'm giving you of yourself!" The image of Eliza was wringing its tiny hands. "I guess only you can solve this puzzle, because I sure as hell can't figure out how to make you remember."

"Why do I have to remember?"

The miniature Eliza heaved a dramatic sigh. "I guess we've talked enough for today. I'll see you tomorrow, my dear." And with that, she blew a kiss and flickered out, leaving Rachel to ponder their conversation in silence until Selex alerted her to the need to eat dinner, several hours later.

Growth and violation

You created my inmost being and knit me in my mother's
womb. I am fearfully and wonderfully made,
a demonstration of your marvelousness.
—Psalm 139:13–14

A few weeks later, Eliza was attempting to interest Rachel in
the other colonists, on Dr. Covington's orders. "I hear Sara
D'Angelo's a few doors down the hall from you," she said from
her perch on Rachel's copy of *The Little Prince*, which Selex
had left out along with a stack of other books. Rachel's mind
drifted to the question of why and how she knew how to read.
When had she learned? Reading was a startling joy, a phenomenon out of the blue, and the prince's journey filled and colored her thoughts. She, like him, was on a planet far from
Earth. Was she just visiting, or was she home? Was she here
because she was looking for something? If so, what might it
be?

Her body startled, and she remembered that she was on the
couch in her apartment, facing Eliza, who was still talking
about people Rachel didn't know. Who was Sara D'Angelo, for
example, and why would Rachel care? Coming back into the
present always made her catch her breath, a surprise every
time, as if her body were coalescing just then, for the first time,
right in that moment. She tuned her attention back into the
ongoing monologue.

". . . five times, at least! Wears me out just thinking about
it. And she was a voice worker like you, but I doubt you ever
met her, she lived in Phoenix. I've watched her vids, kind of a
crazy cat lady after she retired, hah, but anyway, you remember the career you had, right? Human Converse?"

Rachel watched Eliza's face, saying nothing.

"They tell me you're way ahead of everyone else on Patience. Maybe you could entice some of these folks to talk to you, who knows? It might jog your memory. You'd be able to try out your social skills, which Dr. Covington tells me are already in place in your frontal lobes." She lowered her voice to an aside. "Gives me the screaming meemies, the way they set up your brain with all that prefab stuff. But anyway, yuck, not my choice. On to happier thoughts." Her volume rose and she held her hands out to Rachel. "Wouldn't you *like* to meet the people you live with?"

Still nothing, though Dr. Covington warned Eliza this might happen. None of the newly ensouled clones seemed to remember anything about Earth or their former lives, nor did they care. Most were adjusting to solitary life on Patience, and no one but Rachel had yet exhibited signs of nascent social curiosity. One step at a time.

"I'd like to hear more about your yard," said Rachel. "Anything new?" So Eliza returned to the only Earth topic that interested Rachel, which was the Calla lilies, rhododendrons, and wild irises in Eliza's backyard in Oakland, and the dandelions that she treated as weeds even though they were really rather pretty, and even though their greens were actually *edible* . . . .

"Sorry to interrupt, Eliza," said Selex, rolling up to the couch, "but Rachel's special friend is ready to see her. I hope you've primed her interest appropriately."

When Rachel heard the word "Rachel," she had no automatic "Ah, that's me!" response, but she'd learned that when Selex and Eliza said it, they always meant her.

"My special friend. Is it Glass?" she said. "Didn't he come back inside after I left the window open for him?" She looked behind her and found Glass curled up on the back of the couch.

"No, it's not Glass," said Selex. "It's Tensel."

"Tensel?" Rachel was perplexed. "What's that?"

"Lord have mercy," said Eliza, "I told Dr. Covington she's not *ready*! What if she's *never* ready? What if she doesn't *want* this?"

Selex ignored her and addressed Rachel. "Tensel's a human, and his genome varies from yours in a compatible way. He's been next door to you the whole time you've lived in this apartment."

"Oh." Rachel wondered what she should feel about this. She felt nothing.

"He'll play an important role in your life on Patience," Selex continued. "Eliza really should've explained this to you. It's her job, after all, and she's better suited to it than I am . . . ."

Still complaining about Eliza, who was confined to her hologram on the coffee table, Selex slid open a door in the wall near Rachel. She turned and draped her arms across the arm of the couch so she could see the new vista, a studio apartment with a layout that mirrored hers, with a green fabric couch just like her blue one. Slumped on the couch was a tall young man with dark hair and a clean-shaven but haggard face. He stared at the carpet, his eyes blank. He hadn't noticed the door open, or maybe he didn't care.

Rachel heard Eliza's wheezy inhale and knew from experience that her supposed granddaughter was about to speak, but Selex cut her off with a slicing gesture. Selex and Eliza whispered, then Eliza spoke at a normal volume, her tone strained. "We'll let you get used to this for a while, dear. Just drink it in. I'll be here if you need me, and Selex too. We're right here. We're not going anywh—"

That seemed to be all the talking Eliza was allowed to do for the time being, because although her lips kept moving, no sound emerged from her hologram.

Rachel shifted from the couch to a recliner that faced this new mystery and sat unmoving, gazing at the man next door. He was breathing, but otherwise he didn't move or lift his gaze.

After 20 minutes, Glass climbed onto Rachel's lap. The connecting door slid closed, and Eliza was released to speak.

"Well," said Eliza sourly, "I suppose that's enough titillation for one day."

*
**

The exercise was repeated every afternoon for a week. The door opened, the man stared at the carpet, Rachel stared at the man, time passed, the door shut. Rachel began to notice that she was having an emotion about the unmoving, unspeaking man next door: irritation. Why should he interrupt her solitude? For that matter, why should Selex and Eliza? Why couldn't these people leave her alone?

She also felt a mild but growing desire to understand what was going on. Why did Eliza visit every day? Was she really human, really on Earth as she said she was? Or was she machine-generated? She wasn't present in the flesh, and so she didn't seem real, no matter what Selex said about VR being *real* by all definitions of the word.

Her own organic flesh was the real her, just as the collection of polymers and metals and silicon that cooked her meals every day was the real Selex. This much seemed clear.

So what was known about the real Eliza?

And was Eliza her granddaughter? Rachel had never been pregnant, or not that she could remember. Her body felt even more untraveled than that — she felt sure she was a virgin. Certainly not a mother, never mind a grandmother.

The growing questions brought a change to her mood. It was harder for her to stay grounded in the present moment, and her perplexity and her heavy heart kept her on the couch much of every day. Her body kept sending messages that it wanted and needed physical activity, and this energy in her muscles and bones felt natural, because she was a young person in a young body. But it also felt unnatural and foreign, because in her heart she understood that she was old. So how could she feel young? And if she was young, how could she have a grandchild? Everything was off, misaligned, wrong way down deep, where it's hard to pin cause to effect.

On the eighth day after her first glimpse of Tensel, the door opened as usual on the scene next door, but the couch was empty. "Things are a little different today," said Eliza. "They tell me Tensel isn't feeling well."

And sure enough, when Rachel forced her gaze away from the couch, she noticed a figure splayed out across the bed. It was Tensel, in sweat pants and T-shirt. He lay on top of the bedspread, his eyes squeezed shut. "He needs exercise but won't get up," said Eliza. "You at least ramble up and down your apartment a few times a day, but they tell me he won't even do that. Velex carries him to the toilet and back, washes him, feeds him."

"Velex?"

"Like your Selex."

Rachel had a new sensation: empathy. The stab of it was so sharp it hurt. "Ow! Eliza, where's his Glass? Doesn't he have an animal of his own?" She pulled her eyebrows down into a frown and felt as if she was using muscles that had never moved.

Selex answered before Eliza could speak. "We had a technical difficulty creating his companion animal."

"Technical . . . ." Rachel said the word slowly, looking at Glass. A new puzzle to reflect on during the hours ahead. Why would the word "technical" belong anywhere near Glass?

The day after Tensel wasn't feeling well, Selex ran her usual morning tests on Rachel, then made an announcement. "You're ready to mate."

"*Mate?*" Another emotion erupted in Rachel, similar to the irritation she'd felt about all these people invading her solitude, but more intense. "You've got to be kidding. What do you think I am?"

"I'll tell Dr. Covington you've expressed anger," said Selex. "It's a good sign, it means you're regaining a sense of yourself."

Rachel ignored this and sat down to think, refusing to get up when Selex prompted her to exercise. "You need to get up now and then," said the robot. "I've told you before, but you seem to need reminders."

"Leave me alone. I'm waiting for Eliza."

"She won't open the link until 2:00 p.m., Patience Central Time. If you need to talk, I can talk with you."

"I've heard too much from you already. I want to talk to a human being, if she really *is* one."

Selex wasn't wise, but she was smart enough to know that it was time to retreat and leave the talking to Eliza.

As soon as Eliza's hologram appeared, Rachel began to speak, more animated than Eliza had ever seen her. "What do you know about Selex's idea that she can *mate* me? What's going on?"

Eliza shifted from one foot to the other, her gaze directed somewhere behind Rachel. "Well, hello to you too. Mating . . . er, yes. Leave it to Selex to make you sound like an animal. I've been telling that stupid machine and Dr. Amir and all the rest of them that it's way too early for this, *way* too early, if it even needs to happen at all, which I don't see why it does, but nobody listens to me."

"What are you talking about? Just tell me."

"Umm, O Lordy." Eliza chewed on her lower lip, deciding how to proceed. "It's like this. Ark's top priority is for this colony expedition to succeed, and to succeed, you have to have colonists. To have colonists, you have to have babies. Creating baby colonists is a big part of your job, and unfortunately you agreed to it in your contract. The Ark Project wants you to have two of them. Babies."

Rachel was silent, and Eliza went on.

"And here comes the shittiest part. You're required to conceive them, well, by having sex with the man they've selected as your best match."

"A man they've selected? Why? Why would I do this?"

Eliza stalled for a moment, then went on. "I'm afraid you might not have a choice. You agreed to it with a biologically binding seal. That's the bad news as Dr. Covington delivered it to me."

"I won't do it, and there aren't any men around here, anyway."

As if on cue, the door in the wall slid open. Tensel lay sprawled on his bed, eyes closed. Rachel moved to take a closer look just in time to see him roll onto his side and vomit over the edge of the bed into a container that Velex held below his mouth. "Would you like some water?" said Velex in a gravelly voice, wiping Tensel's mouth with a cloth towel. It was the first time Rachel had heard Velex speak.

"But why can't —" Eliza began, but Selex muted her mic. Rachel could see that Eliza was talking heatedly and Selex was replying, and then Eliza's voice was audible to Rachel again. "I asked not to witness this," she said. "There's nothing I can do, Rachel, I'm so sorry. They promised me they won't hurt you, because you're a valuable asset. I told Selex if that's not true I'm going to fly out there and dismantle its robot ass piece by piece until its butt won't even —" Her hologram image flickered out, and she was gone.

Rachel felt her anger deflate as Selex slipped one robot arm under her knees and the other behind her back, and then she was in the air, being carried. She remembered the glass of juice Selex had handed her a few minutes before. Had Selex done something to make her this complacent? She was watching herself from a distance as the robot turned to fit her through the doorway, carried her across the room, and propped her on the bed next to Tensel's inert form.

Tensel's eyes were squeezed shut, and his skin looked cadaverous. Rachel felt a vague curiosity, because she'd never seen him up close or been in his apartment. She also felt fear, but her mind was graying out, and she couldn't remember why this sick panic was filling her belly.

Then a wave of vertigo hit her. She blinked, shook her head, and opened her eyes to a wholly different kind of bedroom scene. Tensel lay on the bed as before, his eyes closed, but he was transformed. The hollows of his cheeks had filled out, his pallor had shifted to a healthy tan, and the expression on his face was settled and calm. He wore a plain gray shirt, a gray blazer, and jeans. His wavy dark hair was clean and dry, and a faceted green crystal hung around his neck.

This didn't look like a man who'd been retching moments before.

Rachel pressed her hands to her head and the room spun once again, then adjusted itself and came into focus. Her body softened and warmed, as if someone else had taken a seat at the controls, cracked their knuckles, and started pushing buttons and moving sliders. Dopamine rushed into her brain, followed closely by oxytocin. Who *was* this man? She wanted to get closer, to know more. His shy, solemn face was asymmetrical in a way she found fascinating, and she pressed her palms against his chest, reveling in her body's first contact with another human. She felt supple and relaxed. Her mind became fuzzy and left the room, but that was okay — her body was now happy to be left unchaperoned with this man. This was real, because she could actually touch him, and he could touch her.

A corner of her mind complained that this wasn't real, that something about it was a horror, but . . . who cared?

She felt compelled to unbutton his pants.

As if responding to commands from his own puppeteer, Tensel opened his eyes, which were a dark gray-blue, like the sky Rachel had glimpsed from her window.

Being here with Tensel made sense, for whatever reason. Everything fit together, and all would be well. A catchy tune started up in her head, something about her body being safe with Ark, safe with Ark, safe with Ark . . . .

*
* *

She woke up in her own bed, staring at her own blue couch, feeling Glass's small body pressed against her back. The thought of the flesh-and-blood man in the room next door made her stomach cramp up with a knotty anxiety: partly leftover physical excitement, mostly disgust.

"O God," she muttered as slow tears rolled down her cheeks. Could it have been a dream?

No, her body wasn't the same today as it had been yesterday. She didn't remember the specifics, but her body knew the essence of it, just as many of her foremothers' bodies had known it.

She wrapped her arms around herself and cried quietly.

Burdened

I saw, also, that there was an ocean of darkness and death;
but an infinite ocean of light and love, which flowed over
the ocean of darkness. In that also I saw the infinite love of
God, and I had great openings.
—George Fox

At 2:00 p.m. the next afternoon, Eliza's hologram appeared in front of the couch and looked appraisingly at Rachel, who was slouched back on the cushions with her knees spread, eyes open just enough to see her small visitor.

"How do you feel?" asked Eliza, though she knew without asking.

Rachel said nothing.

"Great news," Eliza continued. "Selex just told me that the innerbots in your left fallopian tube are reporting the presence of a fertilized egg, and it appears to be dividing and moving toward your uterus in a normal way. That means you're probably pregnant already." The miniature Eliza paced back and forth from the wadded up tissues on one end of the coffee table to the dirty coffee mug on the other end, rubbing her hands together like a scheming old wizard.

It no longer seemed bizarre to Rachel to see a tiny person walking through her coffee-table junk. Just another day in her life, which now apparently included pregnancy. The idea of having a baby was as wispy and unreal to her as her memories of what had happened to her yesterday, next door.

It didn't help to feel as if her head were being excavated with an ice pick. She'd had enough of Ark and its tests and procedures, and a new thought came to her: Ark apparently had many uses for her, but what use did she have for Ark?

"You know," she said, "my body doesn't feel safe with Ark."

Eliza stopped, startled. Then she smiled. "That's a good one!" She stopped laughing and looked at Rachel. "No, I guess it's not funny. You know, I hope maybe *I'm* keeping your body safe, or at little safer than it might've been. I can't say I've gamed the system, but at least I'm starting to figure it out, and they'll leave you alone for a while now that you and Tensel have, you know—" She paused with her foot in Rachel's Boston Fern, which was thriving in its little pot. "Anyway, the hard part's over, and it's in their best interests to take care of you while you're pregnant, so let's let them do it. Just let Selex take care of you, okay? No more conjugal visits with Tensel, or not for a long time, anyway . . . ."

*
**

Time passed.

Deep on the inside, Tensel felt burdened, like a sapling buried under winter snow. But closer to the surface of himself, his young body and mind overflowed with energy. Time had passed and he was alert, no longer catatonic as he'd been during those first months after the Merge. He wanted to be busy. Vague thoughts about work stirred in his mind — no memories of what he'd done as a soul physicist back in San Francisco, but something about the feelings work had given him: the rush of being in the zone, absorbed in a task. Competent and strong. Too full to notice the emptiness.

It was time to look for those feelings.

"Velex, I'd like to alter your programming," he said. He was talking with the robot these days, though he still maintained a stony silence whenever his Earth sponsor, Caryatis, appeared near his couch and tried to engage with him.

"Interesting, but impossible," said Velex. "If you try to override my programming, you'll activate my defensive subroutines. They'll defeat you. At worst, you could injure yourself."

"Okay then, tell me what I should do. I need a challenge. I'm going crazy! You tell me the other colonists will soon have jobs that fit their skills, and I supposedly have 12 more years of education than anyone here. So what's my job?"

"Your presence is unplanned, as you're well aware. Sorry, but no job in this colony matches your specialized skills."

"That's ridiculous. This colony depends on technology: the terraforming maintenance, the agriculture, the embedded sensors, the medical bots, and you yourself. It's all about technology. How could a technologist such as myself not have anything to offer?"

"As I said, your presence is unplanned. The colony was designed to function without local human-based technical expertise. The expertise we need, beyond what's in our database, comes from Ark."

"Maybe we're too dependent on them."

"I scoff," said Velex. "The colony would fail without their extensive daily intervention."

Tensel grabbed a windbreaker and sun goggles and went out the back door, leaving Velex to his chores. He walked a straight line into the desert scrub, ignoring the paths, and soon he was out of sight of the village buildings. He walked roughly parallel to the river canyon, and in another hour his long legs had taken him up to the peak of one of the low mountains that bordered their valley. Rugged terrain lay in front of him, and he stopped when he reached the edge of a wide chasm.

Yelling every profanity he could think of, he threw rocks and sticks out over the chasm. When he ran out of things to throw, he sprinted along the edge, wondering if he might trip and fall into the gap, but his strong young body kept him out of danger.

Thirsty and exhausted, he headed home.

"So Velex," he said as he collapsed onto the couch, accepting a glass of water, "can you think of an activity that would occupy my mind in a meaningful way?"

"I have lots of programs you haven't tried yet," said Velex. "Chess, Pyramid, and virtual athletic games you could play by yourself outside until other colonists are inclined to join you: soccer, bocce, —"

"Damn it, that's not what I'm looking for! If you keep pushing that crap on me, I'll figure out how to take you apart."

Velex, having learned from his extensive study of human literature that discretion is often the better part of valor, dropped the subject.

*
**

The full-spectrum lights were starting to brighten around the edges of the room. "Thanks for your cooperation!" said Selex as Rachel walked from her bed to the toilet in her flannel nightgown. "The fetus in your uterus is now eight weeks old, and during your exam this morning I infused it with nanobots. Over the next several years, the nanobots will deliver one half of each pair of a thousand pairs of entangled particles to the child's organs. It's fascinating technology, if you'd ever care to hear more. A companion procedure has just been carried out on a compatible male fetus on Earth. That fetus, of course, received the other half of each pair."

"You certainly like to tinker, don't you," said Rachel.

"Aren't you interested in your son?"

"I don't want to know the baby's gender," Rachel sang from where she sat on the toilet. "It's more 'fun' that way, I thought I told you that. You asked me what fun feels like. Well, this is it."

She flushed, washed her hands in a stream of warm enzymes, and turned on her electric toothbrush. Maybe the noise would drown out the robot's next irritating comment. Selex rolled right into the bathroom and parked herself behind Rachel, within kicking distance, she noticed. Why couldn't her bathroom have a door on it? To Selex, the concept of privacy seemed as peculiar as the concept of fun.

Selex upped her volume enough to be heard. "I've mentioned the fetus's probable gender four times now," she said. "You choose to forget that you already know that this fetus has a 98 percent chance of presenting as a male."

Rachel began to hum along with the whir of her toothbrush.

"Would you like to know more?" Selex was almost shouting now. "Its body type and coloring? Its probable health outcomes and intelligence?"

Rachel spat and slapped her toothbrush back into its charger. "No. Thank you." She pushed around Selex and headed for her pile of gardening clothes. Whatever was growing inside her body, she didn't need details about it. It belonged to Ark. If they wanted it to thrive, they'd have make it thrive. She wanted no part in it.

A shadow was drifting across her mind and into her heart, and she told Selex to leave her alone. She needed to think, and she didn't want help from a machine or the corp that controlled it.

Selex's announcement about the entangled particles bothered her, which in itself surprised her. Did she actually care a little bit about this baby? The Ark Project controlled her life, and now it was clear that Ark controlled her baby as well. This troubled her.

She put a hand on her belly, ever so slightly curious about the tiny human taking shape in her uterus. Was he really in there? If so, was it okay that Ark had so much control over him? Did *she* have any control? Did the nanobots and their strange payload make the baby something other than human? And what about her own body? Was *she* fully human?

She opened her back door and walked into the enclosed garden that Selex had helped her create, providing her with seeds from the *Svalbard*'s seed bank. She took a direct path across the spinach, her bare feet crushing a few of the fragile seedlings and making gashes in the dirt. She'd planted fast-growing yucca around the edges of her enclosure to create a screen and mark her boundaries, even though her neighbors on either side, Tensel and Dante, never seemed to come outside. She pushed roughly through the young shrubs and opened the transparent door that led out into the desert scrub and Patience's bright atmosphere.

She paused, remembering that she didn't have her sun goggles or her shoes, then pushed her way out onto the path anyway, senseless of the small, sharp rocks that dug into her feet. Passing the silent apartment buildings and the empty refectory, she left the path instead of continuing across the bridge. She made her way uphill along the edge of the river canyon, following it south until the village was out of sight. She stopped at an enormous boulder that leaned half a meter over the edge of the canyon, which in this section of the river was a tall, rocky cliff.

She crawled onto the boulder and sat, letting her legs and feet dangle over the edge, looking down past her feet to the bottom, where the river was narrow and flowing fast through a section of rapids. She closed her eyes.

Eliza had told her what she'd been like back on Earth, long ago, in her other body. She showed her passages that she, Rachel, had supposedly written in her journals about Jesus, about church friends, about her prayer life and her longing to be close to God. But here on Patience, none of it made sense. Even the idea of good and evil felt like a human construct to her, and though she hadn't said so to Eliza, she'd privately decided that there was no good and no evil. As a clone, she didn't need to be burdened by the old superstitions; good and evil were no more than ideas that natural-bred humans invented to help them categorize and make sense of the events in their short, painful lives.

But now, gazing down into the canyon with its ancient rocks, she understood that evil did in fact exist. She didn't feel like the same person Eliza was always talking about, but if that old Rachel was gone, where had she gone? Had Ark killed her? Had Ark taken her apart and bolted the pieces back together, soul bolted onto body, without success? Had Ark done both of these unspeakable things to the original Rachel, killed her and savaged her?

The idea was accompanied by something sulfurous and wispy, a confusing presence that slipped out of view the moment you turned your eyes in its direction.

Evil.

And from what she'd learned about the original Rachel's family on Earth, is seemed possible that her own son, Sam, had participated in this evil, whether he knew it or not.

She thought about Selex's automatic obedience to any command that came from Earth. She thought about the Ark Project and its agenda. She thought about her forced episode with Tensel, and insight arrived: Ark was about profit, and profit came from the promise of long life for Ark's patrons back on Earth. *Her* long life wasn't the point. She was a test subject, no more. A machine, selected for this work because of her qualities. Different from Selex only in the type of care and maintenance required to keep her functioning.

Yes, evil existed.

Old and weary, her soul ached. There's a time to die, and she was long since past it. A quote came into her mind. "All things are wearisome, more than one can say." Where had she heard that? Maybe it was from the old Rachel, wise lady that she must have been. She opened her eyes and looked down between her feet, realizing it wouldn't take much. She could slide forward and let gravity help her down to the bottom of the chasm. Maybe the fall would kill her, or maybe she'd die slowly of dehydration and exposure. It would be painful, but the pain inside her was becoming overwhelming.

Time passed. She didn't notice the heat, or her thirst, or the brightness burning into her retinas. She didn't care.

She almost fell asleep. Next to her, a wind-blown acacia tree leaned toward the river, clinging hard to the rocks, and it seemed to Rachel that *she* was the tree, clinging to the edge, alive despite the improbability of it, and not wanting to let go.

Like the tree, she could thrive here on Patience. *This* was her home, not Earth.

She remembered her plants, and Glass, and the baby growing inside her. These were good. Her life, her being alive at all, was good. Ark had put her together, in a crude way, but something else had put together the intricacy of her body and soul and mind, her humanity, the mystery and rightness of her existing at all. Both evil and good did exist, but she now saw with perfect clarity that good was larger — overwhelmingly larger—than evil. Evil existed, no doubt about it. It was as big, as sickening, and as malicious as she'd sensed it a few minutes before. Evil was part of reality, like a drop in the ocean. But there was an ocean.

She sat with this for a long time.

What had sent her this hopeful message? Was the sender goodness itself? Or maybe *love*? Maybe *life* was the right name for it? Or *God*? Whatever it was, it wanted her to live.

She was thirsty, and now aware of a sharp pain in her eyes. How long had she been in the sun on this hot cliff? Had it been hours? She picked her way down the rocky path, squinting, making her way home on blistered feet.

Once inside, she felt her way to the sink to get water, and her eyes wouldn't adjust to the dimness of her apartment. "Selex, my eyes." Her voice was hoarse. "Help me." She lay on her bed and let Selex scan her, put drops into her eyes, and cover her eyes with bandages. She tuned out the lecture — "I told you never to go off the path barefoot; better yet, don't go off the path at all; you know you have to wear your sun goggles until the atmosphere's 'baked' and the glare fades; I can't take care of you without your cooperation . . . ." Usually the robot's monotone delivery of what was meant to be an impassioned parental scolding made her smile, but not today.

"Leave me alone until dinner," she said.

"I haven't administered the analgesic. It'll only take a moment."

"I don't want it. Please leave."

She listened to the machine roll onto its docking station and took a long, slow breath, feeling a stinging in her eyes and a growing pain behind them, but also a deep calm. Her despair was lifted, and she had hold of a clear and simple truth: she wanted to live, and there was goodness and love in this world. Goodness and love existed, and she was part of them.

Whatever had rescued her from the chasm wasn't a feeling, and it wasn't an action. It was simply goodness, or love, and she could choose to love back or not. In a way, her choice was irrelevant. It would love her either way.

Thinking about this, she fell asleep.

*
**

She dreamed she was on the edge of the river canyon. Someone shoved her, and she fell. As she fell, she discovered that she had wings. She flapped them, but she was only a baby. These were tiny wings, and they wouldn't hold her up. She was falling, terrified. Her life left her and spun around her, falling out of her reach as she grabbed for it, and she landed with a thump. Why so soft? I should be dead, I should be at the bottom. Then she realized she'd landed on a ship, an ancient schooner, and she was being lifted up to the top of the next wave.

She woke with a sense of calm, thinking about the dream while Selex checked her eyes and replaced her bandages with a light layer of gauze. She remembered a quote she'd read in one of the mystical gospels Selex had given her: "The light shines in the darkness, and the darkness has not understood it." Exactly. She didn't understand what had happened to her the day before, and she didn't understand the dream, not in any objective way. But a light had dawned, and her experience of waking up within this light was more significant, more life-giving, than understanding could ever be.

She went outside to check on her garden, as best she could with sore feet, blocked vision, and only a sense of light and dark to guide her. With her fingertips she explored the uncurling leaves of the tomato seedlings, the peas filling out their pods, and the wispy greens that gave away the locations of the carrots. Glass gave a quiet, chirping meow nearby, and Rachel put a hand on his back and her other hand on her own belly. "Well friends," she said to those assembled, "we're all Patience natives, it seems. This is our home."

*
**

One day, trying to jog Rachel's memory, Eliza told her a story that Eliza had heard from Sam: Sam was an 8-year-old imp who didn't want to have his hair cut, and Rachel wanted to cut it. Sam's 10-year-old sister, always an advocate of freedom, hid him under her bed until Rachel found him and dragged him out. He screamed, Rachel cried, Miriam preached about justice, and in the end Rachel gave up. From then on, Sam was free to do whatever he pleased with his hair, so he hadn't cut it again until after Rachel and the Temenos were long gone. To bring the story to life, Eliza showed Rachel short vids of Sam as a young man with a big grin and big hair, then as a middle-aged man with short salt-and-pepper hair and a neatly trimmed beard, accepting his Lisa Randall award.

Apparently that middle-aged man now lay in cryogenic suspension alongside Miriam and a woman named Jessica, all hoping to see Rachel again someday.

As usual, the story and the vids didn't stir anything in Rachel, beyond her agreement that Sam's dark, wide-set eyes did look like her own, and that his smile maybe matched hers too, in some abstract way, as did Miriam's. She felt especially large and warm and awkward in her body that day, which made it impossible to forget her real child, the one physically present with her. She knew Eliza would be disappointed to hear this, so she stayed silent, watching Eliza's gesturing hands and letting Eliza's words wash over her.

She had a funny idea that Eliza was her own grandmother. It was her private fantasy, and she kept it to herself. She knew Selex and Dr. Covington would see it as a psychological problem, or a misunderstanding to be explained in mind-numbing detail, or both.

The next night she had another dream, and this one was full of humans. People who were unfamiliar to her, but important.

"I'd like to meet the other colonists," she said to Selex as she ate breakfast. "I know Tensel's next door, but Eliza told me about other people who live near me too." Knowing Selex as she did, she braced for a lecture.

"Ah, excellent," said the robot, launching into an explanation of the 14 theoretical substages of macro quantum pattern reattachment and the significance of social initiative to the process.

Rachel clenched her teeth in silent vexation, waiting for the part that interested her. "No one gathers in the refectory yet for meals," said Selex, finally getting to it. "You can start eating there anytime you like, though you'd be by yourself for now. Dante, next door, is barely verbal, but he spends 10 minutes outside at dawn every morning. I can wake you in time for you to intersect with him. I think you'll like him — the predicted friendship coefficient of your pairing is relatively high."

The robot took Rachel's breakfast dishes to the sink and began to clean them, turning most of the sensoria on her head toward Rachel as she continued. "Anya, who you worked with at Human Converse back on Earth, is alert and active, but shows no interest in leaving her apartment. We'll see how that goes. Bob lives across the courtyard from you, and he's friendly and verbal. He's frequently out and about, but he doesn't follow a pattern. He'd be difficult for you to find . . . ." Selex's commentary trailed off for a moment, then continued. "In fact, because of a small equipment malfunction, we're not sure where Bob is at the moment."

"Huh. Okay, anyone else?"

"There's Tensel, of course. He refuses to interact with his Earth sponsor, but he talks to Velex a lot now. He walks each evening at sunset, and you could join him if you'd like. Maybe he'd talk to you or listen to you, but I'm unable to make a friendship prediction for your pairing. It might or might not go well."

"I'll start with Dante."

But that evening close to sunset, she went into her garden and stood between her half-grown yucca plants, peering through a view port in the translucent enclosure. She watched as Tensel, wearing shorts, a T-shirt, trail shoes, and sun goggles, left his apartment and set out on the path toward the bridge. She put on her own goggles and opened her enclosure door to watch him cross the bridge and fade from view.

She was still watching when a vague silhouette reappeared and came toward her in the dusky light, growing and resolving into Tensel's tall form. He must have seen her as he approached his apartment and went inside, but he didn't give any sign of it.

At dawn the next morning she met Dante and discovered that she did indeed like him. He had thick dark hair that stood straight up on his head like a brush, and a half smile on his face as if he were enjoying a gentle, happy memory. He wasn't wordy, a nice change from Eliza and Selex, and during his 10 minutes outside he and Rachel exchanged a simple greeting, then stood looking at each other.

Dante nodded and went back inside, and Rachel returned to her garden. She was satisfied, as if she'd just eaten a nourishing meal of the exact right proportions. She and Dante understood each other, though they'd only just met.

Later that morning, she took a walk along the path next to the river canyon, and a sprightly man with curly blond hair, a beard, running shorts, and a forest of hair on his legs appeared out of nowhere from the bushes next to her.

"Phew," he said, with a joyous, lopsided grin, "Intense!"

Rachel stared at him, thinking that with horns and cloven hooves he'd make an adorable faun.

"I'm Bob. Alright, yeah!" he said, still congratulating himself on whatever he'd just done. "Top to bottom to top in one straight shot. *Again!*"

"I'm Rachel," said Rachel. "Please be careful, I've hurt myself going off the path."

"The *path*!?" Bob laughed, sweating afresh and still breathing hard. "Rachel, those little engi-rocks you're standing on are a machine's poop trail. The *path*, on the other hand, is what we make for ourselves, and for each other, every day. That's our reality here—that's the gift Patience can give to us."

Walking back to her apartment, Rachel thought about Bob and what he'd said about the path. She'd met him on Earth, according to Eliza, and Eliza had shown her photos—an older man with an excess of belly and a dearth of hair. Was this the same person? She felt as if she knew Bob well, and it had nothing to do with anything that ever happened on Earth.

*
**

That evening when Tensel came out of his apartment, she was waiting for him. "Mind if I join you?" she asked, and he gestured for her to lead the way down the small footpath that led away from their building.

They stopped on the bridge that led to the machine shops and barns across the river. They watch the golden light play on the water, creating crescents of light that skipped across the surface, and she understood why Tensel did this every evening. It was a beautiful moment, numinous and evocative in a way that made it intimate, almost embarrassingly so. She put a hand on her belly, a reminder of the intimacy she'd been forced to share with the man next to her. But that first, forced sexual contact between them wasn't intimacy — intimacy was standing here, together. Intimacy was this deep sense of familiarity, of being one with an inseparable community, a *knowing* that happened when she was with Dante, Bob, and now Tensel.

Eliza and Selex had told her about the Temenos, but the idea of being a disembodied macro quantum pattern within an organic database was abstract, and she had no concrete memories of it. But now she wondered if their time together in the Temenos had formed the colonists into a community in a way that no one had predicted, and that Ark could never grasp.

"I love being outside," she said to Tensel as they walked homewards in the dusk light. "I want to be outside on this planet every day for the rest of my life."

"Your body was engineered for this place."

Rachel had never heard his voice, or not that she could remember. It was a gentle tenor, and he spoke slowly. "It should feel right to you to be outside," he said, "natural, in a deep and inexplicable way."

This man was biologically 19 years old, and his body looked it. But within him Rachel saw an old soul, much older than the 31 years he'd lived on Earth before their journey to Patience.

"Yes," she said. "Deep and inexplicable."

Hacking

We look at life and cannot untangle the eternal song:
Rings and knots of joy and grief all laced and interlocking.
—*Ramayana*, traditional

"After you give birth, it'll be time for you to select an occupation," said Selex, watching Rachel squat unceremoniously to pick up the rake she'd dropped.

"An occupation? I can only imagine enjoying one line of work on this planet." She held the rake in front of Selex's visual processor, and Selex, not strong on innuendo, waited for her to continue.

"Farming."

"Excellent idea," said Selex. "I see farming as the highest probability fit for you, because your garden exceeds the size and productivity of every other colonist garden in the village, even controlling for your early start date." Rachel hadn't known her garden was the best, and she felt a flush of pride. "You can start working through the training modules whenever you're ready."

"Modules?" She started to rake, still facing Selex. She knew Selex didn't care which way she faced while they talked, but she couldn't stand the feeling that she was being rude, even to a robot. Damn pre-fab social skills.

"They're quite informative," said Selex. "In them you'll learn all you need to know about cooperating with your fellow farmer colonists to produce short-, medium-, and long-term crops from the soil of Patience. After approximately a year of soil conditioning, which will begin with an application of—"

"Thank you, Selex. I hope to save the boring parts for later. Please don't spoil it for me. So . . . ." She paused her rake, trying to look casual. "What's Tensel's occupation going to be, by your lights?"

"My lights aren't very bright on the subject of Tensel," Selex replied, "but Velex believes he can't be anything other than what he's always been: an engineer. He's already tried to hack into our mainframe, and he's attempted to alter five of Velex's subroutines."

"Ha! That's a good one. When he's done with Velex he can start on you."

Selex let out a convulsive chortle. "You're being humorous."

Rachel smiled. "Now *you're* being humorous."

That evening when she joined Tensel for their walk, she asked him about his occupation and how he saw himself fitting into the community.

"I'll do what's mine to do," he said as they picked their way down one of Bob's steepest trails to the river.

"Selex says you've been hacking."

He smiled gently. "Hacking. The geniuses who planned this trip didn't expect any of the colonists to know what a mainframe is, let alone how to tinker with one. As you might remember, I'm not supposed to be here. They wanted you to be dependent on Earth."

Rachel nodded, thoughtful.

"And what I'm doing isn't hacking, by the way, it's coding. If you were doing it, it'd be hacking."

"And why's that?"

"Because you're not supposed to be doing it. I am."

"How do you figure?"

"We're back where we started: I'm doing what's mine to do."

They were wading in the river shallows, watching for fish. She looked at him, taking in the changes since the day Selex had first shown her the sickly man next door. He'd put on weight and muscle, and the light of Wolf 1061 had turned his skin a warm brown. He'd let his hair grow long, and he was wearing cargo shorts that showed his knobby knees and long shins. Around his neck he wore a tiny camera that he'd uninstalled from his bathroom and repurposed, and his pockets were filled with pliers, fishing line, a magnifying glass, and other small pieces of equipment. His eyes glowed with a grim joy, and Rachel knew she was looking at Tensel the way he was always meant to look.

*
**

Rachel tried to explain to Eliza her nebulous half-rememberings, the feelings and states of mind that seemed to come from her past, but not from Earth. Eliza listened, but held firm to her theory that Rachel would remember Earth in vivid detail and the Temenos as a dream — an *interesting* dream, maybe, but unreal and irrelevant to the minutiae of daily life.

"Everything's new for me," said Rachel. "I don't remember the Rachel Anna Deimos you talk about. Isn't it possible I bear no relationship to her?"

"But you *are* related to her, and to *me*. You look like Rachel Deimos, and you have her genome and even her epigenome, as best they could manage. You seem like the same person to me, and you possess her soul. Or so they say."

"Rachel's soul. I don't know what that means, not when you talk about it as an object to be 'possessed,'" said Rachel. "All I know is who I am. I have my own ideas, my own thoughts. I don't remember Rachel Deimos, and to be honest, some part of me wants to move on. I want to let her go."

Eliza let out a gasp, and her tiny hologram recoiled. "You can't let her go. I need you!"

"I'm sorry, Eliza. I love you, I really do. But you need your grandmother, and I'm not her."

*
**

Rachel ate dinner with Tensel that evening in his apartment, and then they sat together on his couch eating strawberries for dessert. Now that she was with him, the turmoil that she'd felt after her conversation with Eliza faded away. Her body calmed and her mind slowed, and a bigger thought than herself returned to her, as if she'd forgotten something that now had space to return. Idly trying to find words for how she felt around Tensel and the other colonists, some part of her relaxed and sank back into a timeless oblivion; a deep rest; a sweet acceptance that comes after long pain and long thought. She felt present and immediate, as if she'd just come home after a tiring trip, or as if she'd returned to bed a few minutes after leaving it, delighted to find the comforter still warm.

Glass had come into the room without her noticing, and he was now curled on Tensel's lap with Tensel's hands cupped around his body. Both the man and the cat were at ease. She watched them in silence for what might have been five minutes.

"Someone's missing," said Tensel.

The idea startled Rachel so much that she dropped the strawberry that was in her hand.

"You can feel it too, can't you?" he said.

"Yes, now that you mention it, someone's missing. Is it my baby?"

Tensel pondered her large midsection. "No. There's something else, or someone else."

They sat in silence until Rachel got up to leave. "Well, goodnight," she said. "I'm tired, and what you said makes me sad. I'm not sure why."

*
**

The next day she spent the afternoon weeding and harvesting vegetables from her garden. She considered the deep sadness she felt about whatever, or whoever, was missing. It seemed to her that even her son could feel it, this absence.

Selex had been explaining the finer points of labor and delivery to her, and thinking about the imminent arrival of her son made her want to touch base with Tensel. She knocked on his door and he let her in, a reading slate in one hand and a circuit board in the other.

"Looks great," he said, noticing the bowl of steaming hot rice and stir-fried bell peppers, mushrooms, and zucchini squash that she carried. "If we eat together, Velex says we should do it in the refectory." He obviously had no intention of following Velex's directives in this or any other matter, and they ate for a while in silence.

"You spoke of someone being missing," said Rachel.

"Yes."

"It makes me sad. I'll give birth to my baby soon. Our baby. He's welcome to join us, but you're right, he's not who's missing."

Tensel didn't need to answer; they both knew the truth of it. They ate in silence for a while, and then Tensel said, "I've asked Caryatis about it."

"Caryatis?"

"She's like Eliza is for you," said Tensel. "They say she's my brother's great-granddaughter, though I don't recall having a brother. At first I refused to talk to her, because Velex seemed so desperate for me to do it. But Caryatis can access Earth resources for me, more directly than what Velex allows. She's a human being, unlike Velex, and unlike the colony scientists back on Earth — they seem more like robots to me than our actual robots."

Rachel smiled. "No doubt Velex has made note of your discovery of humor," she said.

"Velex, a machine, tracks my so-called progress in the pursuits of humanity. Interesting, isn't it?" He smiled, ever so slightly, and Rachel felt warmth fill her heart. It was a joy to have human companionship.

After they finished eating, she put her bowl on the floor, and Glass ran in through the connecting door from Rachel's apartment to lick the bowl clean. Tensel watched in silence, then put his own bowl on the floor when Glass was ready for it.

"So what does Caryatis have to say?" asked Rachel.

"Well, some of the macro quantum patterns that the original Ark team inserted into the Temenos weren't viable when we arrived. They were absorbed, in a way. People like Jax, who was apparently your friend on Earth. Quite a few of the colonists who *paid* to be brought along were absorbed, in fact. Caryatis's idea is that our missing 'someone' is those folks. We got to know them inside the Temenos, and we experienced a loss when they were absorbed. That loss was our strongest emotion during our years in the Temenos, and so it's the first emotion we're remembering."

"Hmm."

"Yes, that's how I reacted. Hmm. I don't agree that that's who's missing. I think those people were absorbed for a reason. They wanted to be absorbed, and who knows, maybe that means they were stronger than us from the start. Or maybe it means their boundaries failed; maybe they couldn't handle being alone inside themselves. We'll never know, but when I imagine it, I don't have any sensation of loss or grief about them. I believe there's someone else, a central figure, an organizing principle that should be among us, but isn't."

Rachel nodded, knowing the truth of it.

"The Temenos is still connected to its own life support," Tensel continued, "as it was during our trip to Patience. Velex tells me they downloaded every viable quantum pattern from within it when they Merged us with our clones. So why are they keeping the database alive?"

"Maybe it's in case we need it again?"

"Maybe. But here's what keeps coming into my mind: how do we know they really took everyone out?"

Missing pieces

Rachel was often irritated at Selex, and nighttime sleep eluded her. Daytime naps in the recliner, feet up, were frequent. Her back ached, in spite of the supply of drugs from Selex. Her young body, which had felt new to her even before the pregnancy, kept shifting, growing, and stretching, and she wondered if she'd ever be at home in it. Her body was changing to support the life of the fetus, which put Rachel out of control: her body was on auto-pilot, in service to a stranger.

Her feelings about her baby swung from one end of the spectrum to the other. Sometimes she prayed for him and sang to him, wondering about his life. The idea of him painted her world in healthy, vibrant colors, and his imminent arrival gave her hope. She looked forward to meeting him.

At other times he scared her and felt like an intruder — what had Ark done to her, and to this baby? Who was he, and why did Ark make him happen? In these moments she felt anxious about meeting him, and even imagined him as an alien using her as its shell, its hiding place. If this baby was foreign to her, then she wanted it out.

She traveled between these poles several times a day — swinging from gloriously present in her pregnancy to pretending she wasn't pregnant, then back again.

One morning after her regular exam, Selex announced that the baby had lowered into her pelvis. "You'll go into labor soon, maybe today," the robot said. "You'll have pain. When you want to stop the pain, tell me."

Rachel brushed Selex's arm out of the way, rolled onto her side, and pushed herself into a sitting position. The effort left her breathless, which surprised her, but she stood up and transferred her bulky self into the recliner and put her feet up.

She opened the catalog from the *Svalbard*'s seed bank, day-dreaming about farming beyond her garden. Soon.

She dozed, then woke to pain in her abdomen. "Selex," she called, half asleep, "I think I'm having menstrual cramps. Could you give me something?"

Selex rolled up to the chair and scanned Rachel. "As you know, menstrual cramps make no sense right now. You're going into labor." Rachel stood up without speaking and let Selex lead her to the medical table. The robot inserted an intravenous line into her arm, and as she began to slip under, some unfamiliar part of her came to life. She'd heard that some people want to be awake and alert for their own death — was that what she was experiencing? Was she about to die?

"Wait! No drugs, I want—"

But it was too late. Her thoughts slipped away and melted into a soft twilight. She knew what was happening, but she didn't care. Selex did this and that, moved here and there, and Rachel saw blood on the robot's hands. Then she fell asleep.

She woke up with a headache, dressed in her favorite nightgown, lying in her bed. She tried to move, but every muscle in her body ached. What had happened? Ah, there should be a baby. Or maybe it had died? One minuscule part of her hoped so.

She noticed Tensel sitting by the bed, watching her. And she noticed that Selex was holding a bundled blanket. She lifted her arm and pointed.

"It happened," she said.

Tensel smiled. "I know."

Rachel watched his face as he stood up to take the bundle from Selex. His gaze softened, and his lips moved into a kind smile as he gazed down at their baby.

"Your progeny is sleeping," said Selex.

"Our progeny needs a name," said Tensel, shifting his gaze to look at Rachel with affection. "How about 'Asher'?"

*
**

The next day, Rachel lay on the couch with her arms around Asher, both of them half asleep. Tensel sat on the floor with Glass in his lap, his back against the couch.

"When Asher was on his way," said Tensel, "I had time to think, sitting there with you. And I wondered again if Asher is what's been missing, because he's now filling a gap in me that I didn't know existed."

Rachel nodded, stroking Asher's head.

"But that theory doesn't click," Tensel continued. His words tumbled out faster now. "I think what's missing is Zoë, or more accurately, Zoë's body with Zoë's soul. She was my familiar transgenic on Earth, and she was with us in the Temenos. So what part did Zoë, an animal, play among us in the Temenos? Straightforward, living in the moment. Grounded, independent. A predator at heart. They didn't extract her soul from the Temenos because she's not human, and she's not 'needed,' but maybe we do need that soul. It seems right to me."

Rachel was quiet, nodding.

"I'd have to reprogram Velex to help," Tensel continued, "which I'm not sure I can do. But Velex is uniquely bonded with me, which *might* give me special access to his processing centers."

They were both quiet for a minute.

"Zoë," said Rachel. "Hmm. You could be right."

Coming to life

They ate in the refectory often now, along with Bob, Dante, an obviously pregnant Anya, a less obviously pregnant Sara, and the dozen or so other colonists who were sociable enough to talk and play with Asher while they ate. Asher was the first baby any of them had ever seen, and nobody's heart stood a chance against his big brown eyes, soft baby curls, and toothless, gleeful smile.

He was on Serenity's lap as she talked about the yoga group she'd started. "We meet by the river, down Bob's main trail from the bridge, every morning at sunrise," she said. "Bob's there every day, but I could use more regulars." She turned to Rachel. "You'd like it, and Asher's welcome to join us."

Rachel smiled. "Asher's welcome everywhere, it seems. Maybe we'll join you one of these mornings."

Tensel was quiet, which wasn't unusual in a group, but he also seemed pensive. "You seem down lately, in spite of Asher," said Rachel as they walked back to their apartments. "I have something you can put in your room to cheer you up." When they reached her garden she picked a dozen California poppies and held them out.

"Yes!" He took them from her hands and looked into her sparkling dark eyes, feeling a moment of joy, but the joy reminded him of something. Zoë.

He'd learned facts about Zoë from Velex and the Earth database, but now impressions akin to memories washed through him: daydreams and feelings about an animal with a sweet simplicity, sleek fur, and intuition about his moods. Why hadn't she been Merged? The answers were logical, of course. She wasn't in the plan, and Merge supplies were valuable. And most distressingly, Zoë's soul matter had decohered in the Temenos, so it might not be possible to differentiate and collect it.

"Velex told me that when I was first cloned they tried to give me Zoë clones as companion animals," he said, "but I rejected them. Makes sense, because they had their own souls, not Zoë's. They must've felt wrong to me in some basic way."

He paused to think. "I don't have any idea how to put Zoë back together, but there's nothing I'm above trying at this point. So if you're in the mood to send good thoughts my way, or pray or whatever, go for it."

"Consider it done," said Rachel.

*
* *

In the field behind the main barn west of the bridge, standing in ankle-high buffalo grass, Tensel threw a baseball toward Velex. To make way for clarity, he let his mind relax and follow the ball as it slapped into Velex's glove, paused, then sailed through the air from Velex's hand into his own glove.

"Velex," he called out, "how much material with an undifferentiated quantum pattern is still in the Temenos?"

"523.8 grams."

Slap. Throw. Slap Throw. Hmm, about 20 times what the goo that held Zoë's soul would weigh.

"And what's the nature of the 523.8 grams of material? Whose pattern is it?"

Velex extended his arm an extra meter to catch a wild throw. "Ninety-four percent belongs to those who didn't survive the journey to Wolf 1061 Patience."

"Jax etcetera, right?"

Velex nodded. "Almost one percent belongs to cloned living colonists — it's material that you and your compatriots left behind when we removed you from the Temenos."

Tensel paused after a catch and stood looking up at the barn, rolling the ball back and forth between his left hand and his gloved right. "Interesting. So we're not fully ourselves?"

"I wouldn't know about that. We're in the realm of speculation here."

"And the last five percent?"

"It's spontaneous material."

"*Spontaneous?* What do you mean?"

"The material's provenance is unclear," said Velex, "so I used the word 'spontaneous.' Do you like it? I'm trying out a new intuition-slash-creativity subroutine."

"Yes, I like it," said Tensel, tossing the ball to Velex and running toward his apartment.

The numbers roughly added up, and what was more likely to transform "spontaneously" than the soul of a transgenic cat?

*
**

In the cow barn, 50 meters from the main barn, Rachel introduced Bob to the herd of light brown Jerseys, all of them with black noses and white muzzles. "Only one has a name so far," she said. "I call this one 'Daisy,' for obvious reasons." She held out a handful of daisies, and Daisy leaned forward for a mouthful, ears down and relaxed. "These flowers are taking over my garden. She'd eat them all day if I let her. Maybe I should invite her for a visit? Cows are happier and produce more milk when they're given names and treated as individuals, so if you're inspired to name any of the others, go for it."

Bob tried to look intrigued. Everyone on Patience would need at least some competence in farming, food prep, health care, child care, or planet maintenance — none of which lit Bob's fire.

"Have you opened your memory box yet?" said Rachel, making conversation as they examined the milking machines and husbandry robots that tended the cows.

"*Hell* yeah," he said, bursting into laughter. "A few golf balls, personalized with an 'R' for 'Robert.' Love letters from some old flame who sounds *very* sexy, but she's not here, which is a shame." He paused to pout, looking wistfully into the distance. "Also a union card I got when I was 18, and photos of my mom, who raised me alone. Stuff like that. None of it rang a bell, much to everyone's disappointment. The golf balls are antiques, though, genuinely used on *Earth*, unlike the blobs of biodegradable goo that Quartex spits out for me to tee-shoot over the chasm. I'm thinking about opening a little trading business. My *heart's* not in it, but, aw, I don't know. Maybe people want each other's Earth antiques, who knows? How about you?"

"Same. I opened it," said Rachel, fingering the gold cross around her neck, its small emerald still in place. "I love this necklace — sorry, I won't trade it — and the family members in the photos look related to me, but it's like I'm digging through a stranger's closet. A half-filled journal was in the box too, and I haven't read it, because it looks so personal. Eliza's disappointed. But it feels right to respect the *uniqueness* of the woman whose genes I share. Know what I mean?"

"Yep," said Bob, hopping into the driver's seat of a tractor and pretending to drive and honk the horn. "I feel you."

Soul power

A computer once beat me at chess,
but it was no match for me at kick boxing.
—Emo Philips

Tensel lay on his couch thinking, with Asher on a striped blanket on the floor nearby. He had no way to learn much of technical value without Velex as an intermediary. He had no direct access to the terraforming control center that orbited the planet, or to the mainframe in the *Svalbard*, which was parked one valley over, west of the village. He couldn't even open the hatch on the Temenos, which was still aboard the *Svalbard*, unless Velex allowed it. He'd sent a message to Earth asking for direct access to the colony's technology, with no response. Figured. To the team at Ark he was no longer the lead scientist of the project, but simply an extra in the experiment. Almost 90 years had passed since Tensel had been on the Ark campus. All his friends there were gone, and Caryatis had a limited security clearance.

"Velex," he said, "what's your primary directive, exactly? Put it into words for me."

"To sustain your ability to father second-generation colonists who are soul-healthy."

Ark saw him only as a means to their ends. At least Velex was honest.

"Why not collect sperm from me and let me die?"

"Asher appears to be a soul-healthy baby," Velex answered. "Being conceived by sexual intercourse might've enhanced his ability to bond with his own macro quantum pattern. The way he was conceived probably didn't harm him, and it might've helped him. Therefore your continued ability to participate in the act of sexual intercourse is a boon to the colony."

Tensel felt a flash of anger. Couldn't being conceived by rape — a *double* rape, really, the simultaneous rape of both parents — harm a baby's soul? He looked down at Asher, who was grabbing at a mobile that Velex held over his face. The cold purposefulness of Ark's human-biology planners made him sick, but he'd been that kind of scientist himself. And could he blame anyone more than he blamed himself? This sprawling experiment would never have been possible if his former self, the original Tensel Brown, hadn't discovered Merge technology in the first place, then ceded it to Ark.

But being angry at that long-ago self wouldn't help. He shifted his anger from himself back to Ark, and from there to Velex as Ark's nearest proxy. As much as he wanted to twist Velex's mouth parts from his gleaming metal head, he folded his hands across his chest and took a slow breath. Calm down. Remember your goal.

He didn't trust any of the bots to clone Zoë, because they'd consult with Earth and probably splice sleeper-agent programs into her genome — if they agreed to clone her at all. He'd have to do the work himself, but for that he needed direct access to all the colony tech, both on Patience and in orbit. And for *that*, he needed Velex to cooperate. It would be hard to argue that he needed direct access to the tech in order to father more second-gen colonists. What other leverage did he have?

"Velex," he said, "do you have secondary directives regarding me?"

"Yes. I'm tasked with promoting all aspects of your health, including your physical, emotional, psychological, psychosocial, spiritual, and psychosomatic health."

Aha, maybe he could use this.

The next day, while Asher was with Rachel and Selex, he gave it a try.

"Velex, I need you to build me a personal workstation. It has to interface directly with the mainframe computers on board the *Svalbard* and in the orbiting machine ships."

"That's not necessary," said Velex, who was assembling a casserole to take to the refectory as part of the group's dinner. "I'm your interface. Tell me what you need, and I'll get it for you."

"I'm telling you what I need: a *direct* interface to all the technology that we brought with us from Earth. All the information that you give to me is filtered through your own CPU. For that reason, I also require direct access to your CPU." And now for the clincher. "I require these things for my emotional, psychological, spiritual, and psychosomatic well-being. My having a direct interface to our technology won't interfere with my ability to father soul-healthy colonists, so I see no reason for you to refuse me."

"I'll check with Earth," said Velex.

"No! If you do that, my psychological state will deteriorate. I don't expect you to understand, given that you're not human, but trust me. There will be damage if you ask Earth for permission. *Do not* check with Earth or your fellow AI bots about this."

Velex was silent for a few seconds, prolonged thought for a robot. Maybe he was leaning toward a yes? "I've consulted with Dr. Amir's assistant on Earth," he said, "and she gave me a firm no."

For a moment Tensel tried to resist his rage, but . . . why? It seemed a shame not to come unglued, as promised. He wrapped his arms around Velex's angular body, picked him up so his rollers left the kitchen floor, and pounded him down. Hard.

"You shouldn't do that," said Velex.

"I know," said Tensel. He cocked one leg back and slammed his foot into Velex's facial processing unit, putting all 100 kilograms of his weight behind the kick. Velex tipped backwards and came to rest against the stove, which was hot, and Tensel kicked again, crushing the robot's sensory processors between his foot and the ceramic oven door. The kick made a satisfying crunch as Velex's lights went dark and his noises stopped.

Tensel was breathing hard. He turned off the stove and sat down on the heap of warm metal, biopolymers, fiber, and silicon that had been Velex. His body bristled with adrenaline, but he was puzzled. *Why did I do this?* Anger, lava-flow anger, had coursed through him as he crashed his foot through Velex's processing centers.

What a rush!

He burst out laughing, then jumped up to kick Velex's remains a few more times.

He heard a knock on the door, and Rachel walked in and gasped. "What've you done?"

"Isn't it obvious!?" He wiped tears from his cheeks, still grinning.

Selex rolled through the door and stopped.

"Can you fix this, Selex?" said Rachel.

"No!" said Tensel, putting a hand on what had been Velex. "This is my bot, and it's my decision what happens to it. I'm not sending any reports about this, and Selex, neither are you."

"I sent my report 1.4 seconds ago, along with detailed specs of Velex's condition. When repair instructions arrive, I'll restore him to his former condition."

"Wonderful," said Tensel, knowing that Selex would take his sarcasm literally. He paced up and down in front of the heap of robot parts, his hands on his hips, sober now. "I don't feel like talking, Rachel, and I'm going to skip dinner. Can you come back tomorrow? *Alone*, if you don't mind." He glared at Selex.

When Rachel returned the next day, she told Selex to stay out. "Permanently," Tensel called as the apartment-connecting door slid shut in the robot's face.

Tensel was hunched over a circuit board mounted on a tiny vice. A circle of wires, soldering tools, screwdrivers, and articulated plastic and metal robot parts surrounded him. Surgical magnifying glasses, which he'd found in Velex's medical kit, were affixed to the front of his face like headlights on a car. Above the glasses, he'd strapped a bright light to his forehead with black elastic, making him look a bit like a robot himself.

He was a picture of happiness.

*
**

Without help from any bots or Ark scientists, Tensel's project took weeks. His goal wasn't to recreate Velex as he was, but to create the Velex he needed.

Life without the old Velex was even more satisfying than he expected. He disabled all the cameras and mics in his apartment so he had privacy, at last. He joined the others at the refectory for meals, learned how to cook a few of his favorite dishes, and found joy in doing his dishes and laundry by hand. The busyness and focus glowed in him like a beacon, and his anger died down. He would fall asleep considering a problem and wake up with an elegant solution.

But working alone had a downside. One afternoon he forgot to retract the blade of his monomolecular utility knife, then reached for it without looking. The blade, one molecule thick, sliced through the flesh and bone of his left index finger, just below the fingernail. No one was there to help, and no one was alerted. He swore and jumped to his feet, rushing to the sink to keep the blood off his circuit boards.

He was shaking and lightheaded. He slumped to the floor as blood from his finger flowed along the grout between the tiles, making an orderly red grid around his hand.

*
* *

Rachel found him after he missed dinner. She knelt in the blood to get a closer look at his blank face, and her own mind went blank. She couldn't think what to do next, but this seemed like a good time to lift the ban on Selex coming into the apartment. As if reading her mind, or maybe because a medical emergency overrode other directives, Selex squeezed past her to take the injured hand between her flesh-fibered hand extensions and press a medical sensor to Tensel's neck. "He's lost blood," the robot said. "He's unconscious, but stable. I'll continue the medical protocol while you recover the severed index distal phalanx." Rachel didn't move. "Rachel," said Selex, waiting for her to look up, "search the apartment for a piece of finger."

She got up off the floor and turned to look around, but all she saw was blood. Gradually she parsed the scene in more detail: a line of blood led to the sink, then away. She searched the sink and inside the drain, then among the loose wires and cardboard and dismantled machinery scattered around the floor. She found the utility knife and saw the red spatter near it on the carpet, but no finger.

A meter-high machine caught her attention — it looked like Velex, but rougher, like a cartoon sketch of a personal AI bot. She was surprised by Tensel's progress, and she half expected the thing to open its mouth parts and speak.

By the time she gave up on the finger, Selex had hoisted Tensel onto a portable medical table and inserted an IV line into his arm. Tensel watched Rachel from under his eyelids as she searched his pile of stuff. "Careful," he whispered. "Don't touch Velex."

When she heard his voice she rushed to the bed. "Where's your finger?"

"I think I flushed it," he said with a weak smile. "But I'm not sure."

"Shall I requisition Earth for the programming I need to build a new one?" asked Selex.

"No! I'll do it myself."

Rachel glanced at Selex. Do it himself? How?

"Don't ask Earth, please," she said to Selex. "Let's wait and see how it goes."

Selex obeyed.

*
**

Tensel learned to use his changed left hand. Working at a snail's pace with his right hand and clumsy assists from his left, he brought Velex online. The differences between the old Velex and this one were obvious — its chassis was angular and rough, and it was missing parts that Selex and the other personal bots had, like the flesh-fiber hand extensions. Instead, Velex had metal robotic fingers that made no effort to appear friendly. It had natural language abilities, but its personality was primitive.

Pleased with himself, Tensel offered to demonstrate to Rachel the "best" thing about the new Velex. "I've been saving an exciting question, waiting to ask it until you were watching."

"Okay, what is it?"

He gave her a look that said, "Watch this."

"Velex, will you please ask Earth for a program that'll show you how to clone Zoë's genome?"

"You know I can't do that," said Velex. "But in the last two milliseconds I created four possibilities for ways we might be able to clone her using the data, medical programs, and materials available in the colony stores, without alerting any of the other bots."

Tensel grinned. "Velex, tell Rachel why you can't ask Earth for help."

"There are two reasons, both of them sufficient," said the new Velex. "First, you've forbidden me to communicate with Earth. Second, I'm no longer physically equipped to do so."

Tensel was beaming.

*
**

Velex set to work building Tensel a workstation, complete with an ergonomically correct chair and bespoke AR headset. The workstation interfaced directly with the colony ships and machines, and also with Velex.

Tensel watched Velex assemble parts, thinking that the robot seemed almost cheerful. Maybe it was a relief to be less of a pain in the ass? He had a fleeting twinge of guilt about the downgrade, but it was a machine, and its personality was synthetic. Besides, it seemed content and had no memory of its previous life. What was the harm?

He'd planned to create a prosthetic fingertip for himself, with Velex's help, but scrapped the idea. His changed left hand was a reminder that he wasn't Dr. Tensel Brown of Ark but a new person, a person he was discovering himself to be.

He had Velex move the workstation into the cloning supply room on the *Svalbard*, which now served as his lab. Each morning after breakfast he hiked to the valley west of the village, his human feet and the robot's trekking rollers wearing a trail into the pass between the mountains. He never felt alone in his lab inside the *Svalbard*'s massive aft section, because the ship hummed with life of its own as it kept the Temenos alive and served as the local datacenter for all the tech on and around Patience.

Today he was prepping to clone Zoë and thinking, as always, about ways to confound Ark's control over the colony. He leaned back and put his arms over his head, then ran his hands through his hair while he thought, a habit he'd had on Earth. No one from Earthside was scrambling to blur any of the colony's code or data, as far as he could tell.

Good.

He cracked his knuckles and returned to his task, remembering the need to move fast. He'd be discovered, but the longer it took, the better. Ark knew that he spent every day outside the village, of course. But thanks to a little help from Velex, the satellites orbiting the planet were no longer able to transmit high-res images to Earth, and the cameras inside the *Svalbard* were malfunctioning as well.

Back on Earth, Dr. Covington and her team decided he was moping around the *Svalbard*'s landing site to act out a leftover psychological process from his time on Earth.

Fine.

Kindred souls

What keeps me coming back is the quiet, the beckoning
silence of the meeting at its best, when each person's
search is deepened by the search of all.
—Quaker elder Raja Lin

More of the colonists started eating at the refectory, and the
growing crowd was what triggered Bob's "aha" moment about
his role on Patience.

"You know what we need here?" he said to Sara D'Angelo,
who was sitting across from him holding her newborn, Thane.

"Well, I can think of a *few* things . . . ." She playfully nudged
Bob with her foot. Sara and Jaden, Thane's father, had a predicted friendship coefficient near zero, and sure enough, they
couldn't stand each other. One of Sara's favorite hobbies was
flirting with Bob.

"Ha ha!" said Bob. "I'll get back to you on that. But what I
was thinking about is . . . get ready for it . . . a *group vision!*" He
stood up and clinked his fork against his glass, clearing his
throat dramatically until the room was quiet save for a few
fussy babies.

"Those folks at Ark keep trying to tell us who we are and
how we should progress in the human arts!" he yelled. "Well, I
say we start figuring ourselves out on our own. And I say we do
it *together*. Let's meet back here after sunset to discuss our
common fate. Let's work on ways to make decisions *without
Ark*. Leave your bots in your apartments and join me. And if
you know folks who aren't here right now, let them know.
What do you say?"

There were murmurs of agreement and a few happy shouts
from around the room. Bob had found his calling.

Every colonist showed up in the refectory after sunset, without a single personal AI bot. A small group had arrived early to move tables out of the way and arrange 430 chairs in roughly circular concentric rows. Bob stood on a chair near the back, clapped his hands and whistled until everyone was quiet, then climbed off his chair.

He didn't start talking right away — he twiddled his fingers in his beard, cleared his throat, and even paced back and forth a few times. Then he made a surprising first move.

"I have an inkling that if we're all silent together — as silent as we *can* be, that is, given our younger members" — and here he paused to beam across the room at his infant daughter Frieda, who was on Suzanne's lap — "I really think that if we did it, the silence thing, we'd discover something important."

"Bob? Are you feeling okay?" called Serenity from where she knelt on the floor stretching her arms behind her back, fingers clasped.

"I know, I know," said Bob, making a face. "It's nuts, but consider this: if someone like me feels an urge to spend time in silence with the group, I'm guessing a few others have felt it as well. Am I right?"

Dante, half smiling as ever, put his hand up. "Yes, Dante?"

"Yes," said Dante, putting his hand back down.

"Any good reason not to try it?" said Bob. "Alright, nobody objects, so let's do it. I'll call time in 15 minutes. Ready? *Go.*"

After the surprise of this abrupt instruction wore off, the adults adjusted themselves into silence. They were fidgety and self-conscious, then more tranquil, and then they dropped into a more spacious place, personally and communally, as if they'd navigated a turn. A gasp from Bob was the only sound that marked this transition.

There were still baby murmurs, stomach noises, rustling clothes, coughs, and nose blows—human noises. They listened to each other breathe and shift as if together they made up one enormous, vibrant being. Whether Bob's request that no personal bots be present was the result of insight or just a personal whim, the wisdom of the idea was now clear. It wasn't that the bots were noisy — they were better at literal silence than the humans — but the fact of their absence was a gorgeous color of silence all its own.

*
**

As the weeks passed, they found a rhythm for their weekly meetings. More newborns joined them, filling the room with cries, cooing noises, jingles, and rustles of all sorts, making "silence" even more of a relative term than it already was. After half an hour of "the silence thing," someone might stand up and say, "I'm frustrated with my seedlings." Someone else might say, "I'll stop by tomorrow." And that was that.

Eventually they realized that shared silence helped them to return to something like the frame of mind they'd shared in the Temenos, where straightforwardness was their habit. It was a discovery that no tech or theory could've given them.

Bob was a natural moderator, offering a gracious, "Well, let's talk about it," or, "Okay, I'm listening," in the face of every divisive issue. His cherubic curls and bright baby-faced smile made it hard to remember that his young body held an old soul, but in moments like these, his maturity was obvious. He printed a copy of *Robert's Rules of Order*, which he called "Bob's Orders," and he kept the printout handy. He never quoted from the book, and many wondered whether he'd actually read it, but that didn't matter. When the tension level rose he stood up, tucked his rules of order under one arm, and paced around near his chair until things quieted down. That printout was like a gavel, and when he carried it, he brought order.

Sometimes by simple consensus, sometimes after much discussion and several votes, the group made decisions about things like starting a childcare rotation (yes, but only for those who wanted to participate), setting a noise curfew (yes, with exceptions for crying babies and equipment malfunctions), allowing locks on doors (yes, with emergency override protocols), and allowing personal AI bots to attend their weekly meeting (a unanimous *no*).

*
**

Lately Rachel inched close to Tensel on the couch when they read together or talked in the evenings, and something about her closeness distressed him. One night she rested one of her strong, graceful hands on his thigh when she was making a point, and a jolt like an electric current went through his body. They were best friends, and they'd even been sexually intimate — technically. But Asher's conception was a complicated and painful memory for both of them. A violation, and a reminder of Ark's domination over them. Territory to avoid.

It seemed to Tensel that their ambivalence had kept them in perfect balance — they were drawn to each other exactly as much as they wanted to stay distant — and so they'd been at ease. But lately the balance was shifting toward attraction, or for him, anyway. Should he ask Rachel if that's what was happening for her too? Was that why she was sitting so close? But how could he start a conversation like that? Having her as a friend and co-parent was natural and comfortable. Did he want to risk ruining it?

"Umm . . . ," said Rachel. She was fiddling with her hair, and now seemed unable to get comfortable with it, or with anything else that was going on on the couch. Finally she settled her hands on her lap. "It feels like a big deal when you and I touch, either on purpose or by accident," she said, "and I've been meaning to ask you about it. What would you think about us, well, touching each other *more*, and on *purpose*? Just a little bit for now, and if not, that's okay, it's fine, really . . . ." He looked at her and saw hope and fear in this woman he'd grown to love, and he shifted to face her on the couch.

"I like your idea a lot," he said. "Actually, I was just thinking about it myself."

There was an awkward pause.

"So . . . how do you think we should start?" she said.

Tensel took both her hands in his. "How about like this?"

She smiled, looking into his eyes. "Perfect."

*
**

Tensel didn't like the thought of speaking to a crowd, but Rachel talked him into it: it wasn't fair for him to alter the colony's tech and clone Zoë without the consent of the group. His work had implications, and all the colonists should agree before he went further.

That evening, he and Asher got to the meeting early enough to claim seats in one of the central circles of chairs, though Asher wanted to be on the floor so he could toddle around and visit.

During a silence after the resolution of a question about pesticides, Tensel stood, hundreds of faces looking at him with surprise. They knew who he was, but he'd never spoken at a meeting.

He had trouble deciding where to look, so he picked the wall of windows on the building's east side, taking in the view of the desert scrub in the twilight, not turning to look at the people behind him.

"I've been using some of our colony's resources," he began, "and I wonder how you all feel about that."

A few people cupped their hands to their ears. "*Speak up!*" Bob advised.

He continued more loudly. "I rebuilt Velex, and I had the new Velex build me a workstation, which used up some of our colony resources. I've also spent time rummaging inside our machines' programming instead of gardening or . . . knitting sweaters." He glanced at Bob, who'd suggested that idle hands could be put to use in the textiles group. "I hope it was okay to use our resources, and my own time, like that."

Silence.

Serenity, who chaired the planet maintenance committee, stood up. "You being able to control our technology is a *beautiful* use of resources," she said, "and no other humans on Patience have that skill. Given the limits of what Ark lets us access, I'm anxious to learn all you can teach me about how the machines control our atmosphere and geosphere. We'd like to move closer to natural, but we'll probably never be able to live without those machines, not entirely." She sat back down.

"I'm with Serenity," said Sara, who stood with her back against one of the piers between the big windows, keeping Thane nearby on a toddler leash. "I say it's fine. It's delightful to be without our AI bots once in a while, for example right now, so I imagine that the more 'private' time we can get from our machines, the better. Tensel can help us with that."

"Okay," said Tensel, relieved. "If anyone wants to talk more about it, let me know. But there's something else, and it's more complicated." He paused, gathering his thoughts. "Have any of you noticed that someone is missing? Do any of you wonder if we left someone behind when we left the Temenos?"

"They tell me Oscar's missing," called Anya, who was sitting next to Dante. "Supposedly I lost him in the Temenos, but it doesn't bother me one bit." She squeezed Dante's arm, and he smiled at her placidly. Everyone knew they were the happiest forced couple on Patience. "So if I don't miss Oscar, who I apparently adored, why would any of us miss *anyone* who was absorbed in the Temenos?"

"Great question," said Tensel, staring into the desert again, his eyebrows pulled together in concentration. He was remembering that Rachel had no recollection of her friend Jax. "But I'm talking about a slightly different 'someone's missing,' feeling. It's like I miss someone who's different from us, not human at all . . . ."

The room was quiet, or as quiet as it ever got, until he continued. "*That*, the moment we all shared just now: it speaks to me of who's missing. It's a presence that was with us as we rested and waited in the Temenos, and we can only access it now as an opaque memory." Now that Tensel had re-accessed the feeling itself, words came more freely. "For me, it's a sense of wanting something but not knowing what it is that I want, and it comes and goes quickly, like a shadow around the corner. I believe I can give that presence a body. I can give *her* a body. *She* can be here with us, full of all the soul that she shared with us while we were in the Temenos."

He gave them a minute to absorb this, then went on.

"Some of you might remember from your reading, or from what your Earth sponsors told you, that my own macro quantum pattern was one of two unexpected patterns in the Temenos. The other belonged to a transgenic cat, Zoë, who was my companion on Earth. Zoë's quantum pattern, being an animal pattern, would've been the 'plainest' among us and the most straightforward. In theory, it would've dominated our patterns, because simple patterns are robust. But Zoë's quantum pattern wasn't removed from the Temenos, because Zoë isn't useful to Ark.

"So here's my proposal: I'd like to use some of our supplies, and most of my time for the next few months, to create a clone of Zoë and Merge it with Zoë's soul, which is still alive in the Temenos."

He saw hope, confusion, and anxiety on the faces around him. Rachel, though, gazed at him with calm joy from the couch where she sat in the back. She gave him a thumbs up, so he kept going.

He explained that 94 percent of what was in the Temenos belonged to those who were absorbed on the journey — Oscar, Jax, and others they'd known on Earth. People understood this, and after some discussion, the group agreed that they should keep the Temenos alive to give those souls a permanent home. Easy enough to do, given the efficiency of the *Svalbard*'s solar-powered life support system and the minimal nutritional needs of the Temenos's organic parts. So far so good.

But when he told them that almost one percent of what was in the Temenos belonged to *them*, the living colonists, the discussion heated up. He explained that it would be tedious to differentiate the little bits of pattern, figuring out which bits belonged to which people, and that it would be even harder to merge those bits into people who were already in possession of mature macro quantum patterns. He proposed that instead of trying it, he should put the "little bit of everyone" into Zoë, along with her own pattern, when he merged her.

Anya stood up. "Who *is* Zoë, really?" she said, "and why should she get our missing scraps of soul? Even if sorting out the bits and merging them into us is challenging, is it impossible?"

People murmured agreement. Yes, why should a cat get their missing bits of soul?

Tensel opened his mouth, but it took him a moment to formulate a response. "Maybe it's possible to sort out what belongs to whom, I'm not sure. I just don't know if it's worth it. I for one don't feel that anything's missing within myself, only that a piece is missing from us as a group."

A few people said they agreed with Tensel, and a few said they didn't. It was something for all of them to ponder during the coming week.

Anya had another question. "Tensel, do you want to do this because you don't have a companion animal of your own?"

"A fair point, but I believe Zoë and her soul are important to all of us, not just to me. And I spend a lot of my time with Glass. In a way, he's my companion animal now." He lowered his eyes, realizing that what he'd just said implied that he and Rachel were together quite a lot. "Umm, phew, I'm getting tired."

Bob stood up. "Yep, I think we're all getting tired. Tensel's given us a veritable *boatload* of mystery to reflect on, and I propose we let it sit until next week. Meanwhile, feel free to keep asking him questions—I know I will—and we'll return to it next week: should we let him use colony supplies and his own time to clone and Merge the animal that might be a missing piece for us as a group? I'm inclined to think it's a good idea, but like I said, this question needs to be waited on. Seasoned."

Tensel sat down, nodding his gratitude to Bob. A boatload of mystery indeed.

*
**

During the week ahead, the idea relaxed into place in everyone's mind and heart, and Tensel was thrilled when the meeting gave a unanimous "yes" to the idea of him re-creating Zoë. He decided not to use a cloning crèche to spawn an adult Zoë —instead, he cloned her the way she'd been cloned on Earth. He programmed the vet bots to harvest healthy egg cells from female cats to use as host cells, then asked Sara if she'd be willing to let her calico, Tigger, be a surrogate mother.

Tigger's last litter was weaned but still living with Sara when Tensel stopped by to talk about the details. The apartment was a noisy nursery, layered with baby paraphernalia and half-grown cats. Sara and Tigger were a good match: since settling in on Patience, Sara had given birth to two boys, and Tigger had given birth to two litters.

Tensel pushed aside a teething ring and sat on the couch, holding his hand out to Tigger. "She's an excellent mother," said Sara as Tensel hefted the cat into his lap, burying his fingers in her thick black fur.

"The vet bots and I will take good care of her," he said. "She'll do just fine."

*
* *

Pacing outside the surgery while the bots implanted 10 cloned embryos in Tigger's uterus, Tensel worried that he might not be able to give any of these kittens away. But if he didn't, how would he cope with 10 kittens? Would they all be Zoë in some way, or just the one who received Zoë's soul? Would even that one be Zoë? Or maybe he should split the soul matter up among the kittens?

He paced faster and began to sweat. What had he done? Was this a colossal blunder?

The lead vet bot rolled into the doorway and faced Tensel. "The surgery was successful," it said. "Tigger can go back to Sara's place in an hour."

During the next two months Tensel visited Tigger every day, petting and talking to her as she purred next to him on Sara's couch. As she grew sleeker and rounder, her clarity and ease about what was happening in her body began to affect Tensel's state of mind.

Maybe everything would be okay after all.

The dairy cows now spent their days grazing on the plains of Patience instead of shifting from one leg to another in the barn, thanks to Rachel's intervention. She and Tensel, with Asher on his shoulders, were strolling among them. They petted and talked to each cow, asking Asher which names he liked best.

Velex appeared in the distance, raising a dust cloud as it rolled closer. "It's happening," it said as it arrived. Tensel hefted Asher to the ground and left him with Rachel, then hurried to Sara's apartment.

Tigger was curled in her bed, breathing hard and purring with a deep, loud buzzing sound, licking two tiny newborn kittens and preparing to push out a third. "Don't touch!" cried Sara, slapping Tensel's hand back from the kittens.

Mesmerized, he watched as the rest were born. A particularly cute one put its wobbly head up and sniffed the air. "That one," he said, pointing. "That's her." He knew right then that he'd have no problem letting other people raise Zoë's sisters. The scratches and bites and curtain-climbing craziness of *one* kitten would be more than enough for him and Rachel.

"Let's hope that one turns out to be a female," said Sara.

"They're all female." The voice came from Daemex, Sara's personal AI bot, who was parked nearby. "This is because they're clones of a female. Even if that weren't the case, any name works for any gender identity, and the evidence for macro quantum patterns being gendered at all is inconclusive. The macro quantum pattern of Tensel's Zoë could probably inhabit a male body, or any other type of body, without complications. Though no one's certain."

Tensel stared at Daemex. "Sara, is your bot always an insufferable know-it-all? I could fix that."

"I'm afraid she is, but she almost always has something interesting to say, so no thanks on your kind offer."

Daemex, who plainly grasped the situation, had no further comment.

An hour later, Tensel removed Zoë from Tigger for a few minutes to put her through the Merge process, with help from the vet bots. Merge had become a fine art since Tensel's messy first trials nearly a century earlier. It wasn't clear how the procedure would affect Zoë's *soul*, but her physical safety wasn't in question.

He returned her as soon as he could, slipping her in among her sisters while they napped in the circle of Tigger's warm body.

*
**

Rachel and Tensel spent most of their nights together in Rachel's bed, moving with care among the memories that their bodies held of each other. Their minds didn't remember Asher's conception, but their bodies and souls did. Slowly, they made their way through the numbness and anxiety that one or both of them sometimes felt when they touched.

"I keep thinking about how they betrayed us," said Tensel one night, his arms around Rachel as they lay together looking out the window at Callista, which was full and low on the horizon. "Ark used us, and what they did could've ruined any possibility of us growing to love each other. They act like we're machines."

She sighed. "I know. They don't care about us."

Tensel addressed himself to Selex, who was parked behind them across the room.

"Selex, what's your primary directive?"

"To serve Rachel and keep her healthy so she can bear at least one more child, preferably within the next year," said

Selex. "In fact, as I've mentioned, you should be moving forward with that."

Rachel turned over and raised herself on one elbow to glare at the robot. "That's Ark's opinion. It's not my opinion or Tensel's, and it's not even necessarily *your* opinion, Selex. You need to butt out." She turned back around and resettled herself in Tensel's arms.

"Well put," said Tensel. "So Selex, what if, to serve Rachel, you had to betray the scientists who control you from Earth?"

"That wouldn't happen. They gave me my directive, so they share my values."

"But what if it *did* happen? What if Rachel's welfare conflicted with Ark's business interests? Isn't your primary directive related to Rachel herself, her person, her physical self here on Patience?"

"Yes," said Selex. "So I suppose that if I were forced to choose quickly, say in an emergency, I'd choose her."

"I'm glad to know you'd keep functioning," said Tensel, wrapping his arms more tightly around Rachel. "You're useful, and I'd hate to lose you. Now please power yourself and all your external sensors down completely until we activate you again. I think we've had enough company for now."

*
**

The day Zoë and her sisters turned eight weeks old, Zoë went to live with Tensel in his apartment, and that Friday evening he carried her with him to the meeting. Not many people had met her, and everyone was curious, knowing that she carried a fragment of every adult soul on Patience, along with the soul of the original Zoë. In addition to all that soul matter, it was likely that she carried an original soul, given that she'd had time to develop something on her own before Tensel put her through Merge.

But none of these things made her act any differently from her playful, adorable sisters, all of whom had gone to their new homes that week too. And yet she was different in a way no one could put a finger on.

"Okay, all ya'll!" Bob called from his spot in the back circle of chairs. "I know we all want to stare at Zoë, but let's stick with the program. We'll start with silence, as usual."

They settled, letting go of Zoë and all their other ideas as best they could, listening into the silence that widened and fattened among them. After half an hour, Dante stood to speak, a rarity. He put his hand over his heart and beamed his gentle half-smile around the room, resting his gaze on Anya, then on their son, then moving his gaze contemplatively over the whole gathering, stopping on Zoë. "Friends," he said, his voice clear and audible, "we should sever our contact with Earth." He nodded his gratitude to the group and sat down.

The idea was startling, but no one was shocked. He'd found words for an inarticulate truth known to every soul in the room.

Zenia, one of the few women who didn't have a child, stood up. "I agree. They've done enough to us already."

"But is it possible?" asked Serenity.

"Yes," said Tensel. "I've found myself reflecting on this exact idea, believe it or not. I'd need to train some of you to help me, but we could do it."

"Well!" said Bob. "Call me intrigued, my goodness. Any more discussion for now?"

There was none.

"Okay, let's give it time, talk about it during the week, and maybe even bring it to a vote at our next meeting, shall we?"

Letting go

soul *noun* \sōl\
: the immaterial essence or substance, animating principle,
or actuating cause of life or of the individual life
—Merriam-Webster Unabridged

Rachel paced up and down her apartment, wondering what she could say to make this easier. The air above the coffee table shimmered as millions of pixels coalesced into a representation of a human form. Eliza was light years away, and today, it felt like it. Why had she felt close before?

Rachel sat down on the couch and waited until the image was formed enough for Eliza to hear her. "I need to tell you something," she said softly.

Eliza's smile of greeting disappeared, and Rachel leaned closer to the small image that hovered among her books. She looked at the face of the woman who'd been like a mother to her. She remembered Eliza's voice helping her to wake up, telling her her own name.

I've grown to love this woman, she thought.

The silence grew long.

"What *is* it?" said Eliza. "*Tell* me."

"Let's start with the hardest part," said Rachel, "and it's this: you let me be hurt, and in a way, you lied to me."

"What?"

"You knew all along that Ark was using me, but every time they hurt me, you encouraged me to cooperate with them. You acted as if it was no big deal, or maybe even a *good* thing."

Eliza clasped her gnarled hands in front of her heart and raised her eyebrows. "Oh my dear," she said, "I *didn't* think it was a good thing, but I *had* to cooperate with them, and so did you. They want to keep you *safe!*"

"Only safe enough to have babies," said Rachel. "What bothers me is that you didn't fight harder for me. I think you could've."

Eliza opened her arms and reached toward Rachel, moving her hands outside camera range. The effect from Rachel's perspective was startling — it looked as if Eliza's hands had been cut off at the wrists. Rachel pressed her body against the couch cushions behind her, instinctively shrinking away from the handless arms. Eliza was beloved, but she was also 13.8 light years away. Rachel could never hug her, or share a meal with her. Eliza could never be more than a virtual presence, and she could never be part of life on Patience.

"I did everything I could," Eliza was saying. "I told them over and over that it wasn't right to trick you into being intimate with Tensel. I wouldn't let it go. I made noise, I yelled, I threatened to quit, but Dr. Covington said the plan would go forward with or without me. For *your* sake, I didn't quit, and I like to think I made the right choice. I like to think you're better off with me than you would've been without me."

Rachel's expression softened and she took a deep breath, reminding herself of the point, reminding herself what she wanted and needed to say. "Yes, it's true. You had to cooperate with Ark, and so did I. They tampered with my body and my soul, and they used you too. I'm sorry for that, and I want you to know that your love and your presence, especially in my early days on Patience, was life-giving and grounding. Here's what I want to say—I want to say—" Now her voice was thick with tears. "I'm saying thank you for everything, thank you for witnessing me as I came into being, thank you for calling me by name, thank you for making me laugh and showing me how to be a human being. *Thank you.*"

"Why are you talking as if everything's so final?"

"Because —" Rachel pressed a tissue to her eyes, struggling to continue, "Because we've learned to care for ourselves, and we won't be in contact with Earth much longer."

"What!? You know that can't happen. Life isn't *possible* on Patience without help from Earth. How could you make it on your own? Ark keeps things running for you — your bodies, your agriculture, your technology. How could you survive without tech?" She lowered her voice to a whisper. "And they're listening to us, you know they are."

"We can maintain our bodies, our planet, and our tech without Ark. And they're not listening to this conversation — you'll probably get an earful from Dr. Covington about the bad connection she had today, and all the static she heard."

Eliza was silent as Rachel's meaning sunk in. Then, "Don't be foolish! What if you're wrong? You think you've learned how to—you think you're able to—"

"This is hard," said Rachel, interrupting. She put up her hand, ready to make the cutoff gesture to end the call, tears streaming down her face. "I'm grateful to you, my dear grand-daughter, and I love you. Be at peace. Goodbye."

She gestured, and Eliza disappeared.

*
**

Rachel arrived early and claimed one of the rockers that lined the refectory's west wall, setting Asher on her lap and his bag of food and toys on the floor beneath her. She watched people gather in twos and threes around the room as she thought back to her conversation with Eliza. True, she'd told Eliza the news before the group had made its decision, but she felt sure how the group would vote—it was in the air.

Tensel arrived, with Zoë riding in a little satchel slung across his chest. People went silent as they passed, some reaching out to touch Zoë's fur. It was hard to articulate what made this little animal different from her sisters. When she entered a room, the light seemed to clear, and each person's spirit made a subtle adjustment in the direction of peace.

They'll get used to it, Rachel thought as she took the lid off a wooden bowl of cheese cubes and handed the bowl to Asher. She'd seen Zoë many times, and it seemed to her that what Zoë brought to those around her was a shift toward *groundedness*. The colonists would still have problems and conflicts, but now everyone could stay more present within events, because a fundamental piece of everyone's puzzle had slipped into place.

She rocked in the chair, letting her thoughts leave Asher while he munched on the cheese and played with the bowl. She wandered into a daydream, and the daydream wandered into territory more like a night dream. A black woman was entering a glass and metal building on an island. She seemed familiar, as if she might've been Rachel's mother, or an aunt. A middle-aged, gray-haired version of Rachel herself. A red-suited usher pressured the woman, urging her to do something. The usher convinced the woman to go into a room, undress, enter a VR body bag.

Rachel wanted to scream a warning, reach into the scene, tear that bag open and get the woman out.

What was happening?

Then she understood: it was a memory! The woman was the person Eliza had told her so much about. Unique, different from her current self. Beloved, just as her present self was beloved.

Her heart warmed and filled with compassion for the woman in the VR bag, the former Rachel, herself. She longed for that Rachel to be free and healthy, but she couldn't reach into the past to fix or change it, much as she wanted to. She could only stitch together memories and remind herself of the truth: Everything Ark gave them or did for them was for Ark's benefit, not theirs.

Why hadn't the old Rachel seen it?

Ark had forced her to receive their story as if it were true, as if it were her own. But now the new Rachel was awake and finding her own story, shaking off the untruths and half-truths that had followed her from Earth into her new life.

She woke up with a start, breathing fast. Her breathing slowed as she returned to the present, and to the room of friends and neighbors around her. The memory was terrible, but its timing was perfect: any small doubts she had about voting yes were gone, even though she carried sadness with her too, thinking about Eliza. She knew that her children on Earth, Miriam and Sam, would come out of deep sleep soon, hoping to meet her.

They'd be disappointed. So be it.

The room filled, and Bob rang a bell to start the silence. Asher started to sing an incoherent song, and the baby on the lap next to Rachel decided it was time to cry. But that was okay. Rachel pulled Asher into her lap and let the sounds wash over her as the group entered into the closest approximation of silence that it could muster. No one had been willing to skip this meeting, so no humans were available to do child care. And no one had wanted to leave their child in the hands of an AI bot that night.

*
**

Time passed, Tensel's thoughts raced, Asher and the other kids were driving him crazy, and he began to wonder if Bob had forgotten to set the timer.

Just when he thought he'd have to go outside and pace back and forth for a while, the kids settled down, and his own body and spirit shifted into a lower gear, as if someone had tapped the brakes inside his busy mind. He let himself relax into this odd lull, knowing from experience that others were feeling it too. Zoë, draped over his shoulder, began to purr, and his peace deepened as she vibrated against his neck.

He felt a flavor of peace that he sometimes felt before a unanimous vote, as if at that moment a sealed envelope were being delivered to each member of the group. Some believed the message in the envelope came from God, the Universe, or another benevolent and personal entity who was lovingly present within and around them. Others believed it came from the group's ability to tap into the deep interconnectedness of all that is. And a few, like Bob, didn't wonder about it at all. After all, being stuck with hundreds of adults exactly your own age was bound to produce synchronicities — they knew each other well!

As for Tensel, he suspected it had something to do with macro quantum patterns and the ability of souls to "entangle" with one another — although, as he'd said to Rachel, explaining a phenomenon scientifically didn't preclude God being the impetus behind the phenomenon or the animating force within it. He intended to look into it during the years ahead on Patience.

He reflected that Zoë's presence among them made group consensus easier than it used to be. Maybe it was because the missing pieces of their quantum patterns made them whole as a group. Or maybe their desire to agree ran deeper now, so people were more willing to fight until the fight was over. And when it was time to decide, people were more willing to "stand aside" and abide by the group decision even if they didn't personally agree. Whatever made this possible, their agreements, when reached, ran as deep as the iron core of the planet beneath them.

The bell rang to end the silence, and Serenity spoke from near the back circle. "I move that we sever contact with Earth.

I think we're ready to vote." Bob rose from his seat and asked for someone to second the motion, and then asked for a vote.

Unanimous.

Even the babies were still for a moment as this new truth permeated everyone's consciousness: they were going to disable the technology that connected them to Earth. They were leaving behind the humans they'd gotten to know on Earth — the link sponsors who'd guided each of them through their first difficult months on Patience, the scientists and doctors who'd advised them and cared for them, blood relatives who were important even if they weren't familiar.

Earth, their safety net, would disappear.

Bob spoke, ending the hush that filled the room. "Alrighty then. We know who will do it, because only one of us has the know-how." He looked at Tensel. "But when?"

Tensel stood up, Zoë still draped over his shoulder. She brought her paws down and faced forward, staring sleepily around her at the colonists. "I assume we all want to be together when it happens," said Tensel. "I can upload the final script tomorrow night, here, from the portable workstation I had Velex build. How about it?"

"Tomorrow night," said Bob, "Let's say after dinner. Great, I can't wait! Any other news? Not that anything could top that!"

Serenity stood. "We're on the verge of our first rainstorm in this quadrant of Patience," she announced to murmurs of surprise. She walked to a window and pointed at the sky. "Maybe you've noticed that the light has a different cast to it these last few days? From what I've been able to figure out, we should have rain as soon as tomorrow evening. Amazing timing, don't you think? Yet another sign that the terraforming's beginning to self-perpetuate."

*
**

The next day, Rachel cut branches from the overgrown acacias outside her garden, trying to imagine rain. Water would fall from the sky! With help from Selex, she ground the branches into chips to use as mulch for her roses. The project wasn't urgent, but it was hard work and it occupied her mind. And preparing for winter was an act of belief: yes, winter would come. Seasons would take hold. Their colony would thrive and grow.

But could they make a clean break from Earth? She remembered the speculative procedure Selex had performed on Asher's fetus, infusing it with the halves of entangled pairs of particles. She'd have to tell Tensel about that event, dreamlike at the time, now returning to her in vivid detail. What did it mean for Asher and the other babies on Patience? Were those particles affecting them? And what about the babies on Earth who'd been infused with the other halves of the particles?

Some colonists had also raised questions about the IDLE-COM, which they relied on for real-time communication with Earth. The IDLE-COM used pairs of biologically active entangled particles that were separated from each other when the *Svalbard* left Earth so long ago. Would those connections persist in some form when contact with Earth was severed? No one knew.

She stopped to watch a line of cumulus clouds that caravanned from left to right across the western horizon, making a mental note to ask Tensel what he thought about all this. The air smelled full, and a light wind was up.

By afternoon, the clouds had piled into towers on top of the mountains around their valley. The sky swung from dark to light to dark again, and Rachel asked Selex to tell her when the sun was half an hour from setting. She understood how weather worked, but in this body she'd never been without the sun in the daytime, had never seen rain clouds or smelled air that was pregnant with water. She knew that weather meant life, but the manic sky filled her with uneasiness. What if it was a mistake to cut themselves off from Earth?

Turning her mind in a better direction, she chose to remember the settled concord she'd felt with the group. "We're in this together," she said out loud.

"Of course we are," said Selex. "I'll always help you, even though the equipment problem is still creating static in our communications with Earth. But I have a great deal of knowledge within my local database, so don't worry."

Rachel looked at the robot, now seeing a useful "it" rather than a companionable "she."

She felt a twinge of regret that Selex didn't know what was happening: the communication static was only the beginning. Tensel had been training apprentices, and one of them had visited Selex to upload a small virus into its operating system. The robot was already under local control, and tonight it would be cut off, completely and forever, from its Earth handlers.

*
**

At sunset, Rachel walked to the refectory and joined the others for falafel, tomatoes and zucchini, cheesy quiche, salads from many gardens, semolina cakes baked by Dante, and an ambiguously fruity drink that Bob promised was "the bomb." The room was loud, and everyone had a few words to say about the clouds, the air, the dark day, the oncoming rain, and their impending separation from Earth. Would they feel different tomorrow? Did Dr. Amir or the other scientists suspect anything? Were the AI bots *really* under local control now? Would Ark send a ship?

After the meal, Tensel hooked up to his portable workstation. Bob and a few others watched, others milled around and talked, and a few sat with their heads bowed in thought or prayer. Rachel bundled a sleepy Asher in a second blanket and carried him outside, beyond the rectangles of light that fell from the meeting-room windows. She lowered her head to listen to his soft, even breaths. "This is your home, kiddo," she whispered. "Get ready for your first rain. And mine."

Tetheus had set, and Callista, small and pale, was barely visible above the horizon through a break in the clouds. Rachel tilted her head to drink it in. The clouds shifted to show the triple star of Rinconda 570 moving fast toward its zenith, the black of space just visible between its one bright yellow star and its two smaller companions.

The trinity of distant lights, framed by clouds, seemed to gaze at her as she thought about the old Rachel. Whatever that Rachel had experienced, it belonged to the old Rachel, secure in the past. This night, this community, these stars, this child, the rain, and the hard work and changes that were coming — all these belonged to the new Rachel.

The curtain of clouds drew shut across the stars, and a cool mist touched her upturned face. A drop of water fell onto her forehead, and she felt her whole self receive it—a sacred touch from the sky. Whispering thanks, she pulled the blanket over Asher's head and turned back toward the refectory, where Tensel waited in the doorway. As she came inside he put his hands on Asher and looked into Rachel's eyes. "It's done," he said.

The storm grew louder. The wind drove the rain sideways against the closed windows, and a flash of light seemed to make the whole building expand and contract in the blink of an eye.

"This is lightning, and now there will be *thunder!*" shouted Bob in jubilation, startling everyone around him almost as much as the lightning had. He threw his arms up and began to shimmy around the room, and when the thunder rumbled a few seconds later, someone turned out the lights.

Each new bolt of light caught a snapshot: two men dancing a baby around the room, Zoë chasing one of her sisters, people on the floor resting their backs against the wall, smiling and talking. Sara lit the beeswax candles that she'd made that week, now that the apiary was thriving, and Serenity lit a fire in the enormous open fireplace at the end of the room.

Rachel, off to the side and staring out the window, imagined each bolt of lightning charging her soul with new life, filling her with energy and joy, a benediction for all that lay ahead. She gathered Asher close to her chin and turned to face Tensel where he stood next to her chair, letting him lean down and put his arms around her and their boy.

This was home.

෭

Acknowledgments

I'm deeply grateful to Lauren Sapala and to my beta readers: Gene Anderson, Tess Evans Clark, Steve Merryman, Dana Cairns Watson, and MaryLynne Wrye. Each of you gave me a precious gift through your feedback and encouragement, and I hope you'll see your fingerprints in the finished product. I offer extra thanks to my husband Gene, who read the book multiple times and lovingly listened much of it into existence. I also offer extra thanks to my dear friend Dana, who gave me detailed comments on the book, twice. I'm humbled by your skills as a reader, thinker, and editor—thank you!

About the images and quotes

The cover design includes images from NASA, iStock.com/Bigandt_Photography, and iStock.com/kirstypargeter.

The quote from Richard Feynman is from his Messenger Lecture 6, delivered Nov. 1964 at Cornell University, available online. The quote from George Fox is from *Autobiography of George Fox*, available online through Christian Classics Ethereal Library. The quote from Mary Shelley is from *Frankenstein or, The Modern Prometheus*, available online through Project Gutenberg.

The quotes from Emo Phillips, Shakespeare, Socrates, the Nicene Creed, and the Ramayana are also, God willing, in the public domain.

Dictionary quotes are from *Unabridged.Merriam-Webster.com*, Merriam-Webster, 2018. Quotes from scripture and from *The Cloud of Unknowing* are similar to current translations, but adjusted by a future translator.

I quote a few words from Wendell Berry in hopes that I'm covered by section 4.78 in the *Chicago Manual of Style: 15th Ed.*, which is about quotations in interior monologues.

All other quotations are products of my imagination.

And finally, although I can't quote it, I recommend Mary Oliver's "Maybe," a poem about the soul. It's in her *House of Light* (1990) and also in her *New and Selected Poems: Volume One* (2004).

If you enjoyed *Soul Boundary*, please support me by leaving a review on Amazon or elsewhere online.

91634562R00183

Made in the USA
San Bernardino, CA
24 October 2018